THE JUNE RISE

THE JUNE RISE

THE APOCRYPHAL LETTERS OF
JOSEPH ANTOINE JANIS

William Tremblay

Fulcrum Publishing
Golden, Colorado

The June Rise was first published in the United States by Utah State University Press, Logan, Utah, 1994.

Library of Congress Cataloging-in-Publication Data

Tremblay, William, 1940–
    The June rise : the apocryphal letters of Joseph Antoine Janis / William Tremblay.
        p. cm.
    ISBN 1-55591-452-7 (hardcover)
    1.Janis, Joseph Antoine, b. 1824—Fiction. 2. Indians of North America—Government relations—Fiction. 3. Indians of North America—Wars—Fiction. 4. French Americans—Fiction. 5. Colorado—Fiction. 6. Trappers—Fiction. I. Janis, Joseph Antoine, b. 1824 II. Title.

PS3570.R386 J86 2001
813'.54—dc21

                                                    2001033475

Printed in Canada
10 9 8 7 6 5 4 3 2 1

Cover design: Elizabeth Watson
Interior design: Richard A. Firmage
Cover photograph of Antoine Janis and Oglala men, 1877.
    Photograph courtesy of Fort Collins Public Library, Fort Collins, Colorado.

Fulcrum Publishing
16100 Table Mountain Parkway, Suite 300
Golden, Colorado 80403
(800) 992-2908 • (303) 277-1623
www.fulcrum-books.com

Preface

It began one morning as I was walking around Warren Lake near my home in Fort Collins, Colorado. When I got to the WPA spillway on the eastern shore, I sat down, staring at a length of rope coiled like a chromosome chain deep in the ice. I found myself back in my childhood Massachusetts at the kitchen table where my parents were squaring off *en français,* their language for secrets.

A landlocked seagull shrieked. I looked up, and out—with a tremor like those just before sleep—west to the Arapaho Range where huge sheets of snow were slowly swirling off Horsetooth Ridge. I was surrounded by the immense distances of the Colorado high plains and the foothills of the Front Range of the Rocky Mountains. Silver clouds floated above bare cottonwoods, taking the eye west in steps, rising—Storm Mountain, Mummy Mountain, and beyond that a Wedgewood sky. Winds I had ignored were sighing, as if to seduce me. I had been living in a beautiful place for many years, and it hadn't sunk in until that moment.

A desire began to grow in me to pay whatever different attentions of scale this place asked. It was then that I remembered the French trapper Antoine Janis. I had known about him for years; it was as though he had been standing quietly in a corner waiting for me to turn to him. Learning about his life might prove a guide through which I could learn more about the Rocky Mountain West. To retrieve not only his life but a way of life much closer to those of the beginnings of this country's history—to repossess a set of wilderness skills involving not only observation but observance—would mean to reclaim a small portion of an almost forgotten immigrant experience in North America.

The log cabin Janis originally built in 1859 at Laporte, Colorado, has been reassembled behind the Fort Collins Pioneer Museum by the Daughters of the American Revolution. I remembered a curator telling me that Janis had been the first white man to receive a legal deed, as provided by the Homestead Act, for 160 acres in Larimer County.

What the sketchy and sometimes contradictory historical sources record is that Joseph Antoine Janis was born in 1824 in St. Charles, Missouri, and was educated in parochial schools there. Sometime around 1840 his father took him down the Santa Fe Trail and taught him the ways of a mountain man. After his wilderness apprenticeship was completed, his father presented him to the Arapaho, Cheyenne, and Oglala at their tribal council grounds in what is now Laporte—the very land Janis homesteaded.

Antoine Janis acquired the skills and knowledge of a fur trapper, a packmule trader, a horse rancher, a guide, a scout, and an interpreter for the United States Army. He married an Indian woman and homesteaded land. However, in the 1870s the federal government issued him an ultimatum: either divorce his Lakota wife, First Elk Woman, and keep the land, or stay married to her and share her fate at Pine Ridge Indian Reservation. He chose to remain with her.

I read *The History of Larimer County* by Ansel Watrous and found a letter reproduced in it from Antoine Janis dated March 17, 1883, and posted at Pine Ridge Agency. Watrous apparently had written Janis requesting information about early settlement in the Cache La Poudre River Valley. Janis responded with but brief reference to his having founded Laporte along with his brother Nicholas and a dozen others. He closed the letter by saying: "It would consume a great deal of time to give to you in full detail, and my health has been such this winter that I dare not undertake the task."

What would Antoine Janis have written, I wondered, if his health had disposed him to answer Watrous's inquiries in all the particulars?

Acknowledgments

Grateful acknowledgement is due (and happily given) to the following individuals and institutions: Sandra Lowry, Librarian, Fort Laramie National Historic Site; Sharron G. Uhler, Museum Archivist, Colorado Springs Pioneers Museum; Karen McWilliams, formerly Local History Archivist at the Fort Collins Public Library; the Fort Collins Pioneer Museum; the staff of the Denver Public Library; Denis Ledoux; Lilianne Labbé; and Lucie Therrien. Thanks also go to the Corporation of Yaddo and the College of Liberal Arts, Colorado State University, for grants of precious time and financial assistance.

For their inspiration and encouragement, I wish to thank, as ever, Cynthia Tremblay, James Work, James Galvin, and Ken Brewer. Thanks also to Jim Foster, Phil Turetzky, Waldo Jones, and Doug Ishi, *compañeros* of the trail. Most special thanks go to Bill Nies, *rechercheur extraordinaire*, who shared his visions of the subtle beauties of Rawhide Flats, Round Butte, Box Elder Canyon, and the Cheyenne Rim.

The "Preface" and "My Lookout" [Chapter 1] first appeared in *Green Mountains Review* (New Series: Vol. VI, #2, Summer/Fall 1993).

Contents

"... they [the Lakota] had asked many times for another interpreter at the fort, one who knew their language and had a good heart for them. A man like Antoine Janis, or his brother Nick."

—Mari Sandoz, *Crazy Horse: the Strange Man of the Oglalas*

LETTER I

"My Lookout"

My health's been such this spring I now can sit against the south wall of my sodroof house here at Pine Ridge to write in the narrow margins of this old account ledger and dare undertake a reply at last to your request for all particulars regarding early days in Poudre valley, with some hope of satisfying my rule never to take a job I cannot finish.

Even so, probably you should have askt my brother Nick. He's the *raconteur* in the family. He'd be glad to oblige, only he's never been much for writing. If you'd come to Pine Ridge you'd find he hangs around the potbelly stove in the agent's storehouse nowadays, smoking his white clay pipe that goes back to the Dutch trade in our grandfather's time, telling you or anyone who'll listen how he come to raise them beams above your head with tipi poles one blue morning.

There was nothing to it, he'd say. It was a kit. Boom. It come on a freight wagon north from the Lincoln railstop and before that way back from Washington, D.C. Didn't have to fell a tree nor get its bleeding pitch upon my hands. Each joist and plank was numbered exactly like them build-ing plans that come with it in a clean white envelope. It was what they called a frame house. I hoisted rafters while my brother Antoine climbed up and spiked them, and, boom, it was done. That's what he'd say.

The facts differ. Nick got the taste for telling tales from the best of them, Jim Bridger, who used to promise them young Army officers he scouted for he'd take them to the peetrified forest way up in Yellowstone country where there was peetrified birds singing peetrified songs and then wonder why them West Pointers never could take him serious. I never climbed up among any rafters, not since I took a ball in my right hip on a horse raid in Crow country at dawn on a summer's day it snowed in Hell.

Nick and I both know a holy man who changed into a coyote under the moon one night, passed south along the ponderosa pine canyons along the Arapaho Range with a pint of water from the Cache La Poudre River in a grass-woven, pine-pitch-hardened jug between his teeth. He paused, buried it with his claws, marked it with his urine, and suddenly Spring Creek come gushing from broken rocks on the eastern slope of Horsetooth Ridge. The waters cut a notch through the hogback and streamed down across the high plains close to where the people camp. Nick's always been such a good-hearted soul. If you ask him he'll tell you without a second's thought where that jug is buried.

I won't. That's the difference between us. I continue believing that to unbury the jug, to break the spell through word or deed, is to end the holy man's boon. Colorado and Wyoming— the entire western states—are dotted with places where holy men done their business for the good of all. Soldiers and settlers, they never known nor paid enough mind to those ceremonies to undo them, so they go on giving life.

These days I look out at the low buttes that run northeast to southwest in White Clay Creek

country not far from the Nebraska line. I watch
the dry wind, that in this season never stops
blowing up clouds of dust, until my mind drifts,
and I'll be switched if I don't see smoke signals or
ghosts along those pine-dotted slopes that haze off
hilltops into these skies below the Dakota badlands my father called *les terres mauvais*.

I tap my pen, unsure how to begin, for mine
has been a lifelong habit of keeping my lookout to
myself. It has proved the wisest way and kept me
alive, more than once. Likely, had I my druthers,
I'd tell my story by dusting my fiddle off, tuning
its keys with a care not to bust a string, and warm
up on some old tune Lady Claribel wrote,

> *I can not sing*
> *the old songs,*
> *Or dream*
> *those dreams again ...*

and let them as has an ear listen and decide what
is the burden of my song.

But what is old age for, except to pile all the
skins and husks of our dearest hopes and disap-
pointments into one dung heap from which we
hope some new life will grow?

I admit my mind's often drawn back to the
land in Pleasant Valley. My father called it
Bellevue. I thought then that the Poudre valley
was the loveliest spot on earth, and I think so yet.
Though I lived there a few years with my wife
First Elk Woman and our growing family, it
seems it was never quite mine. You no doubt
know the place, a quarter-section along the north
bank of the Poudre below Bingham's hill in this
shady grove of cottonwoods—cool in summer,
green, and sheltered from the wind—though it
does not give a view of the plains north to the
Cheyenne rim where trouble might come from.

Sometimes in my mind I walk that land along
the river on a night black as a beaver's winter coat

with only my horses' warm smell to guide me to where they stand inside the lodgepole corrals. I make the sign of the barn loft beam and root cellar stone, the fence post and the well crank, saying goodbye to each thing with a touch. There's no voice but the river's, carrying the mountains down, grain by grain, mumbling over smooth rock the way we restless men fight the itch to pull up stakes to someplace else by whispering endless prayers, without ever once admitting that our only gods are those of the hearth who make us appease them with our lies about wanting nothing more than settled contentment.

Yours of September 1883 asking me to give names, dates, places is writ in such fair hand I hazard your pen's light touch the mark of a man sharp enough to know it's impossible to say who did what pursuant to which dream, without one's lookout figuring in, some.

Mine began when as a boy I first felt this hunger open in my body from missing my father. He was gone far from my native St. Charles west into the Rockies trapping beaver, often so long gone his features grew dim in my recollection.

It was a gray day in March I was out spading the garden after school hoping my father would come home for my tenth birthday when I heard a voice down the river bottom singing loud and jolly the mournful words of *une chanson canadienne*. It was him! I threw down the shovel and ran across the cow pastures along the box elders to meet him.

Un canadien errant,
banni de ses foyers

he sang, and as is the way of that kind of *répons* I repeated the line, calling back to him like an altarboy with his *et cum spiritu tuo*.

I knew from some hello in his voice that he heard me. When he sang the next verse,

Parcourait en pleurant
des pays étrangers

I knew he saw himself a man exiled into such
strange lands as I could not yet imagine, among
feathered and painted *étrangers* on the prairie.
And, as he continued singing the song,

Si tu vois mon pays,
mon pays malheureux,
Va dire à mes amis
que je me souviens d'eux

I gathered that he was the sad soul lost, asking me
to be the one who remembered his song to old
friends on the road.

That was the first year he took me camping
along the Missouri River. We sat drifting
downriver in a canoe around a big bend where
Pelican Island came into view with its tall willows
standing among the wracked timbers and brush
and debris of many a flood.

Where do you think's the best spot for us to
bed down? my father askt me.

How about right here among these willow
brushes along the shore where we can watch the
water run and the sand will make a soft place to
lie, I answered.

That's alright *here,* he said. But out west,
you'd want a place like that one on a little higher
ground where you could fight off some wild
Pawnee with red feathers tied in his scalplock and
a gleam in his eye for your traps. He mought
come aswimming silent as some watersnake and
rise up in the shallows changed back into a two
legged man dripping out of the black river some
moonless night.

I swallowed hard at that moment as I imagined the blackened face of that Pawnee with a
stone hatchet in his teeth and a snake's eyes, ready
to crush my skull while I slept. Would I wake at a
twig snap, would I sit bolt upright in time enough

to pull a sidearm from my horse-blanket pillow and blast him far away where a skulking Pawnee with a lead ball in his heart must go? I was such a boy.

As we sat by the fire I looked at his face, studying the line of his chin lately made bare when he shaved his whiskers off in honor of my mother. I could picture broad valleys of timber standing there in his eyes, and I could hear long slow winds sweeping across dried grasslands in his breath. Yet about him was a silence born of some reluctance to speak, some shyness I could have expected from a boy more my age.

Until the year I can take you west with me into the mountains, it falls to you as the oldest to be your mother's little man and do for her around the house as I would if I was not making the family's living trapping beaver and only once a year trekking back east with William Sublette to cash in our plews at St. Louis, he said at last.

I wondered then as I would often have occasion to if I could be as answerable as my father askt. I was more given to wool gathering. In yet but a few years I would get awful tired of my father in some mountain camp saying, *Arrête de rêvasser et commence à travailler!* I remember that often as I stared out the school windows of L'Academie du Sacre Coeur in St. Charles, pausing in my struggles with early Church history under the nun's stern eye, I tried to picture back to my great-grandparents, who'd lived in Trois Rivieres, Canada.

My mother moved in a dress as black as some curate's cassock from kitchen to well to garden to town through her own seasons, but she never spoke of them, my forbears—neither Janises nor Thibauts—so I began to carry this family silence about as if some bad thing must've happened back in Canada that came with being a Janis. I figured young I must learn to bear whatever expense of spirit comes from not knowing when one's story rightly begins.

All I ever caught sight of in my *rêveries* were endless blizzards that roared out of huge ice caves in Siberia across the Alaskan straits and across the Yukon wastes through the wide plains of Ontario, shaping dark Quebec pines into snow giants, their limbs rising and falling in the wind like steady breathing under a white flying cloud moon that flashed away from my mind when Sr. Mary Immaculta's ruler skun my knuckles.

My father said, You're a big one, and I reckon when you've reached your growth you'll see me eye to eye.

He then took my hand and placed his up to it, palm to palm, finger to finger, and they almost matched. In that moment I was a Janis. I had his narrow shoulders and hips. Years later, as I rested after a day of tramping toward timberline, I remembered staring into my father's eyes lit by the fire's glow that night and seeing them shine like the cold green fire of this hanging lake on Iron Mountain's graveled slopes.

On Pelican Island was the first time he told me stories about his other life in the Rockies. When he said *montagne,* I askt did he mean like the river bluffs? No, he said, but picture them upstream, where the water's turned by sheer rock wall, as made of cloth. Cut them out the way your mother cuts homespun to make shirts, by a pattern she learnt from her mother. You can put red color bands in the rock, any trick you have to help you perch the cut-out pattern upon the original in your mind. Widen the base into one long line, rising up from and falling back to the land. Now, do it again, one on top of the other, he said, and I builded them, the word *higher* drifting in my body.

I dreamt of walking on their slopes, feeling on my footsoles how they must have risen, the plains an earthen shawl thrown off their shoulders. I kept among shadows of ponderosa boughs at the edge of mountain meadows, feeling what I now can only call a modesty that my dream body should not be seen. Yet I did feel eyes upon me, making my hair stand when it came to me how it takes a spirit to see one.

Once I felt those eyes my skin touched alive with moonlight that also fell on blades of grass, tongues of sweet aspen, and pine cones. Each scale sparked stars like lit candles above the distant peaks.

The night sky I gazed into, the ground I walked on, the heavenly and earthly parts of this dream were given to each other, as if the stars and mountains were teeth of gears like an anchor winch on a sternwheel riverboat that turned earth and constellations in one great slow circle—both the above and the below, the gods and our beloved dead.

The next morning as we knelt to wash near a quiet pool along the island's bank, my father told me the Cheyenne use pools of water to gaze at those they call the underwater people. Do you see the riverbottom? he asked. Can you see the weeds that grow there as prairie grass? Can you see a band of horsemen who cross those prairie grasslands following buffalo herds? Imagine, if they sense some gazer's attention present in their sky, they can leap up and become eagles, spiraling on dust devils to spy who changes the light they live in. It could be you, Joe Antoine, your head bending over to look at them, huge as a stormcloud. When I asked him what use they made of that underwater land, he said, Those two worlds are—to each other—places where prophecies get born.

I now wonder if it was to enter this mystery of unknown lands—as if they held both the origins and destinies we sought—that my brother Nick and I, and all of our generation, pushed west across plains and mountains, drawn by a secret hope that at some fork in a river we could not then foresee we would find a profile rock whose features would show us who we are and what we're meant for on this earth.

Yet, as we westered further, what we sought vanished further from us, and so the ache grew inside us, and we did not know the axe to chop it out of us, til gaunt from seeking we seemed to stand so boned in our souls we looked more signposts than men, skeletons who point to those promised lands that glow forever sunset gold and red.

My lookout is woven of such stuff like wooden latticework of trellised roses through which I see with the wilderness eye my father gave me so I could make a living on my own hook, and with the city eye through which I see who built what, hearing in all the remembered sounds of hammering and hauling in Laporte and Camp Collins these mysteries we served, as if shadows cast by the very future we tried to secure changed what light we lived in, and no flight we ventured could reach the horizon of.

In those days I played a popular song on my fiddle whose words went like this,

I love the man
with valor clad,
who left his clan
to make this land
of golden sand
renowned and free.

But from my lookout the ox-drawn wagons stretching in a line back across the plains of Nebraska, Kansas, and Missouri appear like white-sailed ships riding waves of dreams settlers were told was "free land" from the Homestead Act. But it was not free and clear, not like the government said.

I come to think all this westering was for a glimpse of God the native holy men live in daily communion with, whose grace is not withheld from this world, awaiting a foretold second coming when trumpets shall sound this age's end and humanity's rapture into those Arms, but, instead, given amply, like a June rise, roaring snowmelt down in cascades to the plains from their gods and from the souls of their dead, one endless and returning stream of lifegiving waters to witness to.

It was not until later in life after I had spent years among the Oglalas that I learned to hear the shape of my father's stories. An Oglala tells stories in circles to make a family of all who hear, with many a refrain like some arrowmaker who sings over and over, so each of the four winds will bless those bonds he ties between flint and shaft in wrapping sinews sixteen tight turns before he knots it off.

Through the stories I've come to believe the Oglala are my underwater people whose fate bespeaks my own, and I am their underwater man, with every part of me, both flesh and spirit. As my father hinted that he led two lives, my eyes often wandered among them, curious, until the day came when my question if I may not have had a brother or sister got an answer. So I have even stood with them, staring and listening into that world where all of us dream and wake anew, ready to break another trail with senses sharp from seeing and being seen.

I'm what is known as a squaw man, Mr. Watrous. Though it means to some half-woman, half-man, less than a whole man, the best step I ever took was to stand at First Elk Woman's side in marriage and learn to share the world that is alive with spirits.

I have always risen early to watch mists, webs, trees, grasses, finches, to see what bright yellow angelwing cactus flowers contribute to morning's light, before the bees begin their day's collections of sage honey. Though I've attended my own plans, how I sought to win the race, and forgot at times the earth's dark other side whose dreamers make the sun shine here, and forgot to note in the sparrow's fall those portions of this dream that keep us all alive, the memories of my childhood dreams where bodies glow with purple nimbuses have never left me, quite.

As I recall the early days of Poudre valley, I see the land fill up quick with so many people all game's soon hunted out and men walk the weary path of daily wages from grain mills, sawmills, stockyards from dawn to dusk, to buy their food from stores as around them Rist canyon's stript of its blue spruce for railroad ties. It seems folks want railroad lines to split a town so they can begin talking of a "right" and "wrong" side of the tracks to be from. Then trainloads of drunk easterners arrived in English tweeds, killing buffalo with rifle shots from open windows of passenger cars for the kind of sport as turns an old hunter's stomach.

Sometimes a wild hare leaps in my brain, and I wonder if the buffalo were slaughtered not on account of the plains tribes hereabout—to take their livelihood and break their fighting spirit, as Army officers said—but on account of the white townfolks who worked the mills. For who among them, if they could ride out on the high plains and make meat enough for a month, would bear a foreman's yoke? As decade has followed decade, the main difference I see between us and those newcomers was that we old trappers had known such free days, and we would as lief die as be squeezed blue by some banker holding a lien over us. In that we were closer to the Oglalas than to our own kith and kin.

At first I felt I could neither take from those mountain valleys nor give to them from my poor stock, but rather I only hoped to be in them as the pilgrim hopes to kiss Jerusalem's stones. For I have seen angels' halos around the sun, and flocks of swallows suddenly become snow, and myself made of thin air, no more than some thought the sky was thinking. The Rocky mountains as they were before the railroad cut them all to pieces took root in me, where they still live, as if inside my chest their million steps of rock and ice rise into swirling clouds.

Neither can I answer all accounts in one sitting nor write more until you've responded to say you've heard my fair warning and give me lief. To pass over ground that holds my dead will not be easy, but I confess this mystery that turns our fondest hopes to its own uses still quickens me. I know you will only take from my tale what you can use. You are not asking to be part of my family.

Most will tell you they want the truth, but damn few really want to hear anything that runs against what you might call their official version of themselves. Most want to be lied to. Is that what you want, Mr. Watrous? I could tell you all the tall tales you ever hoped to hear, with beginnings and middles and everything all tied up at the endings like dressed birds over an open fire, but I've little evidence that that's the way things go, except to say I've seen that our passions do play themselves out.

I can not tell any part of it unless I can tell it whole. From my lookout here at Pine Ridge where I'm in retirement and have little else to do but ponder, I suspect that what we know about what we do balances with what we must believe— that we're part of some greater good we can't see because we're inside it—or else we can't go on. All I ask is that when the time comes for you to commit your thoughts in ink you will recall that the Poudre valley was paid for, every inch, in blood. When you sum that, remember not to tally white blood only.

March 17, 1884
Pine Ridge Agency

"In the Wilderness"

Thank you for sending me the draft of
that piece you intend to publish about me. I note
specially the passage in which you inform your
future readers that I named the Cache La Poudre
River. I know your source for the story that at
twelve I ran away from home and was there in
1836 with my father is Ab Loomis, but Ab is one
of those who think that facts must never stand in
the way of a good story. Well, I guess that's your
lookout.

As to my arrival in Pleasant Valley and who
named the river when: First Elk Woman always
says I had every skill of the Oglalas yet needed
none of them to guide me there. Your date is in
error, Sir. You have me walking that land before I
ever laid eyes on it. If your date was correct, I
would've been a boy about the age I was when my
spirit flew in dreams to those sheltering hills with
their own river music I would in later years play
my fiddle to, stringing some tangled creole lace
between the melody of an old quadrille and the
rhythms of bowing where what I think and feel
meet as what I know among the grasslands that
then were black with buffalo.

I was sixteen when my father took me down
the Santa Fe. It was as if he had been dead for
many years and now by some miracle he was back
among the living, come to sweep me away from

St. Charles like an angel of Election. And it wasn't
long before I tried to say goodbye to my *memère*,
who wouldn't look at me I had so disappointed
her hopes in me to serve God. I won't go on
about this; it is an old story. As I was good in
school and learnt enough church Latin to serve as
altar boy, my mother thought I might take Holy
Orders and make her proud, since it was the best
French families only that sent their firstborn sons
to take the black robe of the Jesuits.

For myself, I'd wanted no more than to play
my fiddle from town to town at country dances,
though the dawn had already rose when I knew
there was no holding a band together.

It was too crazy, each man pulling from his
own bottle of dreams, so that once too often I'd
woke in a barnloft where the night before we had
folks stomping out their *joie* only to find myself
wincing with a blinding headache. I'd open my
hurt eyes to long beams of sunlight striking
through the air alive with dancing grain dust to
find myself alone like old Saul unhorsed on his
road to Tarsus with bleak prophecies in my mind
that I'd have to find my living elsewhere than
music. And the young players were all like me.
Having taught themselves music they could only
play the wildest swamp hollars because they was
only a sign of what they needed and had not got.
The night before they'd pledged their bond to
stick with the band, and now come morning they
had run off with what little change the folks
thereabouts could give us for our tunes.

To my brother Nick I promised I'd be back
someday for him, and shook his hand gravely
beneath the big boxelder tree that hung its shoulders over the roof of our mother's house as if he
and I were already men, men who know that life
is little more than a trail of long goodbyes.

It wasn't dawn when my father and I begun at

a walk from those same Second Street provisioners
that helped outfit Lewis and Clark. We went at a
walk, uphill with three pack mules each of trade
goods for our trip to southern Colorado. We
passed the newspaper offices, then the Town Hall,
stables and barns, until we reached the hilltop at
the road leading east to St. Louis and west to
Kansas City as first light hit us, and turning back
in my saddle I could see early lanterns in houses
going out one by one, as if, with the last flame's
quick extinguishment, it was too late to turn back.
When I glanced over to my father I saw him
turned in his saddle looking back too, and I askt
him, Are you sorry to leave so soon?

Well, he said, I figure living in St. Charles is a
lot like being hung by the neck. I reckon if you
hung there long enough you'd get used to it.

First day out we ferried across back coils of the
Missouri I'd never seen, and as day passed into
day the trees thinned and thinned and as standing
water grew scarcer and scarcer, I felt more and
more naked under the sun and the sky kept
getting bigger. The earth turned from a rich
riverbottom brown to thin dusty red and smells of
the creekwater turned dry. My father called it gyp
water, some alkali that seemed to make horses
crazier and their nostrils flare when they smelt it,
as if the wild roaming life still called to their
mustang blood. Many's the time when I sat alight
my pony, and I'd stroke her long neck to calm
her, yet was afire myself with what next might lie
beyond them western hills.

Days tramped into weeks as we crossed
Missouri into southeast Kansas from the Flint
hills down toward the Arkansas. I watched my
father's beard grow back so fast it was like being
startled at quick flights of spooked quail as they
break from patches of sagebrush, and we both
came to smell of horses and campfire smoke. If I

wondered what was doing back in St. Charles on
Saturday nights when cajun musicians gathered in
some saloon to hoist a jug and strike up tunes, I
didn't say. I watched my father's eyes, which drew
mine to the habit of scanning near and far.

Great towering afternoon storms blacked the
skies and boomed down forks of lightning, so that
when we spotted the Great Bend he called out for
me to follow him down the willow draw that
shallowed out near water.

This here's country where you can't lie down
when it's raining for fear of drowning nor stand
up for fear of being struck by lightning. With the
trade knives and skillets and cooking pots we're
packing, he said, if we're the highest thing on this
prairie, that lightning'll follar its nature and strike
us down. Ever smelt a pack animal struck, fried in
its own skin, smoking and still twitching on the
ground?

A shiver went through me. He and I lit down
off our mounts and loosed the ropes on them
mules and let the bags jangle to the earth like
dropt tambourines. We squatted, our buckskins
soaked and cold with rain, under this riverbank
hollowed out somewhat like human eyebrows by
floods.

Once we leave these prairies, he said, if you're
not to become *le pauvre perdu*, I'll have to take
you on *le grand tour*. You'll learn to make a map
in your mind. Where we're going, there are no
maps nor easy wagon tracks like those past what
the natives call *Quohatolla*, breasts of the earth, or
others call Spanish Peaks, the twin mountain gates
to Mexico.

When we did at last come upon Bent's fort I
spent my time walking up and down its ladders
and stairways trying to straighten my spine. My
backside was rode hard. I'd counted forty-three
camps across that ocean of grass, hearing nights

the high yip of coyotes lighting skies silver in those hours after moon set, and later the wolves' voices, deeper, their chorus more human in its please to the moon coming by that silver ghost the earth breathes out in the deep nightwatches of the prairies where there's no time to brood about St. Charles.

Learning what travel across the grass lands had to show me took everything I had—not wasting water, for example. My father'd said he wouldn't give me any of his if I lost my bottle, and he meant it. I can't tell you about thirst except to say that after nearly a day of going without I begun to hear this croaking and once when I turned to look I saw a huge dark green toad flying with gray leathery batwings just behind my left shoulder, and I started raving so, he had to slap me back to this world. Isn't it always that we remember beginnings with such sharp recall?

Another night on watch I saw as if the air were water and I a gazer into the underwater world, this long company of riders in silhouette against the night sky, the moonlight glinting off them as if they were made of pewter, carrying lances at odd angles to each other, trekking across that valley where my father and I camped on the plain between the Arkansas and Cimarron, an Indian of no feather I'd ever seen leading them on foot. I dared not tell my father what I'd seen for fear he'd call me mad, yet it was not the last time I would wonder at the sight of some procession of horsemen moving silently across the night prairie toward what strange destination I never quite knew, or wanted to know.

What I remember best was how I came to measure our motion west into the torch of sunset. More and bigger angelwing cactus with longer spines day by day and then yucca spines with their bell-shaped seed pods—forty-three days like Noah

blind in his ark until he knows that when at last
mountains lift his hull nothing beneath his feet
will seem like it was before his Creator sent the
flood, for he has suffered a sea change.

I'd been doing what an apprentice does,
making myself one huge callous to stop my
bleeding, to stop remembering home, to listen to
nothing but my father's voice whispering in my
left ear as I took practice shots with that old
Lancaster rifle he gave me, *Windage times distance,
boy, and aim off target to just that many points.*

Then the morning came when I noted my
father smiling his little secret smile. We were
climbing one of the grassy and treeless hills out in
southwest Kansas through a rising fog, and
suddenly he kicked his horse's ribs, bolting
westward, and I followed at a canter, jerking rope
on the three pack mules in my charge, until I
reached the crest and caught up with my father,
who was now at a standstill, gazing off to the west.
When I looked the same direction as he, there
they were, the Rockies, all purple in the long
slanting dawn light.

This is the place I call First Sight, Joe
Antoine. I almost couldn't wait to show it to you.
It was then I remembered that my father had told
me when I was ten years old about how they rose
up from and fell back down to the land. On the
highest peaks snow was shining pink, and they
looked so cold, so distant, and so long from south
to north—an impassable wall—they reached
down into my chest and took my breath away. I
was suddenly seized in my blood with the sense
that to live at the foot of such mountains would
be like living at the foot of God's throne. It would
take some getting used to if I was to get on with
my daily life.

So I spent a day exploring the fort's many
rooms, the store decked out in bright red

Hudson's Bay blankets, silver buckles hung from masonry nails driven into beams. I stopped to take apart a cunning round spice box, boxes within boxes, cinnamon, sage, and thyme. Under William Bent's stare, I put it back together. Then I tramped over to the blacksmith's shop under its thatch roof that gave out onto stables and paddocks with a low adobe wall that would prove some value if ever that place were attacked, more likely from Mexican soldiers come over Raton Pass than from Kiowas or Comanches. I could see for myself without my father telling me that the tribes thereabouts had come to want the iron skillets and other things the Bents traded them for skins. I saw a small band arrive. They was greeted by Yellow Woman, Bent's Cheyenne wife, and led down to the riverside where they set up tipis. Soon the womenfolk were strolling inside Bent's fort, fingering the bolts of bright red yard goods in the store.

When I went strolling, I saw ristras of chilis hung from viga beams, the huge iron beaver-pelt press standing on its center ground like some iron scaffold. As evening drew on gathering shadows among boxelder and cottonwoods and willows that lined the Arkansas I saw three señoritas walking toward the fort. They were wearing bright red chemises and turtleshell combs in their hair like redwing blackbirds that flew among cattails in the marsh just north of the fort, and in a minute they were promenading outside on the raised veranda near the cantina. They jingled silver bangles when they walked, a little drunk I thought, smelling of lavender and sage and whiskey and sassydancing among the few soldiers and trappers in the night air.

I sat with my father in the open air at nightfall, and the fort cat jumped on my lap and I petted it and sweet-talked it about being the best mouser in the territory, keeping to myself that she might've been the *only* mouser in the whole territory.

One tall man stuck out in the crowd. He sat alone at a table with a bottle and shot glass, downing jolt after jolt. I couldn't keep my eyes off his face. It was scarred all along the line of his forehead with white jagged claw marks down the left jaw. He saw me looking at him and drew himself up to standing and wove his way over to me and my father seated at our table just outside the cantina where men inside were laughing as they played billiards on a huge table I wouldn't have thought could be drug out this far west. He stood over me, glowering down with this one-eyed baleful look that sent the icy touch of death right through me.

Hey, bushway, who's the babe? he askt my father.

This is my son, Joe Antoine, my father said, quiet and careful. I rose to shake his hand, but he just stared at me until I dropped my arm.

Well, if you want your son to stay your son, you mought's well tell him to mind where his own stick floats and not cast his long glance that-a-way t' me.

My father jumped from his chair on instant! He whipped out his belt pistol and in one swift movement jammed its business-end in that big man's throat.

Listen here, Phil, my father said, you touch this boy when we're out on the beaver party, and I'll blow yer head off. Hear me?

Phil looked down as best he could at my father with the barrel of an Army issue pistol driving his jaw up and nodded. As best he could though it must've hurt his Adam's apple, he said, I ain't afraid to die.

Maybe so, my father said, but that ain't goin'

t' help you live any better. You best git back to your bottle, Phil, and kiss the girls a good one before dawn comes and you have t' crawl back to whatever hole you come from.

Phil just smiled at my father, then at me. You got no call to heap insult nor injury upon your bedfellow, Antoine. We'll be t'gither a long ways till winter when them nights don't never seem t' end, and you never do know for sure where retribution might come up behindt ya.

Who is that man? I askt my father after the tall man had withdrawn himself back to his table and slammed himself back into his chair.

He's one of the men we've come to pull together into a hunting party, my father said. I want you to stay clear of him, you hear? Leastwise til you've growed enough to stand some chance against him. I advise you never to go anywhere without your peacemakers.

As I sat that evening watching darkness come on with nighthawks sweeping the low skies with the white v's of their underwings, I saw my picture of my father begin to change—or should I say it began to fill in—so that now when I think of him I wonder if what he loved more than anything was staring a man down with gun in hand. Nothing else fed his heart so much, I believe. Everything else fled from him.

Years later, must've been that crazy summer of 1865, I came across one Oglala brave out east of Fort Laramie on the prairie down off his horse picking through the dropped scatterings of what I figured was Col. Carrington's column which had just arrived in the territory from Leavenworth with a marching band and officers' wives picnicing like they was in some city park and not the wilderness where the best light cavalry in the world might swoop down on them with iron retribution in their hearts. He picked this bent

cornet up, liking its shining brass, I guessed, and
held it to his chest to consider it for a necklace
piece, and finding it ridiculously large he threw it
down, then picked up and threw down empty
canteens, a broken Waltham clock that'd been
thrown off some wagon to lighten up the load
until he was so disgusted he sent up one sad howl
that made a pack of coyotes answer him, and he
mounted back up onto his paint and only then
did he smile a smile like my father's when he'd
give over his aching for something, anything, that
would give him peace, and he kicked his horse
into a gallop across the pure happy emptiness of
eastern Wyoming.

Once we head due west, my father said that
night on the fort roof, up through LaVeta pass
toward the Rockies, we'll traverse paths animals
have trod since the sixth day of Creation, which
Utes and Shoshones have worn however light past
timberline and on up to the high tundra to seek
the spirits who live upon the fragrances of tiny
blue flowers that grow only there and who in
showing themselves as animals or whirlwinds let
men share in the power of all life, which they in
turn give their people in songs, dances, and eagle
plumes to renew their medicine bundles when the
whole tribe must atone some broken vow, ward
off bad luck, or from a vision make new ceremonies that seal their hearts as one to their gods.

We carry power to our families back east, too,
he said, peltries that keep them housed and fed, as
you well know, for after all we are *voyageurs* who
go among *les sauvages*, but we are not *of* them.

Yet I think maybe we're like them, like that
young buck long ago who left the girl he wished
to marry for his first hunting party. Can you
picture a clear lake? he asked. Can you see weeds
that grow on the bottoms there like prairie grass?
Can you see a band of Cheyenne hunting, follow-

ing buffalo herds? I stared at the shadow of grasses and the stalks of cattails in my mind.

My father then knelt down and by full moonlight drew with the point of his skinning knife on the packed dirt that was the roof we rested on what the story he was telling looked like in Sioux picture writing. He made two heads with braids but without feathers for the young man and his friend. Then, in widening coils of pictures, he said, They traveled across the plains and made three campfires. Each night this young man made up songs about the beauty of that girl's eyes, he said, as he drew bubbles that rose from the young brave's mouth and filled them with whole notes. He filled hisself with so much longing he talked his friend into leaving the party and heading back to main camp.

They walked alone until they come to this lake and made a fire, though they'd nought to eat. Just then a great wave rose up out of the lake and plopped two fish flapping on shore. His friend wouldn't touch them, as they was mysterious. But that young man cooked and ate the fish. When he knelt along the sandy beach to take a drink, another great wave rose up and drug him under.

Don't feel sorry that I have been swallowed by the mystery, the young man said to his friend before he was taken to the bottom of the lake. Bring our tribe to camp along this shore, and bring my bride-to-be, if she will come with pipe and tobacco and a buffalo robe to float them on. His friend ran day and night until he fell into camp and told everyone what happened.

The girl's father said it would be alright, and the whole camp moved over to the lakeside. Next day, they sent the young woman with her father's pipe and tobacco and the buffalo robe float into the water. Then the young man rose out of the lake, took the pipe and tobacco and buffalo robe, and sunk back below the waters. That night the tribe was waked by rumblings in the lake. When they walked to its shore to find out what that noise was, they seen sparks and smoke coming out of the water. Next day after that they found their camp surrounded by buffalo, and they had a great hunt and filled their parfleches with meat enough to last a whole winter. They saw him, the underwater man, rise up, making sign that means *fill your bellies.*

That young man never did reach home, my father said with a sigh, nor did he ever rest in the arms of his young woman. He lived in that lake and turned the longing in his soul for his lost bride into medicine, so every time the tribe camped there they found another big buffalo herd. They called him "underwater man," the one who gave his life to the great mystery in that lake so his people could prosper. Sometimes, they say, as if there's some underground stream he travels by, he changes which lake he lives in. My father then scratched out that coil of pictures he'd been drawing.

What kind of story is that? I askt him. Are you telling me I must give my life up?

It's what the Lakota people would call *hanblo-glaka,* he said, a story that tells of spirits and great deeds which give heart to the people. It's not that you must give your life up, Joe Antoine. But sometimes you have to let yourself be taken into things huger than you, things that hum with the power of all life, with what Lakotas call *wakan.* To feel those huge powers take you away as if you was a little boat carried off in their bloodstream from time to time is what I come to believe life is all about, and it has nothing to do with practical things like if we survive. We don't survive those meetings with these forces. Something changes inside us, we ain't the same thereafter.

Like as if you was trying to cross a river, the
Arkansas, say, up in the mountains where it takes
its source, and it's a June rise. You have maybe a
strong horse but the current's so wild, the river's
suddenly so deep the horse steps off, plunges, and
you're ripped out of stirrup and saddle, swept
downstream toward white water and killer rocks.
Imagine I'm riding on the river bank trying to get
rope on you at just the moment you hit a sinkhole. You're trying to swim yourself free, stroking
hard, hard, but you're tiring, you can't swim free,
it's too powerful. I'm shouting to you over the
water's roar, *You have to just let yourself go down!*

When that happens, you feel small and alone.
But then the spin of that sinkhole water will take
your body as if it were lighter than some lucifer
stick, tumble and spin you out a ways downstream, and only then will you know you been
given your life that day.

I guessed at what my father meant by giving
myself up to things huger than me from playing
the fiddle, as I'd sometimes got myself into shifts
where only the music's flow took me through
changes I feared would wreck the song that was
coming to me from somewhere beyond—as if in
my brain was some echo of the first song of
creation Orpheus played before he failed his test
of faith on nearly the last step out of Hell and his
voice invented the requiem. This *wakan* my father
was talking about was beyond skill.

He said, It's what makes the river to flow, the
winds to blow, and the earth to grow living things
out of its bosom. It's *Skan.*

But more of that later. What you need now is
knowledge, he said, which you can pick up by
paying better attention. You'll note mountains
give a changed face from south and north. To
learn all sides is more of a *travaille*, but then you'll
never get lost in a land you've toiled over, when

you're opened completely to its huge lives. Time now to turn in and sleep the sleep of those who have yet to know grief, he said with a little laugh.

That first year my father brought me to the wilderness, Sublette showed up with wagons to resupply our trapping party along the Green river. My father told me in the old days there was big meetings, *rendezvous*, with scores of men, whiskey, horse racing, gunfire, wrestling. But this occasion was quiet. Once these men got their hands on bottles of liquor, they sat apart, alone, brooding, and getting meaner by the minute. Most of them knew that the beaver trade would soon end. I remember best playing some old reels on my fiddle.

The men—some, like Sefroy Iott, five years older than me, some, ten years older than me like Sam Deon, Eldridge Geary, John Provo, LeBon, Olivier Morrissette, Ravofiere, and Joe Merrivale—they did a stiff-legged *contradanse*, and clapped their hands until they began to catch the spirit, and smiled out their *joie* that usually came out only in the rhythms of their work, like how they spoke in lover's whispers to their mounts as they rubbed them down with hands full of fresh grass.

After all sounds of merriment died down my father came to me by the campfire, swigging from his stone jug, as I rubbed down my fiddle with an oiled cloth before putting it in its case. I had never seen my father so much in his cups.

You sure hump up a heap of noise off that catgut, boy, he said.

What's the matter? I asked him. Don't you like music?

Well, he said, I guess over the years I got sick of working for men like Capn Ashley who'd say, You frenchies, you're just like the blacks. You like music and dancing and making babies with the dusky maidens, don't ya? You work hard, but you can't be trusted to kill under orders, so you'll never amount to nothing on this frontier.

My father opened up a leather case and took his compass out of it.

We keep a compass, he said, in memory of all who went before us without it. Just the pole star to pin the center's northern wheel, generations of men and women who watched night skies, trying to remember the moon's changes each month, just where the Pleiades rise on the eastern horizon when spring comes and where they set when it turns for fall.

See how it fits the palm of your hand, he said. If you lose it, you can still find your way. I will teach you, but I must also run this crew of ragged men who don't have the oldtime *coeur de voyageur*. He tossed his glance over toward Mountain Phil, who lay sprawled on the ground, snoring drunkenly in a tangle of arms and legs near our campfire. It lit his half-scalped hairline and showed his sunburnt forehead, scarred as if it was the rock wall against which Moses broke those tablets on which God's commands were writ.

A man like him, my father said in his night voice, if he gets a jug of whiskey in his belly, there's no *telling* what he'll do. I been working with him long enough to know he had to run away into these mountains, parts unknown, to escape the hangman's noose.

An edge had come into my father's voice I'd never heard before. As I looked at his face then, it seemed to have swollen to some monstrous shape.

Why are you telling me this? I asked him. You talk like Mountain Phil's the bogey man.

En douce, he nearly whispered. I'm trying to save your life by teaching you what you'll face out here. What we're doing makes for strange bedfellows. The only way you'll live to tell about these

days is if you're quicker, more watchful, to get the
drop on them than they of you. Hell, a man like
Phil's a mean drunk, and there'll come a time
when I'll have to hop on a rock and snort the air
and shout, I'm a wild mountain ram! I love the
wimmin, and I'll break the nose of any man who
won't do what I say! I'll have to turn into a force,
all gristle and buckskin.

He jumped up and shook his head like some
bighorn ram in rutting time, and then he smiled
and began to sound like himself again. Sorry
about shootin' on your music, he said.

I've been at this trade *beaucoup longtemps,*
considering the hazards. I was *un homme de bateau*
on the old Mizzu before I first came out here with
Cap'n Ashley in 1826. I have my place in the
ledgers of men who fought the Rikarees and
Mandans up the Dakotas. See how these sixteen
compass points make *un rose en fleur?* This
damper lever lets its needle swing free. You have
one in your mind. Everyone does, though some
forget. Some day when you're in a bad fix, remember to let the needle in your mind swing free.

But my mind did not swing free, not at that
moment. Mountain Phil's sneer froze me solid. I
found myself going way deep inside myself, asking
a long chain of questions that flew in a stiff breeze
like strips of colored cloth in prayer flags from the
poles of some Sioux burial platform. If my father
was warning me against these men, and he was
one of them, what did that mean? That he was
warning me against himself?

I wanted to tell him that I loved him and that
I could see nothing wrong in wanting to be just
like him. But there were things a young man did
not say to his father in those days without risking
his regard, which was precious. Nothing in the
wilderness was possible without it. Now that I
look back, I know I would have kept any silence

so my father would never turn to me with a look
that said he'd decided he must bear shame at
having a son who froze in fear the first sign of
danger. I had felt to my quick that cut from my
mother, and, though it was now more than a year
since that day I told her I had prayed everyday for
one whole year for a vocation and found none,
her slice still burned fresh on my heart.

Yet what if my father like so many of these
men was himself no more than a hopeless drunk
who came out west where a desperado might find
a place for himself? What if back home in St.
Charles my father would have been no more than
a barfly? A man who couldn't farm, couldn't pay
his bills, couldn't stay out of the hoosegow on
Saturday nights to save his life and his family's
honor? Lucky for me, I was too busy working to
long entertain such thoughts.

He started me out at the bottom, *un mangeur
du lard,* waking before sunrise with wrens chirp-
ing up the new day. I made fires, carried water,
saddled horses, loaded mules, learned my les-
sons—mainly that I did not want to be at the
bottom any longer than I could help it. That feels
pretty awful. My father, as if to make up for
almost never being at home during my childhood
years, took to schooling me on every point in a
dogged way that set my teeth on edge. He said
there was a right way and a wrong way to do
everything, and I had better start learning. He
even claimed there was a right way to eat ants
should the day ever come when I was down to
ants or starving. I couldn't help but sneeze with
laughter. He got mad.

What're you laughing at? he says to me. Here,
see? You pick them up and toss them down to the
back of your throat so you won't have to chew
them and taste the juices of their bowels on your
tongue.

That's plumb ridiculous and disgusting, I said.

Eating ants the right way is not the point, he says to me, pulling himself up to his full dignity.

Well, then, what is? I askt him.

Think about it, he says. It's not eating ants the right way, or even striking a lucifer, or picking your teeth the right way. It's not just for you that you do these things right, but to have pride in yourself, so you know you're not a little boy but a man who knows he can not only do things right but that he *is* right. *Comprenez?* I don't want you to learn one right way of trapping beaver, though there is such a thing, as you well know by now. You also no doubt have figured out that the days of the beaver trade is nigh played out.

What I want you to understand goes beyond that. I've taught you how to handle horses and mules, and surely we will never see the end of the day of the horse, Joe Antoine. But even if that day should come, what I'm trying to teach you will keep you steady even as you change, as change you must because the world changes.

Think about it. How is it possible for men to get way out ahead of civilization in going into the wilderness with nothing but a few simple tools like flint and magnetized steel? It's not just the skills of foraging, the knowledge of what wild plants is edible, the knowledge to survive even on ants if we have to. It's got to do with knowing how to learn, how to read a dusty trail as deep as a priest reads a dusty book.

It goes even deeper than that, as I've tried to show you, down to the roots of who you are. You need to have pride, even if you seem a fool puffed up, or you will never be able to believe your life is real. People say, Don't take yourself too serious. I say, yes, that's good advice, but you got to take yourself serious enough. Look into yourself. What is the place where too much is balanced with not enough?

Par exemple, I ain't sayin' there's only one right way to cinch a pack animal, my father went on, but you've got to either find your own way or follow mine. Like all of his kind this mule has a nasty temper on account of he's smart enough to know he's got no future. I'd be probably like him if I was in his shoes. Haw! He can somehow puff hisself up, then some way down the trail he lets his breath out, and the cinch goes slack. Then this mule sheds his packs, and there you are gathering up your equipment on your hands and knees, and that mule's just laughing at you.

So it's your choice, Joe Antoine. You either have to keep out a sharp eye, and make smart, quick moves before he takes his breath, which is maybe your way, or kick the wind out of his ribs, which is my way. *Entendre.* We can't waste daylight waiting for you to pick up traps and repack.

I tried from that day on to grasp his meaning, paying good attention to the little details of what I did, even in cooking. For breakfast I'd whip up corn meal, flour, baking powder, one dollop of molasses, one spot of salt on my palm the size of a dollar, adding cold water till I had thick batter I fried up as pancakes in skillets greased with beavertail fat. I made sure not just to burn some meat but to roast it, and, when we had it, I brewd some green Rio coffee, packed up my traps, mounted for that day's ride, knowing it would have been harder still if this party was soldiers and had pitched tents. These men slept out in good weather and never once got sick. For years I was always down below camp along some creek washing pots, but something had changed, for now I no longer felt like some scullery slave. I

cooked, and learned to take quiet pleasure in how
the men's devouring my dishes with grunts was
their way of giving compliments to the chef.

Then one morning as first light began, I saw a
figure step from the rising fog—I didn't know
what it was at first, perhaps a doe, perhaps a spirit
forming out of the very air—which slowly became
an Arapaho woman walking into our camp with
her nose split up by a knife and uglified with long
scabs. She had the look in her eyes of someone
running from the nine fiends of Hell. My father
took pity on her, and gave her my job, though at
first she would work by my side and give me
smiles and ideas my father said I was too young
for.

What is it St. Paul says? Better to marry than
to burn? my father askt no one in particular.
A cut nose is the price any wayward wife pays
among the Arapaho. Her husband probably
decided to surprise her one day and found himself
the one surprised, he laughed. But for me it was
no laughing matter, for when I brushed up against
her as we made camp or skun out our day's catch,
I did burn.

From the first day she came to us there was
claw and fang among the men till Mountain Phil
took her to his blanket. Provo and Randall
growled like dogs but dared not trade blows with
him for her favors, for they knew he never fought
but to the death.

From time to time I've met such souls as
would take what they wanted, with no regard to
life nor limb, nor anyone else's supposed rights in
the matter—bad men I guess you would say, Mr.
Watrous, for whom it's not even brute strength or
better weapons or a smarter plan to get the drop
on others so much as just the will to force others
to their bidding. When the time comes I'll tell
you more about such ones as have crossed my

tracks. But I'd as lief be among such wolves—be they Scotsmen or Sioux—as among those who claim to be your friend, then use lawyers' fine words hidden like steel traps beneath what they call 'the fine print' to strip you naked. With a desperado, at least you know where you stand.

So, we turned our faces upland towards the San Juans through spruce forests, valleys where at night coyotes boast from hill to hill, keeping the moon's hours as it climbs the sky, setting at dawn when nearly iced beaver ponds give off mist whose drift made it easy to stay downwind as they spilt their waters into creek flats where so many elk fed I dreamt once I found an antler in a thicket of wild currant.

Its prongs pulled me like a dowsing rod toward a bull elk drinking from a brook, whose rack was the father of the one I held. I ghosted into its bones, looking out its eyes, seeing red traces of bee flight in rippled air as through a fog of blood. The pines were surrounded by a purple glow like in my childhood mountain dream. When I woke, my father said my face gave off a strange light I've always imagined was like the purple nimbus in my dreams. It went out that day, as if it was more brightness than I could then bear.

I learned to step where he stepped first time a timber rattler rose to strike me. A rhythm in my body took over, almost matching his stride, so I could walk with my head up, seeing as he saw, my mind free to feed the sun's direction, probable hours of daylight left, streams, lakes, into a map he showed me how to imagine so I'd know where the mountain passes lay, what months they were open and passable, where streams could be forded, how much water, grass, wood or buffalo chips— bois de vache, he called them—would be found at every camp, what valleys were free of snow in winter, where the drifts lay, where game trails led, which could take wagons' wheels, where tribes were at any time of year, so I could make my living trapping beaver, picking any spot where they gnawed an aspen stand near their lodge, anchoring the traps midstream with a six-foot dry stick, mounding up mud where I set iron jaws open in water deep enough to drown it, else it would crawl up on some creekside and chew its foot off to escape. I baited the pan with a drop of castoreum to fool the creature's senses with *l'amour,* or with what my father called *le semblance,* as of a more mysterious twin brother marking this nook as its own. Then I splashed my scent traces away from the creek bank, and later in the day would return looking for those sticks floating on the water to show me where the beaver's body lay.

When we stalked, my father called it observing silence. *S'observez,* he would say, with his finger to his lips, which at first confused me, for I was used to thinking of that word as meaning how carefully one would look at things rather than as in Church observing a litany or ritual or holy day. But it *was* religious almost, the way we moved, lifting our toes above and between windfall tree limbs and stones, our eyes fixed on the beaver's midpond swim with aspen branches in its cheerful-looking and industrious buck teeth.

Silence was our best friend, and I could not break it slapping black flies or mosquitos be they ever so thick and thirsty, for, as my father said, there's nothing to be done about blood-sucking insects out west. They're so big and mean, if you drive them off they just head for the hills above you and throw rocks.

My father gave me a sign—his left hand palm down above his right hand, a mime that brought to mind how beavers raise their heads at the least noise, as well as what might be thought of if we weren't observing silence and thus not tapping left fingers on the back of the right hand—their way of slapping mud or water with their tails when they sense danger.

One time I was on midnight watch. I was trying to prove to myself I could stay awake without needling myself with fantasies of being surrounded by deadly enemies. But night is blind and forgiving to what goes on in it, and I got to feeling more alone than what I could live with. So I watched shooting stars off in the northeast heavens where Perseus stands with Medusa's head, all killer snakes held out to save himself from turning to ice. I remembered school days when I read that though severed the head still had powers to turn the ones with blood in their eyes into statues of themselves, and thus eternal stars are his sculpture. I was seeing Perseus as that whole volume of sky he makes his godhood out of—and meteors the Medusa's drops of blood—when I heard a low spruce branch whish back through air and saw a feathered head moving across a line between moonlight and treeshadow.

Had I never been asleep? I'd had visions of the mountain forest at night before. But I began to move like my father taught me when we stalked beavers. There were two of them—One Feather and No Feather, I quickly dubbed them—and I waited until they were just at the edge of camp to whistle loud enough to wake the camp, loud enough for my party to rouse up quick with loaded rifles in hand, loud enough the two indians turned to look back at me, long enough my father rusht up to One Feather and strippt him of his bow and arrows before he could wrestle over it.

In the rekindled firelight they sat staring inward like to some underwater world, two Ute boys my age or younger, with blood-red, berry juice-stained faces of an age to be trying to make names for themselves. I was too, I have to admit now. They barely cast a glance my way for the one they'd heard of, the one they had to deal with, was my father. When we got them to sit beside the fire they began signing. The beaver sign first, then with the right hand straight out from his body, One Feather made the sign of go, only he extended his right arm out into a long go that said *way, way gone*—like down the spirit road. I could read it! My father watched his eyes more than his hands, though seeing One Feather point to him, then make go signs, my father shook his head *no* and pointed to the ground.

One Feather pulled his fists apart and then turned his hand into a bear paw, claws bared, and drove them home in a gesture toward my father's chest. He pointed at my father again, then drew blood with his two fingers running out of his nostrils down his chin, and formed his right hand into a cup and made to drink from it. *Go ahead, kill us. Your blood we drink.*

Se calmer, my father said as he raised his hands and shoved them down several times. You boys must learn to keep quiet. He pulled himself up, went to his trade-goods pack, and returned with two polished steel mirrors and gave one to each. When he sat crosslegged again before them, he pushed his right hand finger forward and pulled back with that finger clawed. *Take them.* My father made that downward crosshanded sign for signing and a circle with his thumb and forefinger to tell them they could use those mirrors to flash messages across whole valleys with reflected sunbeams. The boys didn't get his instructions, they just looked at themselves in the mirror and liked what they saw. My father made them the go sign, and they did, backing away, watching where he flung their weapons for them to come get the next day when we'd be gone and no blood spilled.

In fact, the next day had begun. *J'ai faim*, my
father said, slapping his belly. The feather of that
young buck reminds me of a time I was hunting
wild turkey. I caught one by the leg, and wrung
its neck, and skinned it up all nice for roasting on
my spit ...

Yes, I said, and ate it?

Naw, it et me! He roared out his laughter
holding both sides of his ribs like he'd been
waiting five years to find anyone as green as me to
tell his old jokes to, and soon the smell of roasting
meat spread through camp like false dawn's
whitening sky.

Human smells drift downwind like wet
campfire smoke tinged with sweat even through
pine forests. I strictly attended each crow's
squawks for what it said. Its call spread out over
the many circles of grass, trees, rocks, ice, sky,
warning the valley's web of lizard, antelope,
magpies lit and bobbing on sagebrush stalks like
purple whole notes about to fly.

That morning, my father told me the following: A Ute, an Arapaho, a Shoshone, some of
them can talk animal—hawk, wolf, bear, coyote.
Those who know how to change into animals in
spells to see if an enemy or an ally is near don't
tell, unless you give them tobacco or herbs you've
gathered from the foothills as their apprentice.

But I've known some who eat souls, especially
of the young. First they beguile them with visions
of a perfect world, where there are rivers that run
upstream and downstream so that the paddling
goes easy both ways, filling them with the dream
of being the genius of these visions, and once they
have them staring at this world of dreams inside
their heads so they no longer pay attention to this
world in which their bodies live, they steal up
behind them and take their souls. Though he is
no holy man of any known tribe, Mountain Phil

is such a one. *Se défendre.* Be careful. Seeking the power of endless life, such ones still must suffer the fires of the body to go out and need the fuel of others' lives to go on and on. And thus they become drunkards of the soul who are blind to how simple grass that rises each year has its own perfection.

Most medicine men and women I've known, they use spirits to make the world less hurtful, less a matter of eating souls. They call out the spirits of a place so lives can be made more abundant— richer grasses, fatter buffalo, bigger herds of horses, more plentiful game, stronger men and women and children, stronger ties between the bands and tribes.

Such is the world of conjurers—some want to trap power, some want to release power, to teach their apprentices and release them so they can practice the golden art of birthing souls—but all use the powers of beguilement. Ordinary men like us who reach their senses out can get just as much warning, though, before some Ute party comes into our firelight, like them two boys just done, wanting gifts or blood. As you can probably reckon for yourself, it's best to avoid gunplay and bloodshed if you can. Out here it just builds and builds like an avalanche down a mountainside. You kill one man and ten others leap up to prove themselves upon you.

The gifts I gave were fish hooks, sewing needles, small pieces of iron to make arrowheads from. I'd open my pack to flash my wares before them, trade spinning like river water gone 'round the bend and come back as rain. Elk robes, buffalo robes, each kept fair account of in writing, though we were only picking up the last few beaver, from Utes mostly, who knew my father's ties with tribes of the plains with whom they warred. It was part of what my father was giving me, his dying trade.

I found for myself a habit of looking back over ground we had just crossed to take a long last look at each tree or creek as I had when a boy dreaming mountains, though not as I might some treasured memento like a cameo locket of a St. Charles girl. This was when I loved the mountain forest and its animals more than human beings. Everything was *there* before my eyes and *here* inside, as if there was no *me* between. It was not hard work to learn the lay of this land and its creatures. When I looked at a lean gray wolf, I saw it—body and soul together in the same moment —not the wolf's body and some token, like its smoky blue eyes, to make me think of soul.

I even faced my fear of heights when my father dragged me out on the *passavant* of wet rock on the sheer east face of *Les Deux Oreilles,* what is now called Long's Peak, and I saw the high plains whole, saw the earth's curve, saw it covered with a deep snow that shone back sky blue and blurred the horizon so I confused earth and sky as tongue and palate of one huge mouth that swallowed me. The winds tore at my buckskins. My father shouted over the roar as he pointed east, the direction of St. Louis. That's where factories wed humans to machines and make them slaves of time, he shouted, while we are free to live on the earth God, not man, created for these few decades when John Jacob Astor and the lords of the earth still have a use for men like us who ain't forgot the old forest way.

I hardly heard him. All my attention was wobbly and zinging like plucked pizzicato in the backs of my knees. Yet I recall in that high place where pins of snow stung my face he said, Adam and Eve's children will soon begin to mass out

here and act out their only story once again,
spoiling every paradise so that those they call
heathens will learn to need a Redeemer.

April 23, 1884
Pine Ridge Agency

"Where Your Own Stick Floats"

So—as I was about to write before light failed yesterday and, as my father used to say, it waxed so cold words froze in mid-air and could be crated up and sent off like freight and later melted down so the words would sound five hundred miles away—the mountains and plains become spots like stone altars, where to this day candles burn in my memory.

Each niche has its story. Yet even these vast, white beauties of winter and *l'hivernaut's* life can come to hurt. In North Park where I watched storms roll in from fifty miles away, their undersides black as they unloosed snow in long slants, we bent back aspen saplings, tied them into wickiups with leathern string cut from buckskin fringe, chinked their bark sides with mud, so we had a shelter where we ate, slept, and scraped the fat off prime winter beaverskins that fetched the highest price since they had longer, darker, shinier fur, free of summer bugs. We stretched their hides on willow hoops for drying by firelight those long nights. I tossed raw strips of beavertail fat into the flames to see them flare as my father told tales.

I recollec', he'd always start, taking on that Kaintuck twang he'd picked up from his trapper friends over his Creole accent: I was with Milt Sublette and Joe Meek one time we run this bear into a cave only to find its whole family in there.

We stops stock still, and backs out, slow. It was keep *our* eyes locked on the bears' eyes or break the spell.

Outside, Joe says, you two run back inside and taunt a bear 'til it chases you out. I'll lug your rifles to the pulpit rock above that cave's mouth and blast 'em when they chase out on yer tails.

Consider this, Joe Antoine, he said laughing: the clever ones draw up the plans and let others take the risks.

I walks into the cave and of course picks out the smallest of the three, and shouts any silly thing. *Oaf! Failed human!* shifting my feet, leaning as if to bolt for light until the bear catches on and chases me outside, where Joe shoots it. Then, the next second, Milt's bear, though it couldn't have been, for Joe had to drop one rifle, pick up another, aim, and fire.

Bearding the bear in its own den is story enough in its own right, seems to me. But if all we're doing is going 'round the same stories, I figure we're lost and mought's well admit to it instead of going off so vainly about the progress we're making. The native tribes are then only lost tribes of Philistines or Midians, worshipping old gods, fit only to be crushed for Jehovah's glory. Psalmists would have only one burden to their song: God wants them to worship Him or die! We would learn nothing from these people. To survive, you'll need sharp-honed senses, and a mind quick enough to pick up every sign—in house, tipi, cave or open sky. Those were the kind of stories my father told me during the winter months around the fire.

That January there come a snow so heavy all game but a few mountain sheep moved down canyon, and we had precious little meat. A notion took me to go over to Mountain Phil's camp that morning after the blizzard to see if the Arapaho woman wanted supplies, as I still fancied her and wondered after her welfare, living as she did with a man like Mountain Phil.

I snowshoed under thin blue skies that shone like the world was new. What high clouds there was gave off this feathery mother-of-pearl glow. Stellars jays fluttered fine sprays of snow-dust from ponderosa boughs down on my shoulders as they twittered and chased one another. Aside from that there was almost perfect silence, a little breeze maybe, a small gurgling of a stream in the places where the water wasn't flowing under ice.

When I reached the edge of Phil's camp I could see him through the bare aspens hunched over a snowpile with his skinning knife in his right hand outside his wickiup, his hair all down over his eyes more like a wild animal's than some man's. When he heard my cough, he sprung up quick, trying to hide the knife, kicking drifts on that pile, but no quicker than my eye, which lit upon the Arapaho woman's naked ice-blue foot sticking up out of the snow. This was the woman whose full lips had once aroused my first lust.

You jist keep yore eyes whar yer own stick floats, boy, he says. It ain't what you think. He took a step toward me.

I askt 'er fer 'er life, and she give it— not like a cow—but fightin' me, knife in hand, cuttin' me good 'til I bested 'er. He took another step.

This were not tame meat, boy. It were her heart brimmin' with the furies that I tuck inside m' belly. Can you feel it still in me?

Nothing I'd ever placed on the map in my mind matched the strangeness I then felt. I heard tell of cannibalism up here in the mountains, but to run up against it was another thing altogether. Facing this man was like standing on cliff edges. I felt my blood freeze solid in my veins. No word I could use would reach him in this fever.

I heard my father's voice reminding me about the compass needle he said I had inside my mind, and something freed up and begun to flow again like a winter stream under a warm chinook wind. I pulled my hammer back until I heard it cock. I'm leaving now, without the question put, I says.

Phil stared at me with his crazy animal eyes. All there is is life and death and the blood that flows betwixt 'em, boy. You bitter git off one clean head shot, fer if you miss I'll be on ya!

I could scarcely find the words to say, Don't follow me.

But he did. He must've hid behind tree and stone, for when I finally turned my face toward my father's camp he jumped me and knocked the rifle from my numb hands, sending it sliding a long ways downhill. There I lay with my face in snow and Mountain Phil on top of me, tearing at my britches.

What are you doing! I yelled.

Let's jist say I'm larnin' you a lesson, he says.

To become his pupil would surely make an end of me, I knew. My lungs burned from heavy breathing, my head seemed to spin as if my whole body was tumbling. Though out of breath from my awkward struggle in snowshoes I reached down to my right ankle where I kept my skinning knife strapped to my legging, pulled the long blade, and with a wide arc back around me stabbed him deep in the side.

Ah! he cried, as if steel were what he'd spent half his life wanting.

As I tried to squirm out from under him, he tried again to lock me in his arms, so I hit him once more, only this time higher up, in the ribs below his armpit. He let go of me.

I gained my feet, pulled up my buckskins and turned to look at him. He was smiling this peculiar way I only ever saw on a man's face but once again, and then a slash of blood flowed from the left corner of his mouth down his black and silver beard and throat. He let out this long breath, and was still. Large flakes of snow began to break upon his face. I looked up, and the sky was black again and a wind was beginning to drive clumps of snow sideways off tree limbs.

I lunged downhill, picked my rifle up, and jogged back to camp to tell my father what had happened.

Didn't I warn you to stay clear of him! he shouted.

It wasn't him I went to see, I said, trying to explain myself. I'm not stupid, you know. You told me often enough what a bad sort Phil is. It ain't as if I harbored some notion that he really was a good chap with a bad reputation, or that he used the arts of beguilement on me as you once said with tales of how he come to have his face all scarred up from fighting bears. I knew he was a mean drunk, but you never said nothing about him being a cannibal.

Cannibal?

He killed the Arapaho *klooch* he took up with this summer, I said, with tears in my eyes.

And he et her? my father askt.

I nodded yes.

O, Jesus, he said.

We went back to Mountain Phil's camp that afternoon, still shaking from cap to boots. Some fool idea lingered in my brain we'd bury him and his Arapaho *klooch* side by side, only when we got there we scoured about the place and could only find small traces of blood but not his body. That storm had already dropped several inches of fresh snow. Had he been playing possum? Had he somehow hauled himself down off that mountain?

This is damn bad business, my father said through his teeth.

I had never seen him so worried. I don't mind admitting, Mr. Watrous, I felt a little crazy trying to account for what'd happened. Was I mistaken that I had killed Mountain Phil? Did that mean some day I would run into him again?

All my questions were answered when we kneeled to look inside his wickiup. There he was, sitting upright on an Arapaho backrest already stiff from that icy air, his eyes still open. My father drew down his eyelids, and we walked away, leaving everything the way it was. Wolves would take their bodies, tear them hip from thigh until their bones were scattered so far I nor anyone would ever find them. My heart leapt up in victory. I knew I was changed, the ice was filtered from my blood, and I saw my boyhood fall from me that day like baby teeth from my head.

Night after night, afterwards, as I stared at flames in the wickiup fire, a heat that glowed in my belly said the die was cast, that I'd lifted my hand against an older man, no matter that he was one of those who just took what he wanted from his neighbors and broke that bond of love Jesus taught. If my heart had leapt up the day before, now it shook in fear, for in those night winds I thought I could hear Phil calling after me like a jay through the trees. Boy? Don't ye be jedgin' old Phil. Ain't no law out here, boy!

I worried myself. If you've killed a man, you're marked like Cain, I reasoned like a Jesuit. Still, I sweated with the idea that it was me or him, even as I imagined Phil's ghost stalking me so the pure white of snow-covered meadows echoed with coyote howls out of their bloodshot-eyed hunger like stragglers on a deathwatch that was his ghostly moan.

I fell sick with these many questions, lay in a pile of skins in fever, waked once in a while by my father who'd pour hot wild-rosehip tea down my parched throat, but mostly, he told me later, it was me raving in a dream of lean cattle, their plodding hooves carrying them inside their duststorm close enough to begin devouring fat buffalo on the prairie grasslands, that herd of cattle like one huge mouth. I let out a scream that even woke me from my worst nightmare when I saw two animals stand up on their hind legs, and it was Mountain Phil letting drop his cattleskins and his Arapaho *klooch* letting drop her buffaloskins, and they came at each other biting.

When I awaked, I seemed to have grown more solid in my body, bathed in the salt of my penance. It was near spring, and my head cleared enough to consider that, though I had no idea what would later befall me, matters like these seldom get tied off in one knot, so I'd best keep my eyes open for the next thread of it to show.

There is a photograph of me with some of my Oglala friends and relatives—Yellow Bear, He Dog, Young Man Afraid of His Horses, Sword and others. I observe in that picture I have the same distant look in my eyes as they. That stare is I believe into our mind's night prairies where the memories of what we've done to stay alive are stored. Like a small fire in our belly that sends up a smoky sadness born from some mystery that in this world where we are all spirits and all rightly seen the children of spirits, we lift our hands against each other as if history were nothing but the chronicle of the thrashings-about of the pain-blinded. I saw it in a fever dream, this line of us, travelers going single-file through thickets. Branches snap back and lash the eyes of those behind, who place their anger not back to where they got it but to whoever's nearest by, who in their turn misplace it. On and on that caravan of us sinners on a holy crusade plods across the land, our weapons shining like pewter lances that shred the moon.

My father headed us from what is now called Seven Utes east through Cameron pass with pack mules all groaning under ninety-pound stacks of pelts, over Poudre falls, through its granite narrows, its wide meadows, its flood plains where yucca, sage, mullein rod, angel-wing cactus were stirring beneath the purple strewd catkins of cottonwoods and willows, and out to Poudre valley with its broad green rolling prairie. It was the loveliest spot I had ever seen.

What Mountain Phil had become was my hardest lesson. My father said, Well, now you know the worst a man can be. These mountains are magical. In them a poor man may be avenged, or a saint turn scoundrel. Some men do well by others. Some do harm. Some do harm to no one but themselves. What will it be with you, Joe Antoine? From what I hear in the sound of your story, you handled yourself like a man against Phil that day. You're going to be alright.

I was proud when my father said those words, yet sometimes since I've wondered if I am alright, or if Mountain Phil did damage to my soul. Like an avalanche damming up my river, he made the watchful one inside me, ever vigilant for someone hurt and panicky, out of control, so that only when he is asleep can I dream those mountain valleys I went through that day, wondering how the Poudre can keep on flowing, how there can be that much snowmelt, feeling I have my human place beside mountains and rivers with lives so much huger than me.

In Mountain Phil I had seen a man who sucked human light down the strings of his eyes and gave me times so confusing all I hoped for was one glimpse of a stick floating on my own waters to tell me where my soul was.

For we do grieve when youth passes, as if our soul split like lips raw from winter air. And we wonder if there's any balm to heal those open wounds. I couldn't help considering that if I'd only kept my eyes on where my own stick floats I wouldn't have struck Mountain Phil with my knife twice. Now, as I ponder that sad event when my own life did not seem real, I recall another story my father told me.

Seems when the Cheyenne first came out on the western plains they scouted up and down the land to learn the length and breadth of it. One day they came across another tribe also traveling across the prairie, and so soon as they both spotted each other their chief fighters galloped up and down among their ranks shouting for all to prepare themselves for battle. Neither one knew the others' intent, so it was wisest to be wary.

Then the young warriors began to shout insults across the distance and stand on their horses' backs as they galloped in a fine display of trick riding, jerking their breechclouts at each other. This would have gotten even more witty and killing except one Cheyenne chief suddenly called out, Hey! Listen to the words these strangers hurl at us. And everyone went silent.

What they heard was their own language, Cheyenne. They made signs of peace to those others, got off their horses, walked up to them, and sat down in a circle and began to light and pass the pipe and talk with these others. How could it be? they asked each other. Do you have a story of a lost tribe? they asked each other. No, they said—and yet they understood each other perfectly.

It was a miracle of speech, and I imagine the coming together of a torn soul to be like that—a moment when your soul becomes one and your life is suddenly real again and what happens is not always war. To your new adulthood, your passed childhood becomes like a lost tribe that speaks the same language and becomes an ally. My father had said, You're going to be alright, Joe Antoine, and now what he meant has come to me.

I stuck my stake on a claim in the valley the first of June, 1844, intending that the location along the north bank of the Poudre would be my home should the country ever be settled. It was where my father'd cached the poudre and named that river back in 1828, not 1836, on a mapping expedition with Capt. Ashley. Or so my father told me. Seems he and his companion, a mulatto named Jim Beckwith, was in danger from this terrible snowstorm and a band of Arapahos that hadn't yet gone south to their winter camps along the Cimmaron. My father thought it best to bury that powder lest it fall into their hands.

It could've been another of his tales, Mr. Watrous, but maybe someday if I'm ever back down your way, I'll take you to that spot where my father showed me he and this black man in his party dug the cache into the Poudre's south bank, if the railroad company will let us on their land.

I took Ab Loomis there once. It ain't much. Across the Poudre from my homestead on this grassy rise, with cottonwood branches fallen down in there and round river stones driven up in there by flood waters, there's a hole some six foot long, four foot wide, maybe six foot deep, like an open grave filled with rotting leaves, giving off a must from its warm dark. When I go there I feel I'm close to my father's spirit, which remains a mystery to me, especially if I ponder the predicament it seems he planned all along to throw me into next.

April 27, 1884
Pine Ridge Agency

"Sign Talker"

You inquire as to my relations with those native tribes that lived in Poudre valley. To tell you how they began is to tell you how they've pretty well rocked along since.

Though my father and I camped miles to the north up Box Elder canyon, we could hear distant drums beat a steady call to grand council along the Poudre, and we decided to ride on down there to see what was doing.

We rode to the west end of Owl canyon, taking a view of the snow-covered Never Summers, and after we turned south past them long limestone palisades that run north and south some several miles—you know where I mean, what you would call the south end of Laramie plains and we called Cherokee pass—we heard suddenly the hooves of maybe thirty horsemen bearing down on us in full gallop, and we looked a glance at each other that said we thought it smart to light out ahead of them, just in case.

As we sped toward Bellevue and its wide grassy meadows where the Poudre river flows out of its foothills winding its way around the big hogbacks that are the first foothills, we could see we had joined without at first knowing it a pick-up horse race among Arapaho, Cheyenne, and Oglala braves.

The whole valley to the north filled with dust from their horses' hooves as they bore down on us in waves, one group now surging ahead, only to fall back and be passed by another, the whole pack yipping and howling grace notes over the snare drum of unshod hooves.

The boys were soon catching up and one Oglala charged past us, feathers flying. But just as we broke around the last escarpment in sight of the large camp on the meadows by the river at the foot of the hogback they used for buffalo runs and could hear crowds cheering, that lead racer's pony stumbled in a prairie dog hole near this block of limestone the size of a sod house sitting where it must've landed after rolling downhill off that escarpment who knows how long ago, and he went tumbling head and heels. He would have been out of the race except with my blood up I spurred my pony on and held out my arm and slung him up behind me, and without missing a beat I swung my leg over its withers and leapt off.

He was still far enough ahead that he entered camp first, and took the honors. Though there was some grumbling among the other racers, it was silenced by Old Man Afraid of His Horses, who said what mattered was who crossed the finish line first, not whether one racer changed horses. A fine buffalo robe was the prize, which this young Oglala tried to give me in thanks. I told him I didn't like being chased down and caught from behind, and that was my reason for helping him.

His name was Swift Hawk, he said, oldest son of the Oglala chief, Smoke. As we strolled together through the busy camp, cooling my horse down under the shade of cotton woods, my father called out to us, *kola!* which meant we had acted together as friends and so won the race.

Seems I'd made a new friend, and soon we were standing before what must've been his tipi, or his father's. The tipi flap swung open, and a young woman stepped out. This is my sister, First Elk Woman, Swift Hawk said. She wore a white buckskin dress with small blue beads woven in, and she had long shiny black braids down her front, meaning she was of an age to be married. She gave me this from-down-under look with bright dark eyes in an oval face that held the expression of an angel of deliverance. Those eyes changed my world. She was the loveliest Sioux woman I'd ever seen. Swift Hawk coughed and nudged me with this look that reminded me it was bad manners to stare.

The rest of the afternoon wherever I went in that camp I kept getting glimpses of her and three other young women among crowds of whole families who came weeping into their arms. It appeared she was mistress of their ceremonies of grief and what they called the day of releasing souls.

When he saw I couldn't take my eyes off his sister, Swift Hawk laughed. I know a great holy man, he said. For the gift of one buffalo robe he will make you a charmed eagle-bone whistle to court my sister with.

Bring me to him, I said, I wish to become a student of his powers. Ah, Swift Hawk says, I see. Your interest in my sister is ... ah, religious! I gave him a smirk.

Well, you will also need a new blanket. If she likes you she will show it by letting you wrap it around her as you talk.

That I have myself, I said.

My father and I were seated that night, facing east, inside the main circle of the great council. Drums that spoke their tribal names—Arapaho,

O*gla*la—stopped. White eagle pinfeathers on
chiefs' headdresses glinted in firelight as if their
minds threw off a glow.

I was lost, staring at one brave's facepaint.
Thirteen red stripes from jaw to jaw, wriggling
like snakes. All I could think was, *Thunder Mouth.*

My father rose to speak. He said I was of his
blood, *hoksila,* firstborn son, and he wished them
all to hear me. Swift Hawk placed their redstone
pipe in my hands. My chest cinched tight as I
stood to speak in the halting Sioux I scavenged
one word at a time like some magpie building its
nest, twig by twig. I signed as I told them that as a
child in a dream I'd made tracks into the high
country to lament for a vision and dreamed as I
kept to the shadows of tall ponderosa that I was a
bull elk that saw the red traces bees leave as they
pass through forest air. And when I woke a light
came from my face like that thrown off by every
tipi in this great *ti-ton-wan.*

We are messengers like the smoke between
parts of the great mystery, I said. How I made
sign for that, Mr. Watrous, is by shoving the heel
of my palm outward from my chin, waving my
fingers like the grouse waves its tail feathers in his
mating dance and raising them up above the fire. I
blew puffs to the four winds, their gods below and
above, making sign for *wakantanka,* my hands
held out before my waist, then widened, my right
hand spiraling upward, tracing a story that might
have said that the gods had once been earthly
beings who rose like smoke to the sky.

When I sat down, my father stood to speak
again. Many winters ago, he said, I gave my word
to Old Smoke that instead of whiskey for buffalo
robes I would train a sign-talker to be with you as
more and more whites come into your lands. I
have kept my word. This young man is the one I
promised.

It was as if he drew his skinning knife across
my palm and set my fate.

My head spun from kinnickinnick. At last I
saw the plan behind all my father's teachings. My
new life was now a crowd of Oglala braves em-
bracing me, calling me Shadow Boy, calling me
Yellow Hair All Mussed Up. That night before
sleep I told my father, Things turn out in funny
ways. I remember when I was a boy Memé would
get tired of me daydreaming down among the
woods not doing my chores. She'd yell, "I'm
giving you back to the Indians!" And isn't that
what has happened? Only it's not her but you
that's given me back to the Indians, though I was
never theirs to begin with, was I? I was yours,
right, and Memé's? Sometimes I think I don't
know who I am or where I come from. I don't
know if I have what it takes to ... What *do* you
expect me to do among these tribes?

Save them....

Save them? And how am I supposed to do
that?

By holding them together, my father said.

I'm a weak vessel to hold such strong waters, I
argued. My dream told me the lean cattle will
devour the fat buffalo. No one can stop that. Why
would you ask me to do this thing that's only
going to get harder with each year until it's
impossible?

What voice have you been listening to, he
wondered. You spoke well tonight. The braves
shouted three times, once when you said "smoke,"
their old chief's name. Listen to this world, not *le
pauvre perdu.* You can name yourself only once.
Who you are is what you choose, and what you
choose is how you see—for that is how you know
what is and who is most important to you, your
strongest desire, what you'll trade all the rest for.

The young men like Red Cloud fight among

themselves. That's what will defeat them, not the army dragoons. Didn't Jesus say, Blessed is the peacemaker? You can hold them together if you have their respect.

What do you think you, me, and the old free trappers are doing out here? Consider this: in Massachusetts flowing river water drives textile looms by pulleys made from buffalo hides, which last much longer than any fabric belt. Between these tribes and the jobbers back East is our place. Between is where we have placed ourselves. If there's no Sioux to trade buffalo hides with, there's no place for us. So we must save them or we cannot save ourselves. Tomorrow, we shall see what we shall see.

Had I been listening to the voice of *le pauvre perdu* with his father six hundred miles away, wondering—since he has had no one to teach him—if he will pass life's test when it comes? Or was it Mountain Phil's voice I heard, ringing through leafless aspens like a stellars jay, frightening me with the face of what I might also become.

I couldn't speak any reproach for my father leaving me at home when I was but a tot at my mother's fire. What mattered most was how I acted now. I knew the Oglala ask four things from a man: courage in battle, grace in victory, straight talk in all his dealings, and the power of fathering. My father taught me to tell my intended what I was—a *coureur de bois*—to see if she could live with that, and then to live by her decision.

I saw you staring at this First Elk Woman all afternoon, he said. You will find an Oglala woman takes well her husband's need to travel. Remember the story I told you about the Cheyenne underwater man.

If you need family history to know who you are, go back to your grandfather Nicholas who left

Canada to fight English troops in Kaskaskia,
Ohio, in the War of Independence. Never let any
man, regardlesss of your accent, tell you you're
not an American. Or you can go back to Adam
who fathered us all and remember Eve, so
irresistable it must be that God wants us to fall
into a woman's flesh and beget more flesh. That is
man's second baptism in fire—he must grunt in
lust and sin and learn to love the future.

You go back to a race of forest people who
danced and made ceremonies like the Sioux, way
before the new priests came, carrying their
wooden cross, marching like soldiers in their
woolen robes. You have dancing in your blood,
and you'll dance with the best of them because
you remember that living tree before the wooden
cross was hewd from its side. Our people went
from dancing to stepping lightly off of wooden
ships into the Canadian wilderness and nothing
really changed about us.

The ones who lived in the European forests
were outside the law of towns and lords and
castles and bent the knee to no one. Nor did they
fear any man's sword. They had the art of disappearing. They were slippery as pond frogs.

All things form one circle under God, so what
is there to fear? That much I have learned from
the Lakota, Cheyenne, and Arapaho. It's always a
good day to die when generous hearts go to live
among spirits in the mountain forests after death.
So, if their gods call them home, they will answer,
I am here. They welcome even ghosts when they
arise. No belief is mad, no custom is so strange,
no enemy so hardened as may not become your
friend. We are all brothers and sisters. You may
rest your head on that.

I opened my eyes the next morning on my
father's face. No less than Red Cloud has agreed

to Swift Hawk's proposal that you be married to
First Elk Woman as one way these Oglalas can
take you into their band, he said.

She is *lela wakan,* one of four virgins who eats
food purified by sage smoke at their ceremonies of
releasing the souls of their dead. Their custom is
kind. They may entertain their recent dead at
their fires for one year before they must say
goodbye. She is the one who drinks chokecherry
juice that stains her mouth the color of the good
road. She places the buffalo robe on the soul post
for those who grieve to hug and say farewell as
holy men chant, *Go sacred as you travel on the
spirit road.* And you are free to bring her bride-
price, which will be my wedding gift to you—six
good horses, a good rifle, and one pound each of
lead shot and dry powder.

The Oglala way is this, he said. Many women
with a man have seen their sisters carried off in
raids by Crows and Pawnee. If a man wants to
keep his woman, he must be ready to fight. This
alone changes things between a man and woman.
A man can see what in a woman is precious. He
knows he cannot get anywhere with threats. He
knows both must agree. Too many dangers lie in
wait outside their tipi to bring them in where they
eat, sleep, and make talk together.

Never speak of making love with her to her
menfolk or they will take a quirt to your face.
Such talk is forbidden. This brings peace within
the family. But first, he said, go walk with her,
take her down along the Poudre tonight of all
nights because on this night after the ceremony of
releasing souls custom says a young man and
woman who are to be married may meet alone
briefly with no scandal to their families. Ask
yourself how you two feel together. Try to like
her, he laughed. It will be for the best, since you
can not well refuse this gift.

It's time you womaned anyhow, he went on. You can shoot plumb center, but an Oglala woman can make game walk right up to your gunsight, what with her singing antelope charm songs. Your lean-to is one poor makeout, leaky, cold, open to the wind, and where's the fire for hot soup when you come in at night half froze to death, your fingers too numb to strike a light?

The tipi she'll bring as dowry is a damn sight better. You want an Oglala woman for your wife when you're out here. She can pack horses, butcher buffalo, make mocassins and pemmican, ride all day, then give birth after sundown. *Elle est une femme de tête, Antoine.* Besides, you'll find it a heap easier to keep your hair if their braves know you're married in. Later, when you go back to St. Charles or St. Louis and some settlement girl like your mother should strike your fancy, why then you can marry her in Holy Mother the Church and live the two lives of *un voyageur* like me.

Now that I think back on it, I see that all along there'd been something building inside me, something that told me I was never going back to St. Charles. So, I summoned all my gumption to say, I don't *want* to live two lives like you. You've given me to these people, I might as well stick.

You don't need me anymore, then.

Those were the last words I ever heard from my father's lips.

I didn't know that then. Instead I busied myself with the task of courting First Elk Woman, and that very night we strolled down by the river bank together until we found this little spot among the willows where I took my fiddle from out my pack and played a slow ballad I knew called "The Ohio," and sang to her. Only it was my version, changing a few key words.

I sang like a rooster who thinks his call is mighty clever,

I askt my love
to take a walk,
And as we walked
we had a talk,
Down by the banks
where the waters flew,
Down by the banks
of the Cache le Poo.

She smiled and laughed at me and held her hands
over her ears. I think the sound appealed to her,
but I played too loud and blushed at my mistake.
She finally said, I like you.

The thought comes to me now that my life
changed that night. I was a man so in love he pays
no nevermind to old sayings, and changes horses
in midstream.

Yet from time to time Poudre canyon's
tangled groves and slants of green sunlight have
lived as aspen and alder in my dreams. Very few
humans have ever entered there. My father's one.
I've seen him chased by this molasses-colored bear
through a grove of cottonwood and across that
graveled bend at that Arapaho camp where Box
Elder creek merges into the Poudre. His arms are
pumping, yet he's smiling, even as he runs in his
thin mocassins through prickly pear, his tongue
lolling out like some Cheyenne camp dog. What
to make of it?

Did he enjoy the chase more than he feared
the slam to earth from behind, that bear knocking
his wind out before snapping his neck with a blow
of its huge paws? Was he that much of a force?
Only once in a while when I've played my fiddle
have I touched the winds that shook my father's
soul.

Was I babbling when I told that council we
are messengers like the smoke? Could I be their
courier between parts of one great mystery? Might
I fail to deliver? A bear might fell me, or I might

not interpret right, or I might lose my heart for the way.

Could I will myself into that underwater forest of human dreamers to set white clocks to Lakota winter counts? Could I give up my former life, my privacy? Give up my plans to hunt for gold for this life as a messenger? Was I mad?

June 9, 1884
Pine Ridge Agency

LETTER V

"Roots or Claws"

First Elk Woman and I were wed this
very summer forty years ago, standing before Red
Cloud's tipi that was painted fresh as that July
morning with two rainbows, two buffalos, two
sundogs.

The only cloud was that my father slipped out
of camp before dawn that day. I could picture
him plodding north to the Wind Rivers through
the valley west of the Medicine Bows, then up
toward the Gallatin to the Mizzu, then downriver
to settle accounts with my mother, smoking his
pipe by the fireplace, playing papa in St. Charles,
living his two lives, paying tribute from these
mountains to what of the old country still beat in
his heart, paying for a stained-glass window of
that Station of the Cross where Roman soldiers
with their whips and swords make Simon the
Cyrenian carry Christ's cross. My father'd told me
that window would be his memorial to his family
name in St. Joseph's Church, so he would be
lettered in St. Peter's golden book, mindful all the
while what Jesus said about it being easier for rich
men to pass through the eye of a needle. Then he
would bring my brother Nick out west as he had
brought me.

This time he meant to disappear, not like that
first year when I woke to find the camp broke for
high timber. I was but a pup and found that what

above all else I had to do was sit down by the smoking ring of stones to calm my racing blood and to find that compass needle that swung free in my mind.

When I could breathe slow and deep, I stood up and took my bearings. All I need do was find the first print and I could track them until I caught up. When I galloped across a mountain meadow with my horse and mules all jangling behind me like a carnival parade, he sang me *Frère Jacques* all day, glad secretly I'd passed his little test. But this was bedrock. I was on my own. He had abandoned me once and for all. My meat was thrown cold. Who would now be my guide, and my friend? *Sonnent les matines.* Morning bells were ringing, indeed.

Red Cloud placed my hands inside First Elk Woman's. She looked up at me with bright brown eyes that swirled with fear—and lust. I begun to breathe hard and fast of a sudden, as if traversing a mountain pass where I could see sharp deep drops and stones with edge enough to peel my skin from my bones so the man I might become could step out, like a medicine dancer who throws down his skin of bear.

A flutter in my chest flew out of me and lit on her shoulder. I knew I would never go back to Missouri. The yoke of her new elkskin dress was colored white and black and red and blue with stained quillwork for each of the four winds of the world. This was my chance to live one life, one love, one land, though I had no sense whatever then of those angels who wrestled inside me.

Swift Hawk and Red Cloud led us on horse-back four times around the Oglala camp with all their friends and relatives walking behind us. When we stopped, it was at our new tipi. We swung our right legs over and slid off our horses and entered, stooping through the doorflap

marked with the sign of Buffalo Woman, surrounded by an oval of porcupine quills, as if to
say, *This is Her lodge. Come in and go out under
Her blessing.* She led me to the honored place,
opposite the door flap, took off my old mocassins,
put new ones on my feet, then she gently pushed
on my shoulders until I lay flat on my back. Then
she held her hands above my body as if she would
touch my ribs. It's alright to touch me, I said. I
won't break.

She laughed. In the old days when we first saw
you white men, the people thought you all were
wakan. But now we know better. I want a man,
not a god.

Staring into my eyes, she said, I see your
father on horseback riding his way north through
Wind River canyon. Laying her hands upon my
ribs then, she asked, Are those roots or claws I feel
inside your body?

As I wondered how she knew to ask, she took
hold of the birthmark patch of hair on my back
with her hands still painted red as she was allowed
to since she had performed ceremonies.

You think I married you because you made a
good speech in council? No, it's this touch of the
beast that grows on your back that I want next to
me on cold winter nights, she said with a smile.

Then she got a more serious look as she drew
herself up to sitting with her ankles neatly together on her right side on our new robes.
Mihingna—this was I recall the first time she
addressed me as husband—if the Oglala do not
prosper, our children will suffer. I remembered
then what my father said about why he and I were
out here between the Oglalas and the people back
East. If there are no Sioux to trade buffalo robes
with, there is no place for us.

At our wedding, she said, I stood with my two
brothers and my father. *O-weh,* I said, then stood

beside you and said, *o-weh-ya,* now of our blood,
not what you were, *o-ya-te un-ma,* outside our
blood. We are *Itesica* Oglala, Bad Faces. We are
called that from the winter Iron Crow calls *itmoni
kici ktepi,* when *Mahpiua Luta,* Red Cloud, killed
Bull Bear along Chugwater Creek. John Reeshaw,
the trader for Pratt and Carbanne, came around
often and gave whiskey away to all Oglala men.
Bull Bear took Reeshaw's whiskey and turned
mean, shouting at everyone to do what he said,
taking women without ceremony or proper gifts.
Smoke, my father—Red Cloud's father, too,
though his mother is different—was put forward
by some in our band as one they would rather
have as chief. Bull Bear was enraged when he
heard that and came to Smoke's tipi, calling him
out. But Smoke stayed inside.

Bull Bear went crazy. He stabbed Smoke's
best war horse—tethered to a post outside his
tipi—until the poor animal fell dead. Bull Bear
might as well have driven his knife-blade into
Smoke's heart. That was in the year Iron Crow
calls *Sunka wakan opanwinge awicapglipi*—They
brought home many horses from raids against
Pawnee camps.

Next summer, Bull Bear rode in with six
young men and began drinking with Red Cloud
and his men. Bull Bear saw another woman he
wanted and before long a fight broke out. Red
Cloud hit Bull Bear on the head with a war club.

Help me keep Red Cloud from bad whiskey.
What he did drunk he may yet undo sober. That
is my hope, she said.

My full brother Swift Hawk and I are older
than Red Cloud. One of our customs says Swift
Hawk should be chief when Smoke goes down the
spirit road, yet Red Cloud has changed our name
and set our path.

I could frame no idea of Oglala tribal politics.

All I thought of was some dark plot to kill the rightful heir I might have read in some medieval history. I askt her, Is chieftainship handed down father to son?

It can be, she said. But the story I told you about Red Cloud killing Bull Bear shows how proud the Oglalas are. They do not like being ordered about by any chief. A chief is someone chosen for his love of the people and his skills. But it's only human that whoever is best at moving camp or hunting or war or medicine will naturally be looked to for leadership. Red Cloud is a strong, fierce fighter, and we are used to war with the Crows and Pawnees, and now with the whites. That's why I wonder if he can long be kept from the chief's *wakiconze* lodge.

Think on it, she said. Red Cloud killed Bull Bear for being mean, bad-tempered, a man who took women. Have you not seen it happen that such men in later years often become the very thing they fought against in their youth? War may not always be the best way.

Had I foreknown how hard it would be to escape being held by the tongs of my pledge to First Elk Woman and her family between Red Cloud's hammer and the anvils of Swift Hawk and Young Man Afraid of His Horses, I might have carried First Elk Woman off rather than be married before her family. A man's not as be-holden to his woman's family if she'll run off with him.

I was given a great Buffalo Maiden day, she said. My father gave a special feast for everyone at my ceremony. The Buffalo Dreamer burnt sage to drive away Iya and any bad thoughts the Crazy Buffalo might give me. He reminded me that a good woman is like the spider who works hard to give her young ones a home and also like the turtle who is a strong shield to her husband because she listens much and says little and also like the lark who makes her whole life a song. That is the hardest thing for me. Often I am tempted to speak out when my elders tell me I should hold my peace.

I was given a new dress, and the holy man prayed over me, saying I would always be the sits-beside-him wife, no matter if my husband should take another, because no word of scandal had ever been held against me, and I had never had to bite the knife. He fixed a plume in my hair so that I would be touched by the spirit of the eagle, and I would receive the blessing of the sun. He gave me a staff of carved cherrywood to help me find wild plums, and chokecherries to make *wasna* and for long life, so that even when I am old I will be the sits-by-the-door woman who keeps her eyes and ears sharp and is still of use to her family.

She put her arms around my neck and held me close to her bosom with a look filled with expectation. What are you waiting for? she askt me.

I don't know what to do, or how, I said. My father didn't tell me about this.

She laughed at my little joke. Since you father didn't tell you what to do, or how, I will tell you. Your duty is to make me happy in as many ways as possible, and my duty is to urge you on.

She took hold of me in such a way that my blood quickened from my toes to my scalp as if my entire body was blushing.

It is also my duty, she said, to laugh at you. I can see even now how *serious* you are about all your manly duties.

Have we begun yet?

Not even, she said. That first day, that first look that passed between us. We begin then. If you had the nerve to speak to me that day, what would you have said?

All I will say further of this subject, Mr. Watrous, is that I have been answering her that question all the rest of my life.

In the days that followed, First Elk Woman helped me find paints with which to mark our tipi, and what could I paint but this vision I'd had in my childhood dream of spirits in the mountain forests. I painted two large eyes above the doorflap of our tipi.

First Elk Woman looked at my artwork and said, Yes, Spirit Eyes, how the world looks at us even as we look at it.

Now that I think back on it, I remember that my father had told me once that I could lay claim only to that name which is my greatest desire, my strongest choice, the who, the what I would trade every thing else for. That was First Elk Woman.

She and I went to live as man and wife happily in our *ti-ognakapi,* or tipi shared by man and wife. That meant that I could follow my own wish to disappear into North Park summers and camp up near Rabbit Ears Pass where game was plenty. I'd have been a complete fool if I failed to see the end of the beaver trade and had taken no stock from it. I went to the mountains so I'd never have to take a hand in the undoing of the Oglalas. I knew that every packmule train of goods I guided from fort to township to Oglala encampment would only hasten the day when their free-roaming life would end.

Winters then we spent alone together in Bellevue fending for ourselves. I trapped and hunted. She turned the hides into soft leathers, stripping off the layers of fat, working deer brains into the dried skins to make them supple. Then in August we'd come to where the North Platte meets the Laramie river. The Oglalas used to call it the Moonshell for the abalone and dentalium shells traders packed in from the Pacific Ocean to

make necklaces and breastplates. On a big trading
day men would arrive from that far west, and
from the south they carried parrot feathers,
medicine roots, herbs, and turquoise from New
Mexico. The whole grassy valley had long been
regarded as a crossroads, even before the Sioux
came out to these plains and lit the seven campfires that are their name, *Oceti Sakowin.*

First Elk Woman's people sometimes broke
into small bands that spread out up foothill
canyons to hunt and fend for themselves and their
horses. In summer, those times when they weren't
trading, they flocked to hunt buffalo, to dance
and sing—some ceremonies they could only do *en
masse*—and they always felt the more the better in
such matters as the Sun-gazing or making new
heyokas, who are holy men who took strange vows
to do everything backwards to custom so they
could break the habit of seeing and feeling and
thinking only one way. They sat by their many
campfires in those broad meadows behind Fort
William to tell stories—some meant as news of
vendettas, wars, recent adventures, some meant as
wicowoyake or "true stories" about their heroes
and gods. Groups of girls and boys walked from
one tipi circle to another looking each other over,
for it was their custom not to marry within a
band.

It was difficult for me at first to have any idea
whatsoever of how they lived from day to day. If
I may use a map to compare: what my father had
taught me was only the barest sketch of their
customs, their spirits, and their gods. What
understanding I came to after years was that
waking in the morning, eating, telling about
dreams, playing the hand game where they
learned to trust their hunches, which was a small
part of finding *wakan,* caring for horses, cooking,
gathering firewood, making and mending clothes,

hunting, stealing horses from the Crow, teaching customs and stories to young children—the whole of it down to the smallest task really *was* their religion. I asked First Elk Woman about it.

Look back, she said, to when you were young, learning from your father how to make your way. Did you love him, need him? Yes, I said.

It is that way with *wakantanka*. That is how humble your heart must be as you pray.

I remembered those days in school when the nuns had us kneel by our desks each hour as we changed subjects from reading to ciphering to history, geography, and the like. That is, I was familiar with pledging each day, each moment, each action of the day, to God. On May Day we would write letters to the Blessed Virgin asking her to intercede with her Son, Jesus. I loved to watch the smoke rise out of sight up to her in Heaven. I had some notion it was a pagan practice, but I felt the power of it, at least for those brief moments we took out of our lives for such observance, as if we lived two lives. Such prayer was an idea we always forgot in the rush of our play. First Elk Woman did not ever forget.

They would sit—First Elk Woman and her woman friends—in the open space, what she called the *hocoka*, between many tipi circles drying strips of buffalo meat with campfire smoke and mixing pemmican, *wasna*, laughing about their guesses as to how those girls and boys would pair up.

Sometimes as I sit outside with pen in hand these days, the smell of woodsmoke from Oglala campfires will shake loose memories, and I re-member the women's smiling faces. They come back to me so sharp I feel a pain in my chest like sleeping hungry from missing the good family feeling of those camps. I don't wish to give myself over to that, Mr. Watrous, but I reckon you must

have felt something like it, or why else would you
be writing a history?

You ask in your postscript of last what it was I
sought among the mountains. I've already written
to tell you about my childhood dreams of the
mountain forests. The longer I lived in Oglala
camps the clearer it came to me that what they
called their spirit world was what I'd seen in my
dreams. During those many years I lived with
First Elk Woman in Oglala camps around what
was then called Fort William, each spring I went
into the high country with my friend Swift Hawk
in that same spirit, as if I entered what my father
had called the Cheyenne underwater world in
search of those spirits whose eyes I had felt upon
me as I dreamt when a boy.

Passes were wet travel. We hung our
mocassins to dry by the campfire, smoked our
pipes after supper and talked. I hardly knew what
First Elk Woman expected of me and often asked
Swift Bird's advice. My father had told me what
Lakotas want from a man. But once, I said to
Swift Hawk, as I kept accounts in my ledger, First
Elk Woman peeked over my shoulder to ask what
that black water was that I marked the skin of
god with.

Ink, I said.

O, she cried, clapping hands to mouth, *Ink-
to-mi*, trickster! So this is who you are. I have
often wondered, for *Inktomi* takes bird or animal
shapes, but can come as a man. So it is you who
have come to shame the people again, eh? Well, I
will keep sharp eyes on you!

A little mild teasing, Swift Hawk said, as
between a couple first getting to know each other.
Inktomi, or *Ik-to-me*, is pictured often as a trap-
door spider, a lesser god, the son of our spirit, the
Winged, a whirlwind so shapeless even humans

laugh at him. He tempted Wazi, chief in the Third Age when the people lived underground.

I tried to picture them underground, but only when I imagined a quiet pool with shadows of cattail stalks and watery grasses rippled by small eddies in the mountain stream Swift Hawk and I were camped near could I see them.

Wazi's wife is Kanka, Swift Hawk's voice said, and Ite is their daughter, so beautiful that *Tate*, god of winds, chose her for his wife. Even so, Wazi and Kanka dream of having the gods' powers. To do more good for the people, right? Iktomi says to them with a sly smile. Yes, give us the charm of making her so beautiful that *Wi*, the sun, will give her a seat beside him at the gods' feasts.

Ah, I said. First Elk Woman has talked about being the sits-beside-him wife.

Yes. That is very important. Keep that in mind, for when *Hanwi*, the moon, first wife of *Wi*, saw Ite seated beside *Wi*, she drew her dress skirts over her head and wept for shame to be so out of place, and even the human people laughed to see her. *Skan*, the god who gives motion to all things, rose to act as judge.

As Ite is so vain of her looks, she is banished to the aboveground world, *Skan* said. And the Fourth Age we live in now began. Ite's face is changed: on one side she keeps her beauty, the other is twisted, horrible. She is known as *Anog-Ite*, double face. May you never see that side.

Her first four sons with *Tate* had become the four winds. With each sin against that first family order in heaven the world cracked apart more, so that the aboveground world would be no more than a mad jumble except that the four directions mark the world off in quarters so everyone can keep their bearings.

Wazi and Kanka also are sent away to live in the aboveground world, there to roam alone until *Iktomi* tempts the people out of their caves and into this world of sky and stars with promises of meat and leather clothes. The Oglalas don't hate *Iktomi,* nor do they renounce his ways, for though he tricked them with words, life in the aboveground world is rich in buffalo. The Fourth Age is when anything can happen, an age as yet untold, an age not fixed forever in stories, an age that needs its interpreters still.

But I'm *not* what she said—*Inktomi,* trickster—I remember nearly shouting. I don't have the magic. I don't have any idea where I would get it. I always think my dreams will only come true with hard work.

It's like this, he said, placing a pine bough on our little blaze. The secret of fire is in the wood. Everything is both what it is and also what it can become. That something pine branches can become is the spirit part. Often when a man will fast and pray and dance long enough to see what a lump of stone he holds in his hand can become he will open his fingers to find it is now a cactus flower. The magic is not the power to change things, to do tricks, but instead the patience to let his will melt so stone can turn to flower as it will.

So also with human beings. Each has one soul in the body that may linger after death, and each has a twin soul that lives in the spirit world, a soul for who we are and who we may become. So also with words, Swift Hawk said. Red Cloud's band is now *Ite-sica,* called Bad Faces, for the vanity to break faith as Ite did, to kill within the Oglala *ti-os-pa-ye.* So also with words, I agreed, thinking on how the word "trader" sounds so much like "traitor."

Swift Hawk and I agreed to head south down to Grif Evans's place in Estes Park, though he

lived a good republican distance from the Englishman Lord Dunraven's holdings. There we hoisted
jugs of snakehead hooch so strong it'd wrinkle a
grizzly's snout.

Word then came by one of his servants that
Dunraven had heard I was in the area, and knowing my reputation as a guide, he wanted me to
take a young English gentleman up North Park.

Here's a fellow, he says, introducing me to a
Lord Alfred, who's made merry at rendezvous with
those roughs I told you of who trapped beaver.

I said, You've got my pelts mixed up with my
father's. Do you want me?

If your name is Antoine Janis, I want you,
Lord Dunraven said.

I took my first job guiding with but poor
grace, I'm afraid. Watching out after some English tenderfoot in thin air kept me busier than a
buffalo's tail in black fly season, what with Alfred
Lord Something gushing about the grand and
glorious "majesty" of this and that, as if these
mountains and their vistas were put here as proof
of some royal power.

I thanked my stars Swift Bird was with me to
put space between the Englishman and me, for I
hoped these western reaches of Nebraska territory,
should they become someday a new state, would
be named Jefferson. The America I wanted to live
in was as far from fine Lords and Ladies as the
Atlantic is wide.

Turns out Lord Alfred was a painter. I led him
up Iron Mountain, where he set up easel and
begun slapping blue paint to canvas with a broad
brush, then chunking peaks out, ever so cunning
with another brush filled with ochred oils, then
filling its foreground with tall pines. We had to
anchor down the whole contraption as there came
a gale blowing up over the dusty ridge like a
drunken jug player.

I looked at his golden wonder of Seven Utes,
his peaks crowned by sun-filled clouds. His brush
work was so flat and polished with strokes of
turpentine that all his edges looked feathered and
made whatever light shone on them gleam back.

I askt him why all the glitter. He said he was
not painting mountains but ideas. Could I not see
their bright shrouds as emblems? Was I so much
the wilderness ruffian I had no sense of the
sublime?

Yes, I told him, but should the sky become a
wall of gold before we think of soul?

I took him by the wrist and drew him to the
cliff's edge so he tilted there, turning white with
fear that I might hurl him off into the empty blue
air. Then I clasped him to my bosom and askt
him, Do you feel that knot in your stomach as
you stand at the last step to Heaven's gate? Is that
not the sublime as well?

It's not just mountains, I says, but what they
might become. I know enough of what you speak
to ask for more dark in your light to make the
feeling in my chest when I'm so near to bursting
with who I might become I breathe quick and
swallow hard. My father was a fine man who
taught me more than I can ever say about the
wilderness, but it is because I have read that I
know enough to suspect those who go about
spouting words like "sublime" with their eyes cast
upward like angels, as if this world were to become nothing but an object of our contempt.

This is what I've come to believe, I told him.
God doesn't want us to hate the world and love
Him the more for it. God wants us to bring Him
our love of the world. That is what Jesus meant by
laying up treasures in Heaven.

That is why it doesn't in the least bother me
that I must keep my eye out for present mysteries
like those steaming piles of bear dung I saw

among the junipers at treeline today. Some things
like how pine carries the secret of fire inside it
shine, even through black bark.

Ah, and more's the pity, he said.

We set to gnawing hardtack when five elk
come bounding up through thickets so close I
gave a *waugh*! Their foreknees locked stock still,
their eyes like lost children's asking if I was some
bear. Then they bolted. Lord Alfred was put out
I'd spooked the harmless things. Those harmless
things could trample your bones with their
hooves, I said, and I don't relish packing your
broken body back to Lord Dunraven.

Swift Hawk laughed and gave me a look that
said he knew my wife's name is First *Elk* Woman,
and I wouldn't care to have her use her animal
shape to come spy on me while I was out in Ute
country.

Swift Hawk began whittling a coup stick from
a mountain ash sapling, and Lord Alfred before
long asked what its design was.

As you see, a bear, Swift Hawk said.

Yes, but within the bear's outline there's
another line, and above that three arcs—what are
they?

The sign of glad heart bear, which you will see
the use of should we chance on this bear, Swift
Bird says. I'll touch the bear with this stick. The
bear spirit in the stick will take my enemy's heart
from him. A bear counts as a man, as more than a
man.

Perhaps our painter hatched his plot that very
moment, for next morning as we boiled coffee we
heard a rifle shot down below treeline among the
lodgepole. Not five minutes later, here the man
comes, panting uphill into camp, and after him a
great silvertip bear, bleeding from a neck wound,
snarling, with his steel claws six inches long
flashing, his iron muscles that can crush a bison's

skull with one blow bulging—the whole bundle
crashing juniper brush, bent on mayhem, and
Lord Alfred up a tree.

The bear drew himself up to his tallest stand,
then walked toward me as I stood next to the
campfire staring into his dark gold glistening coat
of fur, into his pain-crazed red eyes, long enough
to break sweat with the shock of standing beside
myself on the verge of becoming who I might be
at last, when he swiped at me, tearing the blanket
from my shoulder, and then the raw sting of my
flesh laid open to air quickened my senses smart
enough. I reached for my rifle, cocked it, shoved
its muzzle to the bear's chest and blew out his
palpitator.

Swift Hawk rushed up with his coup stick and
tapped the bear whose meat I'd thrown cold. The
Englishman began to climb down. Perhaps my
blood was up, for I told him then, If you take
another step before nightfall, I'll do you as I've
done the bear.

Swift Hawk began to chant. He sang all day as
I skinned the bear out. Laid on his back and stript
from his coat of fur he was indeed very much a
man, and more than any man. I took his claws the
way my father showed me, cutting all the way
back to its first knuckle. When I remembered how
my father treated me when first I was learning the
wilderness I found myself humming an old tune,

O fils du roi, tu es méchant!
D'avoire tué mon ours rou-ge,
which translates to something like,

O son of the king, you are very bad
To have taken my redskinned bear,
and I told the Englishman, You can come on
down now.

Sorry about the bear, he said, when he'd made
his way to where I knelt skinning.

It's just I don't hunt bears anymore.

Why is that?

I've got too much respect for them is all. One time back in St. Charles when I was a boy I helped old Kitey Taylor butcher out some hogs, and I worked well into the night, so it was under this full moon that I drove my mother's buckboard back toward home along river road with a load of hog heads, livers, jowls, feet, and backribs when I passed into shadow under some willows and heard some sound I'd never heard before— somewhere between a grunt and a howl—and suddenly there was the biggest bear that ever lived this side of Judgment. It had been a long time since a bear'd been seen in that town.

I never knew a bear could run so fast, so I threw a hog's head I had stashed at my feet off the wagon to hopefully appease his hunger so he wouldn't chew on me. Bears are partial to boys, y'know. But that bear he gobbled up that hog's head and come running after me again and pretty soon I'd thrown every scrap of pigmeat I got and he still keeps after me so hard he clumb up the back of my buckboard, clumb over my seat and onto my horse's back, where he begun eating from the withers down, so the wagon stopped dead in the moonlight.

I thought I was a goner, and I began to pray, Lord, do something now, for old Mr. Bruin will soon make a dessert of me. But just then I felt my wagon lurch forward. Seems that bear had eaten himself down through the horse so it'd settled in his harness, bridle, bellyband, and hame straps setting right on the whiffletree. So I just drove him home into my mother's barn, locked him in, and seeing's how his belly's full of jowls and backribs he just settles down to sleep, and I got the shotgun, came back and blew his brains out.

You no doubt take me for a complete fool,
don't you? Lord Alfred said, looking at me sideways.

Hell, no, I said, with a mock hurt in my voice.
That bear, he furnished meat all winter, but long
before that I traded his skin for a new horse, so
that bear had furnished me out all right and that's
why I don't anymore like to hunt bears. If they'd
just leave me alone I'd be happy.

The Englishman at last let himself smile, and
that was an end of the whole business.

That night Swift Hawk changed his tune,
some simple ditty about my hunter's heart he
would chant the tale with at the Moonshell. If I
could hazard to render it, it was the same one-
two, one-two rhythm of a rabbit dance:

O, Yellow Hair
He shot a bear.
He took his claws,
He shook his paws.
O, mama, O, dad
Better never make him mad.
O, Yellow Hair.
He shot a bear.

Over and over he sang, so long Lord Alfred
asked me in a whisper whether Swift Hawk would
ever stop. He will, I told him. He's not a singer so
much as a dancer. That's how he reaches his gods,
jingling his silver ankle bells from Santa Fe to the
change in loudness drummers weave into steady
tom-tom beats.

Swift Bird comes from a race that dances. It's
harder work than hunting or raiding other tribes'
camps for horses, and you know that because
some of the men stop dancing before they ever
stop hunting or fighting, and then they go to fat.

The young men do it right in front of everyone in the village. They lament for a vision that
will help them fight with a light heart, relaxed,

skillful in feinting and swinging almost inside the
Army bluecoats, for if they stay outside in range of
cannon they will all die. Then the butchering of
women and children will begin. What Swift
Hawk does in his dancing is beg for a vision to
give soul to his people with, so they will sing
together his spirit song.

Listen and you'll hear how they leave breaks
of short silence as if to give rest to the air the way
a dancer will leave off from sparking life out like a
sixfoot bolt of lightning stuttering into the
ground, his mocassins beaded white and black
with the buffalo sign, his little soul dancing inside
the great soul, bouncing on the balls of his feet,
sometimes touching his toe to the dust, tapping
little puffs, the bounces counted by flicks of his
wrist where in his hand he holds a clutch of eagle
feathers shook out before him. Swift Hawk
dances, with his buffalo horn headdress brown as
Missouri river water, dipping and spinning so low
you can't see the man for that skin he hides
himself in.

Years later, I heard tell there's a painting in a
St. Louis saloon that shows this towering bear
standing over a man with a rifle blasting through
its chest. Is this painting all aglow with gold? Does
it show the bear's spirit part changing?

July 14, 1884
Pine Ridge Agency

"Saves the Peace"

To answer your question as best I can:
Yes, I did spend time, plenty of it, with First Elk
Woman on the Moonshell. She wanted to be
close to her family, and she had always had some
standing among the Itesica Oglalas, at least with
ceremonies. So we lived often around the fort,
especially in summer, though Swift Bird and I
went out several days at a time hunting buffalo to
provide fresh meat to our families.

Once, when we came back from hunting, the
camp was quiet except for a young woman crying
out her grief as she wandered and fell, weeping
and pulling her hair.

When I stepped into our tipi, First Elk
Woman was quietly weeping. She stood up, came
to my side, embraced me, and said, You should
have been here yesterday. Traders came into camp
and begun to hand out whiskey like in the old
days, and several of the young men thought it was
funny to get drunk and scream and fall down and
say nasty things to some young women, one of
them a daughter of Old Man Afraid of His
Horses. Old Man Afraid come out of his tipi and
begun scolding the young men, and they took up
their rifles and laughed and tried to shoot him like
he was a target they were practicing on.

Old Man Afraid has too much spirit for them
to ever hit him if he did not want to be. Besides,
they were so blind drunk they couldn't hit any-

thing they were aiming at. But one stray bullet hit a little boy in the face, and he fell dead to the ground. Now there is lamenting in our camp, and I must be away to help the grieving. More and more of the people sing the death song these days. The world has gone crazy.

This whiskey is a sickness that brings sadness and disorder among us, and we do not yet know the holy man who has medicine strong enough to cure it. Perhaps Crazy Horse. I see him riding away from camp almost every day. People say he goes into the Paha Sapa to lament for a vision. But, until that day he finds his spirit song, we women have to do what we can to make camp safe for our babies.

So, there had come a day when First Elk Woman flat out told me, The next time you ask me to go with you into the mountains, I must say no, even if you throw me away. Our time living on our own in the mountains is over. With men like John Reeshaw trading in Oglala camps, what can be expected but trails of blood and sorrow? They give poor value in trading stock and make up in whiskey what they withhold in coffee, sugar, all the metal things that the people who hang around the fort have come to want so bad.

I told her what was in my heart. I don't want to be a trader. I want to live by myself with you in the mountains where I know I can provide for you. I want no part in the undoing of Oglalas.

At least with you, she said with a look that said these would be her final words that day, the people will not be cheated.

Then she stooped through our tipi door flap and was gone on her errand of bringing comfort to the bereaved young woman whose cries we heard throughout our talk.

So, as they say, Mr. Watrous, the honeymoon was over.

I would have to add many new strings to my
bow to stand a down-hammer chance of making
my way in this new world, getting on with what
was left of the trading companies, leading packmule trains south to forts—Walbach, St. Vrain,
Cherry Creek, Bent's—south and east along
rivers—Cache La Poudre and Big Thompson,
Cherry Creek, and Arkansas—heading out in
early spring when Lakotas were massing on the
Moonshell.

First Elk Woman said she'd be proud if I
led small bands in winter as an *akcita,* or shirt
warrior.

You cannot have it both ways, I told her. If
you want me to be a trader to save your people
from being cheated, then I can't go that far, I
can't also be a shirt warrior. I can only be *with*
your people but not *of* them. I can't let the shirt
warriors tell me when I can travel. That will be
my virtue with U.S. Army officers should Fort
William become a post one day.

I say "shirt warrior" to a man in Fort Collins.
Should I perhaps rather say "sergeant at arms"?
Words. People in Laporte used to lay great store
by what they were called—"homesteader," "set-
tler," "squatter," "nomad"—each name carries an
order that goes back I guess to before Rome. Who
gets title to the best land, who the next best, how
wealth turns to law, how those without title live as
outlaws, how law turns to armies to hold those
rights the ancient poems say are given from the
gods.

So I began to earn some small fame leading
packmule trains up and down the foothills and
only once a year betaking myself alone west into
the mountains. And I began to hatch this scheme
of finding gold enough to buy those lands the
Itesica Oglalas claimed as theirs from way back
when they first came out onto these plains.

Ever since Jacques La Remie trapped beaver in
the mountains west of the Moonshell, tales had
been told that Arapahos and Utes knew sacred
places up the Cache la Poudre canyon where
seams of gold in rock walls threw back sunlight
that kindled junipers with jellied fire from which
they picked up nuggets large as an angel's tears.

I hoped to stand before that burning bush,
unaided by Swift Hawk or anything but the sun
that shone the day I was born lucky, on the first
cusp of the Ram, or so said that strange woman I
talked to once, who took up in this derelict
keelboat down along the Missouri just north of
St. Charles. I used to go exploring to see if there
was a lost treasure in its hold. Of course, I never
found ought in its black hull but squeaking rats,
but one day as I walked near I spotted a wisp of
smoke curling out of its galley window, and as I
made my wary approach saw this woman of about
my mother's age step out upon its deck. When
she saw me, she smiled.

You may come aboard if you wish, child, she
said. It's alright. I'm just brewing some willow tea,
and if you promise to be on your best behavior
you may share some with me.

And so I entered the dark room lit only by a
nub of candle and flames of a little stove she had
made from a large tin that said "Dill's Best" on it.
You are curious about this old boat, she said.
What is it you wish to know? Where your fortune
lies?

We New Orleans creoles are taught to read
the leaves as natural as you are taught to read your
catechism. The gospel says, Lay not up mortal
treasures that thieves may break into, nor rust
decay. But we do anyway, don't we, boy? I've
thought about it a good deal, she said, and sometimes I get a strange notion that God sits upon
His cloudy throne—cold, dry, alone, waiting for

us to offer Him the tribute of our good lives, expecting us to be wiser than He made us—but Satan is right down among us covered in muck and mire and wet weeds like we are—sweating, hoping, lying—Satan shows he *wants* us and he's here down at water level and below with us.

She wore a respectable dress, shiny black as a curate's cassock, though there was also something—an odor, a dampness—about her, as if she'd fallen off a Mississippi sternwheeler and washed up there, as if she somehow belonged to the river, or the river had somehow yielded her up. And it was as if she wheezed when she spoke, so it seemed to me, a boy awed that this grown woman would speak to him.

Do you believe in ghosts, she asked.

Yes, I whispered, I do.

Well, you are right to, she said. They breathe their unfulfilled desires among us, child. Distance means nothing to them. They spin like the white ball on the roulette wheel. Round and round they go, she said, as she stirred thin tea in her tin can that swirled around, then settled. And where they stop, nobody knows!

She laughed a big full-bosomed laugh that ended in a long fit of coughing. Dream what you need so the wheel turns your way. Awake, you know what *is*. Dreaming you know how what is *feels* inside. Do you want to know that?

Yes, I said, staring at her big wide eyes.

Ghosts remind us of what remains undone. A flash of sweat into the what-might-be can change things sometimes. You get what you give. That is justice. Luck? Let me look in your eyes.

Ah! she said, drawing me closer to look down into the wet leaves at the bottom of her tin pan that glinted with some few watery sunbeams that poured through the slats of the galley walls.

I see you standing in the midst of some

village, all fire and smoke, you with that look on your face as if you stood at the mouth of an open grave from which huge spiders crawl. You will have equal measures of good and bad fortune, but when time comes for reckoning you'll see your life was full, for you were born on the first cusp of the Ram, and your mother called you Sonny-boy before you knew how to speak. Did you know that?

I nodded that I did, but I could not guess how she knew.

Though I came back the next day to talk again with her, she was gone, as if she had slipped over the gunnels and returned to the river from which she had come. Still, I have never forgotten her. She gave me the belief I would be lucky.

Once, when I came back to Fort William busted after one of my gold-hunting jaunts with nothing to show for it, not even fresh meat, First Elk Woman scolded me for coming home empty-handed, then stepped through the tipi doorflap and was gone. A long time passed before I shouted.

Fear I had lost her pushed me. I hunted every crescent of tipis. It was nightfall. No one would speak to me except Swift Hawk, who took me down to the gravel banks where the Laramie and North Platte merge.

If you're going to be stingy, he said, First Elk Woman will take Mollie and Maggie and young Antoine in her arms and vanish. Don't even think of tracking her. You'd follow the wrong ones. She can become her name.

I lit out on a hunch southwest through Morton's Pass searching for her, making good time as I was alone and traveling with two good horses. That first night before I turned to sleep I unpacked my fiddle and played an old tune that

came to me from the night's still, distant skies
under whose stars I had never felt so alone:

    À la clai-re fontai-ne,
    m'en allant promener,
    J'ai trouvé l'eau si bel-le
    que je m'y suis baigné.
    Il y a longtemps
    que je t'aime,
    jamais je ne t'oublie-rai.

It was the closest I could come to spilling out my
troubled heart into night's healing silence, singing
the words that say,

    At a clear fountain
    where I was walking,
    I found such clear waters
    I went for a swim.
    I have loved you
    for a long time,
    never will I
    leave you evermore,

until I fell asleep and dreamed I saw her in her elk
shape, climbing across the prairie at the foot of
Elk Mountain, stopping to drink at a clear spring,
lifting her muzzle to listen to me singing,

    I lost my love.
    For no reason
    I refused her roses.

The elk girls came to me in the dream and said,
Do not follow us. We are near our grandfather elk
and all our family. They are powerful and angry
with you, and may kill you if you follow. Then
they curled up next to me.

    The dream had seemed so real, I was so glad
to be with them, that when morning dawned and
I woke to find myself alone on dewy grass lands,
the sinkholes of my eyes were filled with water
and I could scarcely hold back my feelings. Later
that morning she let me see her human shape after

I'd spotted three elk calves grazing in high meadows.

Often, when I picture her, that's what I see, her as she was then, standing, her hands cradled below her belly, fingers clasped. Her hair—it was many things, a forest of sage, dark, alive. I believe at the sight of her that day I forgot any thought my father had ever put in my head for wealth enough to go back to St. Charles and buy a stained-glass window at St. Joseph's in memory of the Janis family, so I would never again fall from her grace, nor miss the view of her as she slept, her body's features like curved horizon lines of the foothills with her face to heaven under the stars and moon.

We trekked back home together that summer of 1851 with the girls, and on our way chased down a lone buffalo cow with three calves. We clubbed them until they fell to their foreknees, tongues sprawled out of their mouths. I shot the cow, then tethered my horse to her tail, First Elk Woman and I working calmly together now, skinning her, me cutting down her spine with my skinning knife, she pulling the blanket-to-be off, gutting its carcass, its huge kidneys almost purple glistening as they spilled into daylight, white piles of stomach, intestines, First Elk Woman singing all the while,

> the men, the men
> are dancing, the women,
> the women are dancing,
> the dance, the dance
> of Buffalo Cow Woman,

as we took all the meat we could carry in our parfleches for the ride back to the fort, which the U.S. Army had just bought from Tom Fitzpatrick to use for a cavalry post to protect those wagon trains heading through South Pass to Utah and Oregon.

Fitzpatrick had traveled east by riverboat from St. Louis up the Ohio to Pittsburg and then overland to Washington to talk President Taylor into setting plains Indian lands within boundaries, once and for all. And with his new commission as Indian Agent that summer he dispatched horsemen the likes of which would later be Pony Express riders to gather every tribe on both sides of the Divide for a great treaty council.

All summer the tribes massed. So many herds grazing so much grama grass, the bands kept moving camps slowly down to the halfmoon crescent of Horse Creek valley. Many, many thousands, wanting Tom's promised gifts that were delayed at Kansas Landing, three hundred miles east on the Mizzu.

We were waiting for the Shoshones, led by their war chief Washakie and Blanket Jim Bridger, but the Sioux camps kept busy with feasts, with horseback marches four-abreast, with *tours de force* of mounted song,
O-ya-te wan he-na wa-ci
they sang,
We are the horse people,
they sang, their horses' manes painted, haunches painted with as many coup sticks of horses taken from enemies as they could boast.

Swift Hawk and I went over to visit with his friend Little Owl. We found him sitting cross-legged before his tipi tracing this silhouette of his left hand over his jaw and right cheek in red paint. Swift Bird told me Little Owl's father died at Washakie's hands. He said, I will drink Washakie's blood or die. I tried to talk him out of it, but he paid no nevermind to me. Have you ever looked into someone's eyes and felt they were mad, Mr. Watrous? There's nothing to say.

When the old Oglala women began to cry revenge, we turned our eyes west and saw by long

trails of rising dust that the Shoshone at last were
coming, Washakie foremost in full war bonnet,
tassels, scalps scraping their dry undersides against
his spear shaft in rhythm with his horse's gait, the
braves next, each with a good rifle, the women,
children, old people, and baggage last, well
guarded, all of them calm, quiet—even small
children—as they looked down-valley, ready for
peace or war.

Little Owl vaulted onto his pony, galloping
for the whole Snake nation. I took out after him.
Washakie watched us race uphill toward him,
cocking his primed flintlock, drawing a bead as I
caught up not a hundred paces from the Snake
column. Little Owl hit his head and was knocked
senseless when I shoved him off his horse. I slung
his body on his pony's shoulders and walked him
down the long hill to camp.

Jim Bridger came to visit afterward. He leaned
his tall frame against his rifle, stock on ground, as
he spoke in his Kaintuck twang.

You saved that Little Owl from Hell, he said.
Washakie would'er killt 'im quick, then all the
fool Sioux would'er got their backs up. There
wouldn't 've been room t' camp here fer dead
bodies. Tell yer Sioux I got the Snakes all good
guns. Uncle Sam told 'em to come down here,
and they'd be safe. But they ain't takin' his word
on it, not altogether. They'll not be caught
nappin'.

Next day Tom Fitzpatrick came by, asking me
to interpret for the Oglalas. He said, Jim Bridger
told me you're a good man, reliable, like your
father.

The treaty was clear. The wagon trains passing
west on what the Sioux would now call the Holy
Road should not be attacked, nor could whites
attack any tribes. Forts would house cavalry to

protect anyone on the road and punish wrong-
doers, white or Indian.

Fitzpatrick, Bridger, and Campbell drew a
map of the boundaries around agreed-upon
ancestral lands for each tribe—Arapaho,
Assiniboine, Blackfoot, Cheyenne, Crow, Lakota
bands, Shoshone—less lands on either side of the
Oregon trail for which tribes that touched the pen
would get fifty thousand dollars in gifts for fifty
years, starting whenever those blasted wagons
should appear from Kansas Landing.

That was the best deal the tribes would ever
strike with Uncle Sam, though he knew that he'd
have to claim sovereignty over *all* his territories.
For even though the English had lost the war
against the Americans, it seemed they never quite
could accept that state of affairs, and they kept
jamming the U.S. government, specially over the
border with Canada. So, Uncle Sam, he figured it
wouldn't do to have Indian nations within the
nation, or who was really boss?

Father DeSmet came by our tipi. Have you
turned entirely pagan, he said to me, or isn't it
time to baptize your babies?

He gave Mollie, Maggie, and little Joe
Antoine each a Sacred Heart scapular to wear with
cord lacing around their necks.

I myself wore a string of bear claws, feeling
their shy promptings acrosst my chest where Jesus'
red heart flowing gold light had lain when I was a
child, so far had I come from St. Joseph's parish
on the western edge of Christendom, where
perfect fatherhood shone with its gold nimbus
around the balded head of Christ's modest and
self-sacrificing father.

Joseph was not going to be the great Jesus
who opened the gates of Hell and took on the sins
of mankind and redeemed them in his blood, but

someone would have to provide for the boy and His mother, even though the boy was not of his own flesh and blood. Such was the man who was my namesake. Such the man I could not help compare myself to.

I had earned those claws in combat with the bear which I felt was a sight different from having salvation spillt on my hands by blood I had not askt for and would have stemmed if I could. Jesus might have played his trump, but drank the vinegar and gall instead. I had my rifle against that bear's Goliath cubits. I hadn't time to whisper Glory Be, but I had listened to Swift Hawk's singing bear language in Oglala accents, deep inside his throat, where the old ones live, and that had made it a holy death. Jesus had listened, too. How else heal the blind and cast out devils and raise the dead? How else did He know the hearts of sinners and madmen and lepers? St. Paul had said about the early Christians of Rome in his epistles, *See how they love one another!* Closest I ever came to that was my feeling for Oglala village life. Pagan and Christian touched on my map of the world.

When I went to Little Owl's tipi I mistook by trying to give him that necklace of bear claws as I had seen the Cheyennes do when visiting Sho-shones with gifts of blankets for a covering of bodies ceremony to lay ghosts between their tribes to rest. Little Owl's ankle had broken in his fall. He was healing bad, his right foot twisted inward pigeon-toed so the people were calling him Crazy Foot already. He might have forgiven me that, though he was now marked with shame—except I shamed him more by admitting through my offered gift that he might have grounds to think me wrong.

September 2, 1884
Pine Ridge Agency

"Locusts Singing"

No, Little Owl was not the only enemy
I ever made. Those years following 1851 found
me and my growing family near Fort Laramie (as
Fort William now was called) where a man from
St. Charles who'd known my father, Jim
Bourdeaux, was *bourgeois* for the American Fur
Company at a post called Gratiot, four miles
southeast down the north Platte.

Perhaps I should backtrack here: Bourdeaux,
Beauvais, and me and my father were all old
Rocky Mountain Fur Company men. Reeshaw
and Bissonette worked for Pratt and Carbanne.
But when the American Fur Company bought
out the Rocky Mountain and Pratt and Carbanne
folded, we all ended up working together for
American.

When First Elk Woman learned I'd be
Reeshaw's partner, his reputation for dealing out
whiskey made her go very quiet. I knew she was
uneasy, remembering the trail of drunken fights
and dead bodies Reeshaw left in his wake as he
moved from camp to camp among the Oglalas ten
years earlier when she was a girl and I was still at
school in St. Charles. Talking about enemies gets
so twisted it makes me wish for simpler days when
it was only me and the mountain forests where I
could feel the spirits in the trees and not be
blinded by the crosswinds of human dreams.

I helped Bourdeaux and Reeshaw haul timber
from west of Glendo to lash together a toll bridge
that spanned the Laramie, and helped them sink
pilings and spike crossbeams over water.

I told Reeshaw, I said, If you don't boil the
pine pitch out of the bark, then soak the beams in
creosote, they'll get waterlogged and rot. First big
June rise we get the bridge will vanish down river.

He was a man of about my stature, but his
face was pocked so bad only a full beard of black
hair seemed to cover an ugliness that made him a
quizzical character in my eyes, as if his mind were
at war with his body. He seemed to think his life
was nothing but a bad joke. What perverse destiny
had made others so stupid and him so smart and
so scarified at the same time? It gave his speech a
hard flatness, and to his face it gave a constant
sneer like a Bible with no God in it.

We don't have time fer that, he says. We
want to be up and collecting tolls now, not three
months from now.

We built a storehouse and collected tolls.
We'd buy played-out ox teams from one wagon
train for bottom dollar—the going rate was two
lame ox for one good—then we'd feed and rest
them until they got their strength back, then resell
them to the next emigrants, so that within one
summer we'd mass up a great herd to drive back
to Westport, Missouri, for a good profit.

Meanwhile, I worked off and on for Agent
Twiss, traveling north to the Powder River coun-
try to trade goods for buffalo hides with Brulé and
Minneconjou bands, though that might well have
been cut short as one summer day when I passed
Twiss's office, the window being open to catch
whatever breeze there might be, I overheard
Reeshaw to say, Send my man Smith out this
September to trade with those wild Minneconjou.

Well, says Twiss, what about Janis? Oh, the Sioux are grumbling about Janis. They don't like him anymore. They want someone else.

I was stunned. I walked to my tipi and just paced outside. First Elk Woman came out. She wanted to know what was vexing me so. I told her what I heard Reeshaw say. Why would he lie like that? I asked her.

As she always did, First Elk Woman stared me straight in the eye. She said, Reeshaw is a bad-heart man. He will try to get rid of you just for being good at what you do, so he can be the whole show. He knows full well I've asked you to trade with the Oglalas so they won't get cheated. That crosses his plans. He's the kind, if he's being nice, beware, he's hiding something.

We both had a good laugh that early June day in 1853 when the bridge at Gratiot started to bow and sag and tilt from the rots like an old sway-backed mare until it fell to its knees one evening and disappeared downriver, washed away during the night with one long creaking and snapping sound that First Elk Woman and I woke from, knowing it wasn't one of our babes waking from a bad dream.

I did beware of John Reeshaw from that day on, though we worked together for Bourdeaux selling everything emigrants might need, from axle grease to coal oil, mostly to Mormons those years coming west on the Holy Road, until one day a Mormon farmer let his cow stray off into the large camps of Brulés and Minneconjous sited by the north Platte, and trouble spun up fast.

Some days, I can hear a buzz in my ear stranger than cicadas whining, like some shift of weather. Sunlight burns yellow on the willow leaves like any other day, yet that awful whirring like a fiddle bow sawing on catgut made my hair crackle. The whir became a column of dust rising up from under Lt. Grattan's small command— three wagons, thirty foot soldiers, two howitzers, stopping at Gratiot, Grattan begging in his whining voice, Antoine, come along with me down the road to the Minneconjou camp. Lucien's drunk again.

Sure enough, Lucien, Grattan's hand-picked interpreter, was racing his horse back and forth up and down the road to the Brulé camp in a volley of shod hoof thuds, all the while shouting as to how that very night he'd eat Minneconjou heart for supper. If I could reach into Lucien like he was some burlap sack and turn it inside-out so I could see what's in there, I hazard what I'd 've pulled out would be how he was feeling—that the Minneconjou were eating *his* heart little by little, the way they turned their backs on him. He wanted them to treat him like he was a great man, but he was just another half-breed to them. He kept himself at a fever with whiskey as if it would give him the glow he lacked to be a somebody among them.

Jim told Grattan plain he should get Conquering Bear the Brulé chief to talk to this Minneconjou named Straight Foretop who'd butchered out the lean Mormon head of cattle. But Grattan's blood was up. He kept saying he would crack it to those Sioux that day. His little army passed our roadway heading south like an angry swarm of bees smoked from their hive.

Jim and I climbed up on the storehouse roof where we could just about see Grattan call out Conquering Bear from his tipi. When he stepped through the doorflap he was already raising his hands to calm that brave Grattan had come to arrest for breaking the treaty which said no Sioux could exact a toll of a cow or whatever on the folks rushing out west across the Holy Road.

Give the white man something of equal value, Conquering Bear called out loud enough to be within our hearing. That way the blue coats won't stretch your neck and burn our camps in taking you.

Why should I put myself in the hands of my enemies? the brave shouted. Why should I die for butchering out a cow that the *wakan* gave us here at the Moonshell? The treaty says no such thing. I would rather fight!

We heard Lucien screaming, He is *defying* you, Grattan!

We saw the smoke and heard a boom of cannon after that shook the roof we sat on with such force it seemed the shingles tore loose and slipped down the slant to the ground below. Down went Straight Foretop and Conquering Bear. Brulés poured out of their tipis and mounted the ponies they'd already called in when they too heard that buzz in the air.

Rifle shots struck Grattan and Lucien, many cannoneers, the men in wagons. Half died on instant, the rest wheeled about their wagons and galloped back toward us. We scrambled down off the roof. They paused only a moment to drop off a badly wounded private, then raced for the open gates of Fort Laramie way up valley well beyond sight.

We hid the boy down cellar where Reeshaw and Bourdeaux cached their whiskey. He was bleeding bad from a bullet hole in his throat, big bubbles of blood popped and spattered flecks down his tunic with each breath through his windpipe. First Elk Woman went with him, trying to stanch the blood with wild yarrow and rags to keep him from betraying his whereabouts to these wild bands that mostly stayed north of the Powder and weren't used to white ways. Some lit out after the surviving soldiers, caught them,

killed them before they reached the gates. Some
came in carrying Conquering Bear, all riddled
with grapeshot. They were already singing his
death song. Braves circled us slowly on horseback.
Their mad grief could only be vented by attacking
Fort Laramie and trying to burn it to the ground,
though its lime-grout walls would not catch fire.
Black smoke drifted south down toward us,
carrying the stench of human fear.

We laid Conquering Bear out on that
pineboard counter and tried to wash his wounds.
So, here we were, with one man dying in the
cellar and another man dying on the ground floor,
enemies. The women kept singing, on and on
from afternoon to evening to night with Jim
trying to calm the braves down.

Look, he said, you've killed thirty white men,
thirty *soldiers*. The great father in Washington will
hear of this soon by the talking wires. A great
army will come to punish Brulés and
Minneconjous and all the Lakotas for this bad
thing that has happened, no matter whose fault.
Here, take these knives, blankets, pots, pans,
mirrors, beads, rifles, powder, shot. Get yourselves
back north to the Powder River country where
you'll be out of harm's way.

In the braves' eyes was that steady long look
that sees the truth of things. They took what Jim
gave and left, though other small parties of men
and women kept coming all night until dawn for
their presents while First Elk Woman kept her
hand cupped over the private's bloody coughing
mouth down in the whiskey cellar. As the last
band of Brulés dragged their *travois* through
morning light, the boy gave out his last.

When we stepped out of the storehouse,
Laramie peak was catching first light, the color of
First Elk Woman's hands. Wind and dust swirled
together above the nearly empty camps, the empty

bridge pilings that still stood, the wagon road northwest to Fort Laramie still marked in skies above the trees by smoke from fires set last night against its walls. Neither she nor I had ever seen a battle this size before.

Do you want to gather our children and follow the tribes north, she asked.

No, I said. My place is here. Go if you want.

She said, I will stay with you.

Behind us, Bourdeaux and Reeshaw walked exhausted out of the storehouse carrying Conquering Bear's dead body. They placed it on the ground and stood leaning their hips against the hitching post and lit their pipes as the Brulé women together picked their chief's body up and carried it off for later burial on a platform of sticks wedged up in the branches of some cottonwood along turns in the North Platte miles from here.

Wal, Jim said, we've saved our lives and lost our livelihoods. Trade'll be ruined for some while. Lord knows how long it'll take us to recoup from this.

We may never, Reeshaw said. We've set a sorry example. Now the wild ones'll think they can come south and just take our goods. We'll need the army to keep whatever the company will resupply us with.

Like as not, Jim said, the army won't care what happens to us or our stores. Whatever few soldier boys're left in the fort'll tell the new commander we put the Sioux up to it.

We've got to do something, Reeshaw said, gazing off at Conquering Bear's body as it seemed to float in a pool of walking women. What if we let out that that poor fool led Grattan into a trap? How can it hurt him? He's well out of this mess.

Reeshaw, I says, I know you're not someone to turn to for help. If I did you'd look at me the way a wolf does a stray antelope calf. But you,

Jim, I expected you to know the only reason the government tolerates us out here is for us to stand between the Sioux and the Army. That's the only suffrance we have, and we've *failed* at it. Maybe we all didn't know how insane the whole thing was. Grattan just marched his troops right into their camp with no thought to how his men would defend themselves, surrounded as they were. We should've *stopped* him, but we were just as stupid as he. There's no use lying.

O, grow up, Antoine, Bourdeaux spat. John's right. We got to salvage what we can, or we're finished in these parts.

We're finished in these parts if the good will we've built up gets knocked down in a pile of lies, I said.

Bourdeaux's words curled themselves in black smoke a long time as a new day began with that strange spinning I sensed the day before. All I now felt was somehow soon I'd quit these men.

When Twiss made me trading agent for Fort Laramie I learned better than to think John Reeshaw could lie about me and be believed over and above the good name I'd earned for years. Swift Hawk was my brother and spoke well for me, so I traded goods for buffalo hides the next three years. I helped Seth Ward and his partner Ed LeGuerrier build a bridge over the North Platte the right way, with tarred pilings, and they began to take tolls from the emigrants at a place called Sand Point.

From time to time I ran that Overland Mail station for them. Seth was a good man with plain common sense and got the license to trade down the Cache Le Poudre, and I'd go down there to the old council grounds where I'd given my first speech to the tribes and trade. I'd find and unbury that written claim I'd hid in 1844. All along, I reminded myself, I'd intended that land for a

home should the valley ever become settled, and
now it seemed I might be the one to settle it.

I once found myself down near Bellevue after
the Oglalas had chased a big herd of buffalo off
the cliff there on what is now called Goat Hill or
Bellevue Dome.

Hundreds of animals lay dead on the rocks,
their bodies crushed by the fall off that buffalo
run. I took wagonload after wagonload of hides,
steadily saving a small fortune despite my paying
the best prices, though the whole while I went
cold inside, waiting for my chance to get enough
ahead to leave Fort Laramie and the cloud of hate
I felt Reeshaw bore against me once and for all.

Ward and LeGuerrier got so many buffalo
hides they hired me to bullwhack a train of
wagons back to Kansas City with twelve thousand
robes. When we drove those wagons down the
main drag folks said they thought at first it was a
herd of elephants, and they came out into the
streets to see if the circus was come to town
because our wagons was filled high above the
wagonbeds and tightly covered with weathered
tarpulins as gray as an elephant's skin.

September 16, 1884
Pine Ridge Agency

LETTER VIII

"Le Semblance"

As you know, it takes six, seven weeks of spring sun for creeks to sing *fortissimo* with snowmelt and swell the two-horned crescent of rivers, north through Snowy Range up Laramie River to the fort where the North Platte merges in, and southeast by Cache La Poudre canyon over its falls and on out to the grassy plains where it forks into the south Platte, bankfull and beat back by rising waters until the earth opens its bag of possibles.

Why shouldn't I be the lucky one? That is the refrain any young man hears, even without listening to rivers.

As I was thus staring into the Laramie one spring morning in 1857, the Cheyenne chief Bold Wolf walked up to me accompanied by a woman wrapped in a crimson red Hudson's Bay blanket. Behind her stood this young man, perhaps sixteen, seventeen years old. I regarded him closely enough to note that despite his hair being piled in a rolled curl on his forehead in Cheyenne fashion and being dressed as a warrior in leggings with white and blue beadwork of horned buffalo head pattern running up the sides, boned breastplates, throat chokers of dentalium, and a white loop dangling from his left ear, what stood out about him was his cold green eyes and general build, narrow in shoulder and hip, which I felt with a shudder I'd seen before. He sure was the most dandified young Cheyenne I ever saw.

Bold Wolf said, You look the love sick moose, Antoine. Isn't it time you took some good Cheyenne woman like Bright Star, my daughter, as your wife? I am not a rich man. For many winters we have waited for her husband and the boy's father to return, and it is now time that you know your father's wife, your father's son.

My brother? I asked.

With just one look at him moments ago I'd felt something pass between us. I suddenly remembered my father's stories were almost always Cheyenne, not Oglala.

I tried to take a step toward Two Bears and stumbled. I wanted to place my hand to his to see if they matched, but felt some reserve.

The longer I gazed into his eyes the more certain I felt that Bold Wolf was right. My father said he lived two lives, and standing here was my half-brother, what my father would have called *mon semblance sauvage*.

I reached out to touch his shoulder. He batted my out-stretched hand away, and on his face I saw this cold blush, what my father would call *la prise en grippe*. I tried to speak to him. He only spat on the ground and turned to walk away, pulling his strung bow over his head so his one eagle feather broke its white tip and slanted off at an angle. As Two Bears turned back to face me, Bright Star stepped between us, looked into my eyes that told me with her eyes that her son knew I was his father's son. He was this Cheyenne pretty boy, an angel Cupid, who drives an arrow through the heart. She turned to him, and then she walked off with him.

I stood there with Bold Wolf, though lost in the crowd of faces I'd been looking for years into—Cheyenne, Arapaho, Sioux—like a man

waiting for an angel to spread its gold wings and
be the sky at dawn, for a spirit in human form, for
that one blood tie who would calm my heart
when I opened the underwater world my father
called "the sinkhole" and let myself go down
where all roots are entwined.

I've become superstitious that way. I've woven
myself down into those tangles to feel flames grow
like struck lucifers from underneath where things
touch, where human appetites spring from the
soul as from life itself.

Two Bears might be my Cheyenne double,
but he wouldn't speak to me. His silence was like
a moonless night I poured all my fretful music
into, aching like swamp hollars I heard as a young
man among creole riverboat deckhands fresh from
New Orleans with dreams of good company and
happy passages home among their brothers on the
Mississippi.

If yellow metal washes from the foothills this
year I'll help you, I said to Bold Wolf. I don't
know if First Elk Woman will take to it.

Why worry what she thinks? Bold Wolf asked.

Blame it on the June rise, but I did give Bright
Star and Two Bears presents of horses, only to
find myself in a world of trouble. When I told
First Elk Woman, I saw in her face that I
shouldn't bring those two into her home.

It would be one thing if they were Oglala, she
said. Then maybe I could think of Bright Star as a
sister.

They won't come to live with us, I said. I
make this Two Bears angry for some reason,
though as far as I know I've never done him
wrong. Bright Star was my father's wife. I could
not lie with her. It would be far too strange. But I
feel I must do something for them. They'll camp
with Bold Wolf's Cheyenne. You will always be
my sits-beside-him wife.

I now started visiting in Cheyenne camps just enough to keep an eye on Two Bears. He rode so hard in races, sang his own song so loud in camp when he returned from the hills with fresh meat, I guessed he wanted to be taken into the Dog Soldier society. There was little I could do for him except to watch how he went on every hunting, scouting and raiding party, though many's the time I thought of what I myself had done back in St. Charles when I was his age—his schooling and mine were so different.

I found that I was now connected to a big clan known for its troublemakers like Fire Wolf, Bright Star's brother, who even then was pining away in the Upper Platte Bridge stockade, arrested for stealing horses. Bold Wolf told me over a full pipe that it really wasn't stealing. Fire Wolf, Two Bears, and a friend found three strays feeding on the prairie and rode hard north into their camp below the Powder river singing thanks for what the *wi'hio* gave them.

Two days later, one was shot dead attempting escape, Fire Wolf was clapped back in irons, and Two Bears got away to spread their story through the *Paha sapa*, the Black Hills, and summer begun at a mad clip with rumors drifting into Fort Laramie about Cheyenne doings—mailcoach drivers winged by arrows, old Ganier scalped, wagon trains attacked and burnt, women, children taken, Almon Babbitt crossing Nebraska to take his seat as first delegate to Congress from Mormon Utah beat to death with war clubs, so that by July here comes General Sumner and two full companies of dragoons from Fort Leavenworth to campaign against many bands of fed-up Cheyenne.

Those days the Cheyenne and all plains tribes had the upper hand. They knew every inch of those grasslands—where the springs were, creeks, covering cottonwoods that provided fuel for campfires, buttes easy to defend if federal cavalry was foolish enough to charge. They never had rifles enough, but they could travel well-nigh invisible and swift on fat ponies, smart as the Cheyenne themselves.

I had no intention of being forced to sign on as scout and finding myself in Sumner's army chasing down Cheyenne war parties. I had no heart for it, especially since Bright Star and Two Bears had come into my life. I imagined if I should find myself forced to shoot my own half-brother it'd be to blast myself. I had a half-brother who would not speak to me, whose only gesture was to spit. I had a half-brother who was a man on fire, who burned with the velocity of sparks.

But as Bold Wolf told Two Bear's story of his friend's death, shot in the back by some stockade guard, I begged First Elk Woman for her understanding this one time and disappeared with her and our children into the foothills on the Poudre's north fork to prospect for gold, though I could still hear my father's ghost voice in my head saying, *It's a fool's errand to be scrabbling up hill and down vale chasing this dream of easy money.* And what was stranger, now my heart was filled with anger against my father, a man I didn't understand half of, though he had taken me into the wilderness and given me his knowledge and his skills and what else I did not know.

I didn't understand my feelings, so I spent a good deal of time thinking things over while I hunted for placers. For one thing, my father did not quite die the way other men do. I had only heard a rumor that he had died. He passed away on someone else's breath like a leaf on a breeze. Each generation watches its fathers wither around the eyes until whatever light in them is left turns to stars in the deepest night.

When First Elk Woman's father, Old Smoke,
died, she cut off her little finger and screamed
death until heaven wept along with her, until she
saw her father's form hung in some cottonwood
floating down the river of stars she called the
Spirit Road, until the song she sang ended when
her throat was so dry her voice cracked.

I made camp with my family along Poudre
River's upper reaches beyond those meadows
where Seven Mile Creek plays in. I would spend
all day kneeling beside creeks, shoveling out
spadefulls of blue clay and gravel, then swirling
pans of washed gravel around, watching the
brown cloud of mud wash out of the pan's lip,
again and again, slowly working the bigger
pebbles out until I had nothing but black sand.

I rolled small mouthfuls of water slowly,
carefully washing every grain away until nothing
stayed at the backside of the pan but a few flecks
of color, not the glint of mica, but dull yellow,
which I took up one by one on the point of my
sewing needle into a leathern pouch, all the while
recalling how when I was a boy that strange creole
woman swirled willow tea leaves in a tin can
looking for placers that would show my fate to be
not so much good or bad as full. If she was here, I
found myself thinking, I'd tell her what I've found
in panning gold—that if she wanted to find gold
she had to act as if there was gold in her pan or
else she wouldn't swirl that creek water with near
enough care to leave those dull gold flakes behind
up on the high side of her pan above those
washed-away fine blue-black sands.

Or I tramped along the hillsides up gulches
looking for a likely spot to begin flailing away
with a pick I had forged from two Army issue
picket pins that looked more like an anchor, or
sometimes only some *risquer le coup,* as my father
would've said, like throwing a coin backward over

my shoulder and digging on the spot it landed, shoveling hardscrabble, outcroppings of rose quartz, mostly.

Gold was there. It glittered, whole wide seams of it, pulsing in the moony sunlight of my dreams, where I heard verses of an old song saying,

La lune qui rayonne
éclairera la nuit ...

Yet when dawn light opened my eyes, I saw those nuggets fade as if they was children of the moon who circled in the sky while old father sun slept underground.

One late autumn day, when I'd drug my tired bones back to our tipi, First Elk Woman fed me and tended my blistered hands with beaver fat, rubbing it into my chafed skin until it come smooth as saddle leather. She knelt by the fire, took a live coal from the bed of ashes, then sprinkled a pinch of ground juniper over it and held her hands in the smoke until her palms were heated. She then pressed her hands into my aching back and all pain begun to spread away like clouds that part.

She took boughs of ponderosa and swished their needles across my back, sometimes with stinging effect, then worked her strong fingers into my shoulder muscles until they jumped at her touch as if she were digging her nails into my body trying to claw out some nugget of pain that had been causing me grief all my life. Perhaps she knew, perhaps she could see what that rock hard thing was in my back.

She fanned smoke from smoldering juniper incense over my back and began digging into my left shoulder harder than ever until I let out a cry. Then I remember feeling a rush of cold air go over my body as if the tipi flap were opened, and I felt somewhat lighter, as if she had took some bone out of my ribs. Where a moment before I had felt spent and breathless, now I rolled over and faced her, ready for some new venture. But what? What was I supposed to do?

First Elk Woman said, I miss my sisters and fear for our little ones too much to stay away from Fort Laramie any longer. All the signs say hard winter.

Trouble had come into my tipi, and it could not be helped. I don't know how long we would have lived that *impasse.* I was tearing up the earth to find gold for Bright Star and Two Bears, or so I told myself.

I saw that day it was this dream I'd been hatching to buy up the Poudre River valley and make it a place where the old French trappers and their Indian wives and families could live in peace was what I wanted to do. And I'd have to come down off the mountains to try to make it happen, with or without gold to back my play.

Early snowstorms came along to make deciding easier. They drove us northwest through Cherokee pine forest until we reached Diamond Peak and saw the Laramie basin stretched out far to the north where snows had fallen and drifted. From thence we traveled under blue skies back to the fort up along meadows on either bank of Laramie River that steamed like censors as we passed, a small caravan in a vast white desert.

No sooner had I tied my horse's reins at the suttler's hitching post than Jim Bridger took me inside to buy me a drink and tell me the story he stuck to till his dying day.

There's bad blood b'twixt me and them Mormons, he said. They're tryin' to snooker me out of my good stone fort up on the Green river. This man Brigham Young holds probate court in his fist, and makes claims to the right of telling jurors how to vote, on the grounds he's some prophet. He says to prevent him from doing so would be to make laws against him practicing his religion. But that's not the way most folks in America read the Constitution.

A reg'lar guy don't stand a chance in Utah, less'n he becomes a Saint. Out in Utah they're like a plague of grasshoppers that eats whole fields of grass to the ground, then sends their children down on ropes to devour the roots. Add their practice of marrying more than one woman and you got powder and tinder enough to touch off this big expedition to Utah by Gen'l Johnston here with 2500 men, horses, wagons, cannon, and supplies to put down the Mormon rebellion.

As for the marrying part, I says, it ain't as if it wasn't done by others. I have no bone to pick with Mormons on that score.

That's not half ner whole of it, Jim put in. The Mormons massacreed Fancher's whole party, down there in the Mountain Meadows. I heerd they got the indians to do the killin'.

I wasn't going to argue with Jim anymore than I'd stand there jawing with an ice storm. I wanted out of Fort Laramie in case General Sumner swung through, so I'd as lief get on with Johnston. Nor did I need his speech to the men assembled on the parade grounds that day we headed northwest to South Pass how this so-called "Utah Expedition" would be a cleansing fire burning the plague of Mormon secession out of the nation. Mostly, I wanted ready cash. In my thoughts was the lush green floodplain along the Poudre. Gold would be found there any day now, I was sure. And I wanted to be there on my own claim for the boom.

Passage west went slow as we bucked brave headwinds blasting in our faces across high prairie desert with not so much as a jack pine to give it pause. We were traveling later than it was wise for any wagon train to, as winter is nothing if not sudden on the steppes, but General Johnston was so able a leader we might have gone to Jericho. When we reached winter quarters at Fort Supply we looked down valley and saw smoke from where Mormon raiders torched Army wagons and ran off their beef herd. Johnston faced men who soon would want for hot food and warm clothes.

Besides that, Colonel Alexander had taken two companies of dragoons upriver to Bear Lake to flank Mormon positions from the north. This, in December, when sudden blizzards could kill greenhorns with no more sense than God gave stray lambs. It put me in mind of those days I spent guiding the Englishman up Iron Mountain. Talk about camp was that the Colonel took spite from thoughts the General soon would replace him.

Johnston dispatched me north to find Alexander's columns and guide them back to Fort Supply. I lit out to track them north at Bear River and found they hadn't rode that way but further west up Ham's Fork, a short march in summer through grassy valleys I'd passed through, seemed like fifty years ago or forever in another life with my father telling me what Green River had been like in 1828.

It began four days and nights of Hell. Dusk come early. Troops gathered driftwood willows for windbreaks and slept in hollows dug in piled snow with small campfires that got swept away by windstorms, all sparks and orange embers and ash and thirty below—so cold you felt your face might crack from the inside out like an egg. During the day I kept watch for horsemen nodding in the saddle. I'd ride up, tear them from their sleep, and alight to march them dropsy fools, pushing them, running them along the trail until their life's blood seeped back into their legs. And

it went on like that. The boys suffered as they lay
at nightfall on the frozen ground, but they said
little or nothing, for they feared the morrow's
march across a treeless, lifeless windswept valley
even more.

Good horseflesh become fresh food for
wolves. More than half the command was frosted.
To halt, though, meant death. Did I sleep those
nights? Was my mind filled with questions about
my half-brother, as if now I had a double in the
world? Did I dream of Poudre valley where there's
a bend along the river's south bank and cottonwoods cast shadows of a summer's afternoon on
pools of river water that called to me,

Come, lie down,
you needn't go on,
this is the land
of milk and honey,
here, just across
this Jordan,

like as if its silence draws nearer whatever heaven
is beyond, which needs our yearning as much as
we need its promise, as if this bend in the river
were a way station, a stained glass chapel called
"Our Lady of Perpetual Rest," with the sky its
blue window, the sunlight on wild grasses its
cupped candles flickering in banks and rows that
would all blow out when dawn broke in cinders to
another windy day.

The fourth morning I spotted smoke curl
from Fort Supply's chimney, and all gave a weak
shout of deliverance. Jim Bridger greeted me and
took me into his store and set me beside his stove
to thaw me out.

Hell, he said with a broad smile, we need a
few of these days so cold that campfires freeze
solid. Later on I can grind them up and use them
for pepper.

I almost made my mind up never to take

another job with the U.S. Army, and now wish I'd made good my resolve. The only man I could respect was Johnston, and wasn't it odd only a few years later to read he was killed at the battle of Shiloh, a hard-headed Secessionist?

I wanted to get shut of Fort Laramie after Reeshaw got his man Smith to testify that Twiss and I paid ourselves $100 each in Sioux annuities, making us out to be petty thieves. Strange how a man will try to blacken your name by accusing you of the very things he's been doing. Maybe John Reeshaw still feared I'd give the lie to his story about Conquering Bear. That wasn't the only trouble. Agent Twiss tried to arrest Seth Ward on the charge that he had "excited the indians" against him. I was again caught in the middle between two men who'd been good to me and who'd now found themselves at odds. When most folks separate right and left into two armed camps, the loneliest place is in the middle.

Summer of 1858, First Elk Woman and I moved our family and tipis down along Cache La Poudre's banks where I'd buried my claim in 1844. As to the Cheyenne, I learned when I visited Bold Wolf's camp to see Bright Star and inquire about Two Bears that General Sumner had caught up with them in Kansas territory on Solomon River.

Our holy men, White Bull and Dark, had most Dog Soldiers believing they'd found medicine strong enough to make the cavalry's bullets fall harmless to the ground, Bold Wolf said.

It was a good idea, he said. We liked it. But when the armies met, the eagle chief Sumner ordered his troops to advance in a sabre charge! We warriors turned to our holy men to see what their medicine would do against that.

Two Bears rode hard before our lines shouting to meet Sumner's charge with our own. Sometimes the Dog Soldiers will take heart from such a man, but they have not yet accepted him as one of their own. The holy men were struck dumb, and the braves bolted every which way. So much for our war with the whites this year.

Swift Hawk came by to bid us farewell. What is this Fourth Age bringing us, he wondered. So many of our good people are lost to us, I begin to wonder what the world will be like with no human beings to keep our sacred way?

It was that night or soon to then I told First Elk Woman, I've been walking Fort Laramie every day for weeks watching the post grow, with new barracks all around the parade grounds, a guard-house for the drunk and desperate, a row of fine officers' houses, a stone magazine bristling with new rifles and with boxes of grenades. I've been talking most of an evening over pints of beer about what the government has in mind for the Sioux, Arapaho, and Cheyenne bands.

It comes down to race, Twiss told me. The tribes are thought of as nomads and outside the law. If a white man claims land, his word has to be taken above all others. That, or the U.S. government would be lying about the Homestead Act, and everything would turn crazy because that would mean it really wasn't the government's land to give.

Well, she said, you're a white man, at least the last time I looked.

So you think I should file claim? I asked her.

I'm just reminding you of something. Think about it, if you want to.

Think about it I did. As I recalled, Tom Fitzpatrick's treaty gave the high prairies south from Fort Laramie down to the Poudre to the Arapaho, Cheyenne, and Oglala. I would ask First Elk Woman and Swift Bird to pass the word to Niwot that if his Arapaho and Bold Wolf's

Cheyenne and Man Afraid of His Horses gave all those lands to a party of whites they knew as friends and family, among them myself, Eldridge Geary, John Provost, Ab Stover, Sam Deon, Ravofiere, we would file claim and the tribes would always have a home.

As it turned out, Bold Wolf's price for his part in the agreement we struck in the shade of a huge cottonwood tree was that Bright Star should come into our home, First Elk Woman's and mine, as my Cheyenne wife. When put to her that way, First Elk Woman could hardly say no, for if it was my idea it was also her will that the idea be put into action.

October 6, 1884
Pine Ridge Agency

"He Conjures the Whirlwind"

Yes, my Cheyenne half-brother did speak to me at last. He came one night to our tipi along the Poudre where First Elk Woman and I were fixing to build our new log cabin with timber even then limbed and stripped and drying from up-canyon forests. I heard thrown pebbles make small drum-thuds, remembering as I woke how often a young Oglala would call out a fiancée for some moonlight rendezvous that way.

Come with me, he said to my surprise when I stuck my head out the tipi doorflap. He'd never uttered a word to me before. What else could I do but follow him? I had to hear more.

When we reached the river, he turned to speak. I could see his lips move, but roarings of the June rise's spring waters was so loud I could not hear him, so I motioned for him to speak again, more loudly.

I've seen you watching me.

Yes, I said, I've watched you for long enough to know your greatest wish is to be asked into the Dog Soldier society.

And what is yours?

At first I thought to say I wished we could be friends, but something caught in my throat, making me pause, making a silence for something, like an old trout in a deep pool who rises to snatch a flying gnat from the air.

I said, My greatest wish has always been to
play my fiddle in a band and travel 'round from
place to place like Cheyenne drummers from
camp to camp to sing at feasts and ceremonies.

He was looking over my shoulder northward,
distracted.

Our lives have been different, I said. There are
no words to tell you.

Do you know what I need to do to get asked
into the men's society?

Steal horses, count coup ...

Yes, but no one will go with me. Not my
father, not him. He was only in my mother's
lodge once that I remember. I remember only
hearing the sound of her voice pleading, Why do
you leave me? Is it to go back to your other
woman, your white woman? Does she give you
sons? Does she help to boil the human smell off
your traps so you can kill more beaver and turn
them into God's skin with writing on it? So you
can give her that paper and then come back to me
for more? I do not remember him saying anything
to my mother. He just reached for his rifle and
pack and crouched through our doorflap and was
gone.

Two Bears's face was hard, his eyes with that
distant look that spoke of some freshly felt death.

I'm sorry for that, I said. But can you understand that he was never home with my mother,
the white woman, any more than he was with
yours?

Will you help me, then? I need someone to
come with me, not to take horses and coup from
the Crow, but someone to sing my deeds until the
Dog Soldiers come ask me to join them. Perhaps
you can even play your ... what you call? ... your
fiddle as you make your song.

First Elk Woman woke as I threw my poncho
and some hardtack and jerky into my sack. I told

her I was going to the Crow camp in the valley between the Big Horns and the Wind Rivers.

I don't like this. It doesn't feel right, she argued. You don't trust this Two Bears, do you?

You know I can take care of myself.

You can take care of yourself if you are well and strong and nothing truly strange happens.

If something truly strange happens, no one can take care of himself. Besides, I have to set something right, I said. It's a matter of this young man's life.

It was late May, early June, the streams were already rising. I rode alongside Two Bears to the North Platte Bridge stockade, always looking for that point where the Medicine Bows bend like buffalo bull humps to the west, till we reached Hell's Half-acre and passed along Poison Spider Creek, which took us to where the rivers meet and we again turned north through Wind river canyon with the walls of Owl Creek mountain rising straight up until we got to Ten Sleeps valley. My father taught me that was where Crow camps would be in early June, and we began to travel only at night so as not to be seen.

Even along the Poudre it was known to snow hard in early June. There had been a hard snow that June when my father and his mulatto friend Jim Beckwith had cached the poudre down in Colorado—all the more so in these northern reaches. A late snow could kill us more sure than a Crow war party out to recoup its treasure in horses. We crossed and recrossed that valley from Meetseetse to Ten Sleeps, but could find no sign of the Crow. So we doubled back through Wind River canyon, heading west again. We found them, after two nights, camped along Fivemile Creek under Pilot Butte's shadow.

The camp curved along the creek, shaped like the bitten moon. What we would need was darkness, and a large cloudhead that seemed to eat the whole night sky of stars sailing in from the west obliged us. We are in luck, I thought. For dead quiet I cut buckskin mufflers for my horse's shod hooves and tied them on. Two Bears would have none of such caution. He wanted to ride right in and just take the Crow ponies.

This is my raid, he said. You do what I say.

Let me at least circle the camp. Then I can ride through from the west, whooping and firing my sidearm to make a commotion while you stampede their herd and cull out as many as you need to get yourself askt into the Dog Soldiers, I said. And he nodded yes.

I looped way around Pilot Butte to keep from being seen and at last faced smoldering Crow campfires from the west. All the while I stopped often to peer into Pilot Butte's shadow for sign of some night watch, hopefully asleep on his horse somewhere near the eastern end of camp standing there at the edge of Fivemile creek. All quiet.

Hey, hey, hey! I heard the whoop and hollar Two Bears sent up. Hell, I thought, it's just like a young buck to go off half-cocked before every-thing is set!

To my eyes, he was tiny at that distance. He wove his mother's red trade blanket over and around his head in false dawn light when even the best night watch drifted some, enough for Two Bears to work his horse 'round back of that herd to drive them straight into the rising sun he hoped would blind the Crow, so we'd ride east into the split between the Big Horns and the Medicine Bows and spur far north to Dull Knife's camp on the Yellowstone River where he'd dance to drums when the Dog Soldiers stacked buffalo skulls like blocks inside the medicine tent, like he'd imag-ined so many times already.

But the sun would not shine clear that morning. I plunged my horse down through center camp with a torch in my hand trying to draw to me the Crow warriors who ran naked in that commotion with the threat of burning their lodges down. They were already arming themselves. It wasn't a true surprise. Yet I could see confusion in their faces. Which to defend?

A minute's hestitation might mean losing herd *and* home. They ran for their horses, then for me. I was looking into the white disk of newly risen sun behind grey-black clouds and riding fast with a June snowstorm at my back when a ball from a flintlock smashed through my saddleseat into my right hip with a splinter of lead that burnt right through my bone.

I galloped my horse through the rest of the camp and on toward Two Bears, who had already disappeared over a grassy rise with part of the Crow herd, but each time a horse hoof landed on the turf I got another stab hurting so bad I'll say no more about that particular subject. Besides, the day's strange commencement soon did outdistance Crow pursuit. They turned to running down the mavericks, the horses that wouldn't herd up, and so didn't get stolen first—for, like any band, without the wild ones they could never rescue the tame.

Much they had to fear from losing their horses. In less not a quarter hour that storm became a blizzard. Green things, spring buffalo grass, yucca with bells on, were swallowed into a blanc plain hardly given the eye behind witchy wraiths of cloud, except that we both knew it well, and had traveled it, for it was the old Oregon trail thousands had taken westward to Independence rock, South pass, to Utah and beyond. Yet at every hitch my hip schooled me that I should be in my bed under a warm buffalo robe with First Elk Woman.

We dared not take the Crow for granted. Horse raids were aplenty among them before. They was masters of pursuit, of surround and recapture, or else they would've gone the way of the Diggers in Nevada, living on roots and lizards, scavengers without a home. So we loped along, we didn't walk. To drive a herd of horses is hard enough when you ain't shot in the hip. It's a pace more than anything, a movement on horseback that dogs them in the direction you want them to go. I was driving them, though damned if I knew what mystery drove me.

The further we drove the paints due east, the harder the wind blew at our backs. I had a sheep-skin coat, and he the red blanket by which I followed the flag of his long hair that he had untied I guessed as a prayer just before he galloped around the Crow herd into the white slant of hard snow and fog. Sometimes he was pink like the *sacre coeur* in holy pictures, bobbing behind many veils of storm cloud. I dared not stop, though my britches were stained with frozen blood. It felt like some light in my body had begun to go out. I just wanted to fall asleep—which I knew was the soft voice of death talking—until I couldn't close my eyes, and I couldn't see either.

Finally I followed only his voice, hey-heying through the drifting snow and fog across miles of rolling valley grasslands, imagining he could hear the horses drive their unshod hoofs into the deepening snow, their breathing loud and labored and rhythmic like air squeezed through an accordian by some cajun musician.

My horse kept slowing as I began forgetting to urge him on. It went like that for hours as the sun swung south around behind us, and the red I saw

then was his campfire, though I could see nothing
else but white blur.

We cannot stop for long, he said. Who knows
how long this lucky storm will last? I slid off my
saddle and winced as I hit the snow. I can't go
anymore, I said.

You will go or you will die, he said.

What else but cold delirium in the blood
made me hear the spring blizzard's high winds as
my dead father whistling *Un Canadien Errant*
across the banks of Poison Spider Creek?

Don't leave me, I said.

He looked at me in the glow of his campfire
that was almost blown to sparks and cinders.

That's what *she* said, Two Bears snorted. I
believed it was finished. For years, when I was a
boy my mother and I lived in shame because my
father—your father—did not return. In those
days we thought any white man was *wi'hio,* that
we had been blessed by his coming and curst by
his leaving. For years, my mother sought out the
most powerful medicine men and had me study to
learn the spells of killing with them, so that if he
ever came back I could get even with him—for
both of us. I learned to tie the winds in knots I
captured in my braids. I learned to make a storm
that can kill.

He gave me a quick quizzical look. I lied when
I said this storm was luck, he said. Do you understand?

I do, I whispered.

He nodded as if to say to himself he believed
me, then he went on talking.

Word came he'd been killed up north at the
hands of the Blackfeet. Two Bears fed buffalo
chips from his parfleche to his little blaze.

It was like my own death. Can you understand? My whole life was drawn and aimed like a

weapon at one man. Now he was beyond my vengence. And then, one day, there you were, looking just like him.

You look as much like him as I do, Two Bears. Don't leave me, I said.

That's what *she* said. But she didn't die, and neither will you if I get you a healer to cure your wound. Don't worry, my brother, I'll be back with help.

With his horse blanket he covered me and curled my body around the little fire as if I were some caterpillar in a cacoon, then he knelt down beside me. I could feel his breathing against my face. He gathered me up into his arms a long minute, he kissed me full on the mouth, and he got up and disappeared into the slants of snow and fog and darkness.

I'd used my savvy to keep a company of greenhorn soldiers from dying out there in Shoshone country in western Wyoming, yet I couldn't promise I'd do as well by myself. I seemed to hear First Elk Woman's voice telling me that something truly strange had happened, and I fought sleep as long as I could, the while remembering what my father had told me years before about giving yourself over to the huge forces that swirl all around us like white water in an Arkansas River sinkhole. I closed my eyes.

What else could it have been but a dream when I saw Two Bears standing at the foot of these sand banks? He grew bigger and bigger until my vision filled with his light hair and his stone green eyes and his mouth opened wider and wider until out of him in great heaves came roaring a company of blue coats in a cavalry charge, all jangling metal from bridles to sabres in a rhythm like tamborines down sandbanks crumbling under shod hoofs and surrounding him, slashing at him with their long knives in a blur of silver flashes. I saw him fall, get up again. I saw three soldiers jump down off their horses and knock him to the ground and kick and stab at him as he laughed in their faces, *You can't kill me, I made you!*

Tipis were burning. I was standing among them and felt their heat on my cheeks. The fire grew bigger, redder, until Two Bears begun to make himself disappear into a dark shadow like smoke that blots sunlight. *Don't leave me*, I cried.

Whoa there, hoss, I heard the darkness say. I opened my eyes and found myself staring into the face of a black man.

You're Jim Beckwith, ain't you?

He spat tobacco juice into the flames he'd built up of Two Bear's campfire and nodded.

How long have I been out, I asked him.

Couldn't've been that long, he said, or you'd be one stiff puppy. I lit out after you and the Cheyenne buck soon after you two raised all that hell in the Crow camp. I always keep my best horses tethered at my lodge just in case of such a e-ventu-ality. Got to get you to a doctor. Who might you be?

Antoine Janis, I said.

I knew someone by that name, he said, stroking a long white scar on his chin. I trapped the beaver with him when I first decided one night to just walk away from the plantation out to these parts before I tuck up with the Crow. Might've been a man your father's age. We come through Wind River canyon together with Cap'n Ashley's party, must've been in eighteen and twenty-seven, twenty-eight, I'm not sure which. We used to hang by old Bent's Fort together and sing and dance with the senoritas down there. He sure did love his music. Fine man. Trustworthy. Not like this Cheyenne buck who's left you out here to die in this blizzard.

He's gone to get help, I said, not sure whether

I spoke of my father as a young man in love with music or my young half-brother.

Jim paused to wipe both handlebars on his long moustache with the back of his gloved hand. Sure, he said, sure. Listen, I can see you're hurt, been bleedin' pretty bad there from the hip. I'm goin' to leave you here a while m'self to rig a travois to carry you on down to the Platte Bridge stockade.

Don't leave, I said.

I *will* be back, he laughed.

He did come back. Said he had to get me to my Poudre river home in honor of my father, who was a trustworthy soul, though his Crow friends might grumble. I just lay in the travois with a hitch in my hip as the sun came out and melted every trace of that June snowstorm by day's end until at last by nightfall we reached Platte bridge's wooden walls and the Army doctor there had me swig down near a pint of eastern mash whiskey and removed the ball from where it lodged against my bone.

In the months healing, as I learned all over again to walk and then to ride, I never did see Two Bears again. Bright Star said he had gone north to Dull Knife's camp with the few ponies he was able to salvage through that storm, and he got his wish to be a Dog Soldier. I figured he was about as crazy about his mother as I had been about my father, and what we both done from time to time in our lives caught in this flood I came to see was part of the history of a long mistake in which it was everywhere said there was no other way but to turn everything into money, including love and death. As I laid up mending, I heard a coyote call, mocking me for a fool to have ridden off with a man I should've known was up to doing me no good.

I'd fallen again for the same fox and coyote story my father had told me about how if I didn't save the Oglala they would all be rubbed out. They say your strength is your weakness, and mine was believing. As I hobbled from stockade to river and back, gaining my legs again I often pictured myself a child in L'Academie du Sacre Coeur, sitting in the corner on a stool, wearing the pointed dunce cap.

I laid all them hitches in my thinking up to loss of blood and fever. If I was still alive, it was because Two Bears wanted it that way. I sit here even today and wonder as I pause with pen in hand. Try as I might, I could not figure that one out. All I hoped was that fate had balanced our accounts.

October 16, 1884
Pine Ridge Agency

"Small Fish"

When in 1878 we removed from Laporte to Pine Ridge, I staked and strung a site for our new house and corrals, a spot between two hills for shelter from these winds that plague this land. My boys—Joe, Charlie, and Nick—built a cabin, half log, half sod that weighed so heavy work went very slow. First of all we had to chunk and dig out a small portion of a hill to set the building frame in.

After two months there I began to feel such an ache in my joints I could scarcely drag my body out of bed, never mind keeping a store as sub-agent at Pine Ridge. My whole spine felt hammered to pieces so if I could've danced I would've shook like a rattle. The new agent and doctor, Macgillacuddy, he looked me over, made me try to bend my back, and said I was bad arthritic. I began to wonder about those years of sleeping out on wet ground. Most of those old fellows I trapped beaver with had died before they reached my age, and maybe they escaped paying the price.

A young Lakota holy man chanced by my house that fall. When he saw my body so locked, he sat on the floor until he said he knew how to help me. Take whatever you want in payment from my little ranch, I told him. Next day when First Elk Woman stood outside boiling linen and I was lying abed I called out to her, What is he up to? She called in to me, Walking from hilltop to hilltop. That night, after supper, he gave me his findings.

Spirits live on each hill who have been visiting each other every day, he said. Your house lies right in line of their flight, and your house is faced so they can't pass through doors or windows. They are angry with you. They are making you suffer.

I could almost picture what he said as if bodies long and drawn out as winds with human faces were sweeping across this big draw. With no delay, though it meant taking the house down board by timber, filling in the earth works, and redigging another hill, I set my boys to moving the house but a short distance.

It took all of a month, but by its end my spine had unstooped itself enough for me to pitch in with driving our horses into their new corrals. The holy man said his goodbyes after I made good my promise of a stallion as his payment. He headed out as far from the agency store as possible, where he could still see spirits.

Songs and trances don't work around these new white people, he said. I have smoked on it, and I now believe that is their power. They eat the magic out of the world. Why the gods do not give the Lakota lasting victory over these *wasichus,* who cannot be strong since they eat only tame meat, I do not know. We beat Yellow Hair at the Greasy Grass, and we beat eagle chief Crook, but nothing seems to make them go away. Now Crazy Horse is dead, and there's a lot of good people lost. That is always so, but more so now than ever.

The Cheyenne prophet Sweet Medicine saw the whites coming with their cattle, taking more and more land until at last they took even our children away to their homeland in the east where they would change them so an old-time Oglala wouldn't know them to look at them.

I write this now, Mr. Watrous, to show you
what my lookout still is. It goes further than
keeping a sharp eye out.

I had survived my half-brother's plan to take
me out into a blizzard of his own making and
leave me wounded and bleeding in the snow until
it killed me.

I had learned to turn the six-foot dry sticks
from floats in trapping beaver to a tracker's stick
in the service of the Army. If I could find one
print even among a scramble of prints I could use
my tracker's stick to find the next by sweeping it
on a pivot and marking intervals of print size and
gait.

But also I had since boyhood sensed that there
are dark, unseen things out on the prairies in the
same way that thwarting the flight of spirits means
trouble. That's what I taught my brother Nicholas
when he came out west, though my father didn't
bring him out. No one in my family ever saw my
father after he left the Poudre River council
grounds. Word drifted south from Three Forks
that Blackfoot warriors killed him somewhere
along the Gallatin. Even Two Bears had known
that.

So I must father my brother in that school
where books were trees, skies, animals, rivers,
where cipher was sums trading brought, even
though I'd begun to wonder if this magic power
that Two Bears had talked so bitterly about, this
power to turn the beaver into paper with writing
on it, was not some kind of religion, some kind of
religious war, that swept all before it in its flood
and ate the souls equally of all who stood with it
or against it, and made of every man, woman, and
child an infidel who did not believe life is better
lived when everything's not turned to money.

The first trip I took Nicholas on was to find
the Oglalas off hunting buffalo west of Fort

Laramie. We followed the river upstream west and south toward the range, looking here and there for sign. But an Oglala camp on the move spreads out a half mile or more, so there's no one beaten path in the prairie grass to follow.

On the third day out we woke to an empty camp. The horses and mules had run off. Nick hadn't hobbled them well enough. We lost a day running the animals down—first mule, then horse, then the whole kit until we pulled our equipment together and found the crusted scar of a travois pole dragged across a dry sandbar heading straight toward a deep notch in the ridgeline of the Laramie range that my father called La Bonte pass.

We got off our horses and walked. What with scree giving way under foot and hoof, that grade soon had Nick puffing. To make the time pass a little lighter, I started to sing, and my brother picked up the tune,

> M'en revenant
> de la jolie Rochelle
> J'ai recontré
> trois jolies demoiselles.
> C'est l'aviron
> qui nous mène,
> qui nous mène,
> C'est l'aviron
> qui nous mène en haut!

He smiled and said, Yes, it's rowing that gets us on high.

When we climbed near the crest of that notch, the ground broke up into boulder fields so thick Nick stopped and said to go on without him. Hell, I said, if you've got one foot to hop on you can make it.

Nick was young and strong. I watched him as if I were seeing myself years ago, looking up often at the sheer granite walls on either side of the pass with his mouth agape, pulling his bell mare, her white tongue lolling from her lathered mouth until we reached the top and sat to take in the view and a drink of water. We had crawled the last hundred feet or so with the animals' reins in our teeth. Nick shook his head in disbelief as we gazed west to high prairies in the *montagne* that stretched outward from the west slope of the Medicine Bows.

I never thought there could be any prairie higher than the one at Fort Laramie, Nick said.

Grasslands stretched for twenty miles or so, with lone buffalo bulls standing here and there among ravines that marked the June risings of dry creeks. When we get to South Pass, I told him, remember this. Look what an advantage it is to know the land. Without wagons, the Oglalas can go straight over notches like these from valley to valley, rather than around through passes like the emigrant trains have to. Army columns might be able to make it through, but they don't know these passes, not like father did.

Coming here like this with you puts me in mind of the earliest days when I traveled with Pa. One of the first things he did was to tell me about the Cheyenne practice of water-gazing to see what the underwater people were doing. He would start to talk, and I would imagine some clear lake or quiet pool along a creek or river where reeds and watergrasses cast their shadows that rippled in the eddies. Can you picture that?

Yes, Nick said.

Can you see inside the underwater world a mountain pass just like the one we're in now? See across the pass where the rock hangs over so far it looks like it will topple? That's where papa told me about the coyote and the fox. Coyote thinks he's smart, but he never did get the best of fox yet, though one day over yonder where I'm pointing coyote came trotting around that rock and thinks he sees the fox asleep. Aha, he says to himself, at last I'm goin' to make a meal of that fox. He won't have time to wake from his dream before I have him in my jaws. But old fox never sleeps during the day but with one eye open, so he saw coyote coming. Around the ledge of rock coyote comes, only when he sees fox he's leaning all his weight and strength to hold up that wall of rock.

Hurry up and get over here and help me, fox says to coyote. This here wall of rock is about to topple over and crush us both if you don't put your back into it. Push!

Coyote looks at fox, sees he's sweating power-ful, and out of his eyes comes the dread of death itself. Suddenly it strikes coyote that fox is really scared. So he raises himself up on his hindquarters and leans everything he's got into that wall. And sure enough, as soon as his paws ever touch the rock wall he can feel a tremblin' deep inside there that spells a complete slide. Stands to reason. Down in the pass is all the shattered tailings of former slides.

Fox says, Good work, coyote. I think I can go down the mountainside among the other animals and get help now.

Coyote, who's sweating powerful himself now, cries out, No, no! Don't you leave! It takes two to hold this rock wall up.

You're acting ridiculous again, fox says. You saw that when you came upon me I was holding it by my lonesome. And to prove it, I'm going to leave off my pushing.

Fox stepped back from the rock wall, and it didn't come crashing down on coyote's head. He let a snort of relief out of his nostrils.

I'll be back with help, fox says.

And, of course, fox never did come back did he? Nick said.

No, he never did, but coyote remembered that rock wall for the rest of his life, for it was another place that fox got the best of him, just like papa did me.

Papa fooled you like fox done coyote?

Well, sort of. See, when I had only been out here maybe four years he convinced me that the Oglalas would all die out if I didn't get all married in and stay with them to serve as their interpreter among the whites.

But wasn't papa right?

Sometimes I think the Oglalas are going to outlive us all, Nick. We white folks, we're just johnny-come-latelies. Only the Oglala have been here summer and winter long enough to become one with the spirits of this place.

Out here there's not one but many gods, I told Nick. These are Shoshone lands, meaning only the Shoshones have learnt the spirits here. Oglalas can get bushwhacked just as easy as white men any time unless they take the trouble to travel invisible or in such large numbers Washakie would think twice before attacking. So there's a limit to how far west they know.

We spred hides by the fire and stretched our bones and watched the sky go yellow then pink purple in layers like spires of ash in some badlands wall.

This is the time I like best, I said. Nothing left to do, and dark coming on. Coyotes start to howl real pretty. You know, I told you this story about fox and coyote and that might've left you with the idea that coyote is stupid. What makes him stupid is that as smart as he is he *thinks* he's smarter. You've no doubt seen how well I keep my ledger sheltered from rain and snow inside this double oilcloth bag. But that's not the only reason I keep it under wraps, for there's been times when I'd come into camp when I was but a pup working on papa's beaver gangs and see coyote sitting by the fire pouring over my ledger if I was forgetable and left it lying around uncared for.

You might think, Hell, ain't no coyote can read, but I assure you there's them that can, but they ain't so all-fired smart. Know how I can tell? Because I've never seen a one of them that read my ledger without moving his lips.

Nick looked over at me with a smile in his eyes. Feels like I've been here a hundred years already, Nick said, settling his head down on his saddle. Then he stared up into the stars.

Out here is a different century alright. Like life always was.

A light snow began to fall. We could almost see the moment when cold rain snapped into flakes as it entered our light.

How's Memé? I asked him.

Still rulin' the roost with that look of hers, Joe.

We looked at each other in firelight and laughed. We both have seen that face of the Virgin Mary when she's beholding her crucified son turned on us, haven't we, Nick?

Up to a point, Jesus was a momma's boy, too. Nick said. Ain't that how the Gospel sets a man free from a woman's apron strings? Comes a point when we must be about our father's business, and there ain't nothin' Memé can do about it but step aside. She can't suffer and she can't die for us.

She ain't wearing down none?

Nah. We come from strong stock. We're a family that's vain about how much hard times we can take. She could outlive us all, if I take your drift.

Does she ever say anthing?

Nick looked at me like he saw something change in my face when I asked. She brags on you, he said. Says father was proud of how you took to the life out here.

I wish she'd have said something like that just once to my face, I said with a sigh.

Do you really think it would've made any difference?

Sometimes I tell myself I would've been better off with her blessing. I'd maybe been sure enough of myself to have enjoyed the chances I've had to take since I left home. Go to sleep, I said. Nick pulled his buffalo robe over his shoulder without another word. He knew I'd nothing more to say on that matter.

About September we'd put up a full equipment of merchandise and head northwest to open bargaining with the Brulé, Minniconjou, or Oglala up between the Big Horns and the Black Hills. Each of us had five or six horses and mules which we'd march single-file, laden with beads, mirrors, vermillion, blankets, shirts, calicos, muslins, hatchets, axes, knives, flintlocks, powder, lead, traps, cast-iron kettles of various sizes—we wouldn't carry the cheap tin ones as they're worthless, though I'd known Reeshaw's men to carry them. I taught Nick to give fair value. Anything else was too dangerous out in the wilderness, for what else has any man to offer but whiskey to heal the wound made by some brazen offer of bad trades? And how could a trader surely keep his scalp in the camp of drunk Brulés?

As soon as one of us had hides sufficient we'd split up, usually Nicholas heading back to Fort Laramie and coming back with more goods so that we'd meet sometimes midway in our travels. It was a breath of home to come acrosst my brother's slender column of smoke rising through a stand of pines into a late afternoon winter sky somewhere askirt pine-stubbled edges of the Black Hills.

We'd pass and repass each other many times, but Reeshaw finally got Twiss over his whiskey barrel enough to let his men go north with "presents" of the Brulés' own annuity goods, and the Brulés made "presents" of buffalo hides, so that by summer of 1858 Nick and I left off trading with the Tetons as we were less and less able to make a living. We were instead leading mule trains with flour, sugar, coffee, and salt down from Fort Laramie to Poudre river and the Big Thompson where we ran this horse ranch across the way from Mariano Medina's stage stop at Namaqua and on south to Cherry Creek.

Nick imagined a Blackfoot sweettooth behind every rock along the Devil's Backbone, ready to spring out and count coup. We stopped overnight at Fort Walbach once on our way to Cherry Creek, and next morning the *bourgeois* there gave us our price on the goods. We were happy we only had to go half way.

Back at Fort Laramie the suttler gave us news of gold strikes at Cherry Creek. You may imagine how we second-guessed ourselves that day! Nick and I bought a jug at the suttler's and had a high old time laughing at ourselves. What would our father have thought of us, we wondered. I dredged up his maxims: *Never stray from first intent!* As night fell on us where we sat in the cemetery on the hill overlooking the parade grounds, soon our thoughts were of his death at the hands of Blackfoot warriors, well over a decade ago.

Once they have you hogtied, Pa told me, it's no use begging for your life. As they sharpen their skinning knives, spit in their eye! What they want is to eat the heart of a great enemy, and it might as well be you. Me and Nick we was both ghosted that night and fell silent staring at stars.

Father used to say *les indiens des plaines vivant tres belle*, I told Nick, poking him in the ribs, laughing. *Our father who art in heaven*, Nick sang like a monk. Our father was a radical, I said. He

wanted to send Cheyenne braves to the military
academy. He would ask the air, How can they
keep them from going off half-cocked? Even their
own chiefs can't do it. But if every American
cavalryman could ride like a Cheyenne or Sioux
they'd be the best light cavalry in the world. And
if there should prove to be a native prophet who
could bring the tribes together, they'd do as was
done in Europe—their gods would become
canonized saints as they convert to Christ. It
would slow the white digestion to learn plains
Indian religion.

You have a half-brother you don't know
about, I told Nick.

What? he asked.

Has the liquor made you stupid? Haven't you
heard a word I said? He had a wife out here, I told
Nick, name of Bright Star, daughter of Bold
Wolf, who bore him a son, this young Cheyenne
buck about your age, name of Two Bears. For the
longest time he never spoke to me. His eyes were
full of anger and hate. I'd understand if he hated
all white men, Nick.

Ha! Nick said. Sometimes I hate all white
men too, including myself. He pointed a finger at
his temple and made as if to blow his brains out.

Our father had another life out here we never
knew about back home.

Stands to reason, Nick said at last, as he slung
the jug over his shoulder for another swig.

Our father was an imbecile saint, we thought,
as we walked under what First Elk Woman called
the Spirit Road, and we had learned to call the
Milky Way.

He tried to tell me once about his dream of a
native prophet, I said to Nick. There'll come a
day, he said, when a prophet will give birth to
their souls. They will become soulful. They will
become a spiritual force in their very silence. They

will rise up and go to white men's towns, and they will stand on street corners and bear silent witness until the white folks won't know what to do, whether to scream or call the Army, but what good will the Army do? What will they charge them with?

Our father died crossing the Tetons, and his heart was clean. Name your wives Marie, he told me, always Marie.

You understand, Mr. Watrous, this story I'm telling you now took place *before* Two Bears took me out and abandoned me in that killer snowstorm of his own making. Now that I recollect that story, it comes to me what a fool I am. Not only had my father used the fox's trick on the coyote on me, making up the rock wall about to topple and crush the Oglala, but also Two Bears had done the same with his blood so hot to be elected to the Dog Soldiers. Seems I can't resist the lie of someone who tells me I am needed. Either that or I'm just another damnfool musician who'll go anywhere for the chance to play.

As for me, I only hoped my children with my Marie would be a numerous new race—I remember thinking of myself as rocking into her the way she would rock into the corn grinding-stone she kept near our fireplace—they would bond the races in their blood with ties of affection—Maggie, Mollie, Antoine, Nick, Zuzell, Charlie, Pete, Willie, and Joseph.

Next day we outfitted another mule train and headed back to Smith's post at Cherry Creek with Eldridge Geary. We found it swept with gold fever. Hundreds of stampeders showed up each day, all eager eyed to "see the elephant" as they called finding color in the diggin's. Some left farms, families, walked the six hundred miles across Missouri and Kansas only to stick a pan in some gravel wash on the creek bed. Not rewarded with nuggets big as apples, they became go-backers next day, drunk enough on tanglefoot whiskey to gas on about how they'd like to string up Horace Greeley for all his lies. Half wouldn't know a gold lead if it jumped out to hit them between the eyes, the other half couldn't tell any difference between mining and simply moving rock. Still, every day it seemed someone found veins of rotten quartz with blossom. This strike was no humbug.

Price for American flour was fifty cents per pound and would shoot up to a dollar, so Nick and I were soon stuffing our possibles bags with coin, enough to begin thinking we'd struck it rich, not in nuggets but the new gold industry.

Once that summer, as Nick and I headed back to Fort Laramie with Eldridge and Swift Hawk and about twenty-five of his band, we came to the Poudre where Niwot, Big Mouth, and Bold Wolf rode up to ask for a parley. We sat as I recall beneath a grove of cottonwoods to smoke a pipe where Box Elder Creek merges into the Poudre, a short walk upstream from where Straus built that fine Kentucky cabin south of Sherwood ranch and stage station. The chiefs asked if we wanted the land between the Poudre and the Box Elder from the foothills east out on the plains.

First Elk Woman, Swift Hawk, and Bold Wolf had spread word from tribe to tribe of this scheme I'd carried from camp to fort like swords I balanced on my fingertips, unsure whether it would work.

Now we began dreaming of a town built for trappers, mostly married to native women and with halfbreed children. We'd call it Colona, for Juan Colona, a Mexican friend who knew my father and had the same dream of this town where the lost ones of the west could find some peace.

In our minds, it would become a greater

trading center than Fort Laramie, where Sioux, Arapaho, and Cheyenne would always be welcome. Later, in 1862, the name Colona was changed for LaPorte, which remains to this day. Only time would strip me of my scheme and show me what a fool's errand I was on. But I am getting ahead of myself, though not unmindful of how mixed up I was.

You begin to see my situation. My marriage to First Elk Woman allied me to her full brother, Swift Hawk, who was—in her mind at least—rightful peace chief of the "Smoke people" Oglalas. Besides, he was my friend.

There came a day when Red Cloud's band began to take down its tipis to move north to the Powder River country. Red Cloud came to Swift Hawk's tipi, seated himself across from Swift Hawk, and said, I know First Elk Woman's yellow-haired husband has a good heart for the Oglalas, but his idea of sharing the land along the Poudre is not right for me. My people and I will never settle. We love the old free roving life too much, and we will fight to keep it.

You who loaf around the fort I think will find it harder than you bargained for, being little white men, cutting the mother's flesh from her bones with plows.

Swift Hawk bid Red Cloud and the Bad Face band safe journey. But the Oglalas were now split into the Smoke People and Bad Faces—the Oyuhkpayes and Itesicas—leaving men like John Reeshaw an open gate to court Red Cloud, who was really only an *akicita* at that time.

My father's words drummed in my head like a scalp-dance rhythm. "Hold them together," he'd said. My plan to build this town I hoped would do that. Instead it backfired in my face. I'd been so moved by Red Cloud's speech I thought even then he was right and our township venture

X
.
141

doomed to fail. It seemed my future did not lie
with Red Cloud's northern bands. I knew from
the way he looked at me from under his large
brows he bore me no personal spite. It was family.

I remember feeling when first I came to the
Rockies that the whole world lay at my feet. Now
that world had narrowed to this town we would
build on the banks of the Poudre. I was not
prepared nor suited for acting out this new dream.
My druthers has always been to go toward the
mountain forests since my father first sat by the
campfire and sang the praises of such places as
where the air's so pure and cold, meat won't spoil
and all wounds soon heal.

My direction had always pointed away from
St. Charles and schools and jails, the world fixed
in deeds and customs. I'd lived since age sixteen in
the world outside that, where a living was to be
won by those with skill and luck enough. In that
I'm not so different from sodbusters who come
from where everything is owned and youth is a
curse to those with dreams but no down payment.
If love was legal tender, I'd have held the deed
entire to Poudre valley. I came to find a *home,* not
settle for real estate, like some folks do.

We started so green we hardly knew where to
file township. Federal surveyors didn't come until
summer, 1862. It was then we learned the hours,
minutes, and seconds the land can be divided into
between eye and rod, though we never did learn
to grease the right wheels to make our dream come
true, nor did we find enough gold to buy northeast Colorado for our Lakota families and create a
town where whites could farm bottom lands and
braves hunt buffalo out on the high plains.

Picture Colona as one of those promised lands
scattered here and there across the west—there
were many in those days, townships where families
banded together to live according to their own

lights—and you'll see where we then stood,
Nicholas and I and all the old free trappers, at
Poudre River where it enters the plains, beneath
this long strip of shady cottonwoods and willows
in broad fields of yellow prairie grasses where we
spent as much time just gazing awestruck at white
fair weather clouds rising above foothills as we did
pitching hay.

One day about that time, a young man by the
name of Joe Mason rode into Laporte. He was
lately from Montana and points east to Minnesota
and Montreal, Canada, wanting to invest somewhere, and he'd heard rumors Laporte might be
the next Cherry Creek. I had this small fortune by
then myself and hoped he'd throw in with us. For
several years I thought he was with us. Turns out
he was only following his own lookout. Why I
ever thought otherwise I do not know.

Why should I put my money in some town if
I'm not going to run it? he askt me later on, when
he knew the set-up and felt he could speak his
mind. I'd got Nick and the others to vote him to
the Town Board, but he did nothing those years
but wait for the federal surveyors to finish their
work. It was like as if I'd found Paradise and not
wise enough to be content I later introduced the
serpent back into the garden, just to test my
suspicion that if we could not survive that venom-
ous bite we could not survive at all. But I am
getting out ahead of myself here.

We was small fish, as they say, and gasping
out of our element. We could not think big
enough to foresee how the war between the states
would beggar America's treasury. Pike's Peak gold
might clear its debts. No Sioux, Cheyenne, or
Arapaho raid must stop the flow of gold from
Denver.

November 18, 1884
Pine Ridge Agency

"Rumors Aplenty"

You have asked two questions. Yes, I knew your father. He was one of many men who came to Colorado first in search of gold but later sensible enough to see that those with the right land would find living good in Poudre valley. He sought my advice on a section in upper Box Elder canyon, whether it be suitable for farm or ranch, as they were paying gold rush prices—five dollars a wagonload—down in Denver for hay. We rode in his buggy that must've come from back east, for when I remarked upon it he said it was made from an open piano-box, with a stick seat and brewster sidebars and a mahogany cup turned on a lathe and shaped by chisel with some skill.

He stopped when we reached a rise near Park Creek to take in the view. The near ground was crowned with a north ridge, colored with red sandstone and white limestone and stippled with green mountain mahogany and wild currant bushes in patterns like a navajo blanket, and in the far ground lay Box Elder canyon reaching up way north and west into Horse Thief pass with red walls like hanging palisades above the grass-lands along the flowing creek. Silence is the only fit praise of such beauty, so it was a while before I told him that in all the years since I'd prospected with Eldridge, Ab Loomis, and Nick all we ever found was broken bits of alabaster which might

prove some value, and enough in gold to break
even on grubstakes.

Regarding your second question about Sam
Deon: he lived on the Overland stage line north
of Provost's bridge in a log cabin that still stands
like mine, only he lived alone. We all helped him
build it. That's the town we wanted—not held
together by anger toward anyone, white or indian,
but by wanting to sponsor each other, to raise
each others' barns, to help build Provost's ferry
with skills we had learned along the North Platte
or the Rio Grande, to help our families, for New
York still wanted fancy furs, and New England
still wanted buffalo hides as belts to drive their
textile mills, and we could either hunt and trap
them ourselves or trade for them. To those who
grumbled about us having an unfair advantage,
as we remember them they weren't willing to do
the work to learn the native languages or face a
grizzly.

It might have kept working as it did in those
early on years, except that later more and more of
the land was bought up by ranchers running big
herds of cows. It was said any man could arrive in
Colorado with one Texas steer and soon thereafter
count himself the proud owner of six thousand,
presumably all offspring of that original.

Regardless, the ranchers couldn't take losses of
their cows being butchered out and roasted by
Oglalas passing through, and who could blame
them? None of us free traders had money enough
to pay back the ranchers, nor could we persuade
our brothers-in-law to stop taking cattle on open
range.

We cut the half-dovetails for Sam's cabin with
broadaxes, sawed long window-holes, narrow
cross loops like the slits of some mountain cat's
eyes that Sam would peer through sometimes as if

to use them to shoot through, perhaps this very minute.

Real scares were few. Rumors aplenty! Some greenhorn'd claim a raiding party was up Spring Canyon stealing horses at the Overland substation in Stout, forgetting it was early autumn and our Oglala wives were up picking berries, wild plums and currants along the hogbacks with their Arapaho women friends who were used to peace inside Chief Friday's camp up near Horse Thief pass.

When First Elk Woman went visiting, her face shined with eagerness to hear from all her sisters. She made them shine, too, and they looked at me, at what a dark figure I must have cut with a jug on my shoulder spiking my heart with whiskey, unsure whether I had sand enough to make this township dream come true, poking Swift Hawk in the ribs to mark my points about what dastard act the government might think of next, so hard he took to wearing his eagle-bone breastplate and giving me long-suffering looks as if to say it was he and his people would pay the price, not me and mine, and I needn't growl so to show my seeing his side of the picture and drown out the soft murmur of women talking some dialect made from listening to hear what sympathy each might need and giving freely to each other what we men took as our right, that comfort which was to him a music.

I can almost hear Deon spit out his words. Wal, he'd say, we'll know if you laid them logs straight if hell's own breath harries us this winter through the chink holes that creak open when you don't use plumb-bobs and do what they say!

Those days I wore a beaver hat so folks would know me as an oldtime free trapper, and so Deon wouldn't live in fear I'd get restless and pull out.

I have never really been a hat man, though. A *bourgeois* wore a crown, not a hat, always the same black beaver plews spun into silver gleamings on the head. Perhaps I would have worn a gray felt hat if it wouldn't stick out. I never wanted notice. Whatever else my life has been, I always have seen it gray, always private, whatever else.

No, now that I think on it, not always. My vanity and my shyness have wrestled forever like twins—like my boys Petey and Willie—fighting everyone and each other, as if what makes the earth we draw our life from is their bodies and what makes the oceans and their rocking is their sweat, and what makes this world go 'round is both their tender feelings and their struggle. Yet it was that night First Elk Woman and I first talked about death and burial that I begun to suffer a change in my lookout.

I don't want a white marble stone carved with my name on it, she said, nor any scripture. If a stone, then one piece of petrified wood about the size of a pillow to lay my head down on. I want only to be taken into the mother's arms as if I had never lived to make a name for myself. This name is what stands between my soul and the mother's arms.

How different an idea was that from my father's dream of buying a stained glass window to commemorate the Janis family name in St. Joseph's parish in St. Charles. From that night, as we lay gazing at stars along the Poudre river's banks I began to ask myself if I too could contribute to this town's very life without asking that my name be put on it. Why was I in this venture for, anyway? If it was the right thing to do, wasn't that enough?

Mountain men and their families came together, laid out this township, and built fifty houses on good lots. The round table of that good company was Sam Deon's saloon and gaming parlor. He brought in Taos lightning, and I played the fiddle with a touch of the devil in my sawing and stomping reels so old they didn't even have names, for those who could recall *le rendez-vous*—Eldridge, Todd Randall, Ray Godwin, LeBon, John Provost, Oliver Morrisette, Ravofiere, Joe Merrivale, Sefroy Iott, who married my sister, Elsonite—in other words, my father's original crew.

The song they loved to sing along on best was one they sang when they worked as riverboat men,

Youpe, youpe! sur la rivière
Vous ne m'entendez guère.
Youpe, youpe! sur la rivière
Vous ne m'entendez pas,

which roughly translates to,

Youpe, youpe, on the river
you can't hardly hear me.
Youpe, youpe, on the river
you can't hear me hardly atall,

something like that—only by now you must have thought of that old lament, *lost in translation.* You lose the rhyme, the puns, the flavor of worksongs.

The way I learnt to play the fiddle, I always have the sound of two strings, making harmony with an open string that doubles sound. That's the strength of the cajun way I learned back in St. Charles as I listened to music on the jolly riverboats moored along wharfs. When I bow it's like I'm strumming a guitar, hitting first beats. I was *un secondeur* really in a band back in Missouri, but I mostly played alone out on these western plains, taking the lead, with Joe Mason clicking spoons in triples on his knee.

Sometimes I sang in French, sometimes in English; sometimes I'd strike up tunes in one and repeat it in the other. If I began to sing,

Allons à la cantin-e
O boire et bien rir-e,
et bien se vivertir-e
o, nous et nos amis-e

I might get everyone clapping their hands in that
tempo I set up, and usually Sam Deon would do
some kind of jig step in his serving apron with
some other men and sing,

> *Let's go to the cantine-a!*
> *to drink and laugh it up-a!*
> *and have us a good time-a!*
> *us and our good friends-a!*

for all of our company now knew firsthand some
sense of old lyrics they might've heard before,

> *O, when someone's married*
> *He sits there lonely*
> *All the time regretting*
> *The good times now gone by*

which are words from a French song, I don't
know how old it is, that says "If I Had Wings,"
which is sillier for those that took their married
life to be a blessing than it is sentimental, except
for the truly drunk.

Sometimes passers-by, Overland stagecoach
travelers on their way north and west, passed
through. I recall the time Joe Meek joined us in
Sam Deon's saloon one night and told us tales the
likes of which I hadn't heard since my father's,
back when we wintered up North Park in our
wickiups when I was a chap.

Joe Meek is the craziest loon I ever met in the
West! my father would say, as if his words were a
battleline he was prepared to fight all day to
defend.

One time we was up the Missouri forks
scouting when our party—Jim Bridger, Joe Meek,
and me—we happened on a small band of
Blackfoot braves swimming a small lake. Joe took
into his head it'd be a lark to fire at them, keeping

their heads ducked underwater, which we did until along comes their whole band who begun to firing on us! We were lucky to escape with our hair that day.

This very Joe Meek took a place beside Sam's potbelly stove and once liquor loosened his tongue he told how he came to take up with *Unmentucken,* or the "Mountain Lamb," as he called her.

He says, After years in the wilderness, I come to fancy Blackfoot or Shoshone wimmin as well as white, and the woman I fancied above all was the one who saved my life, and Milt Sublette's, too. It was he she first married, so you kin see my per-dicamint. Usually free trappers and Shoshones rocked along together well enough, but a band of them jumped us, and Milt, still nursing a knife wound in the thigh—but that's another story—couldn't outrun 'em, so I says, Let's us ride right into that Snake camp and make for the peace tipi, as they do not fight inside it. So we forked our horses and lit out, not stopping till we jerked up our mounts stock still before the biggest tipi in the village, threw ourselves from the saddle, and ducked in through the blessing of the doorflap to sit ourselves by this small fire.

Bad Left Hand and his fighters come in and set down beside us, offering us tobacco, saying we mought put our guns away as iron was against his medicine, which was a dam' lie, fer when we slud our rifles under the tipi hide his men jumped us with steel knives. Still, Bad Left Hand proved a good ole boy by holding out against the idee of slittin' our throats. He got up and left bye 'n bye till about sundown when this great stir shook camp. The braves guarding us ran out to see a tipi burning. Then Bad Left Hand rusht in beck'ning me and Milt to follar 'im. We splasht through Green River and took to willow brush. There we found a Snake girl holding horses for us. She was the loveliest girl I ever seen, and she became my best friend's wife. When we lit out east for Yellowstone river to find our party, she come along.

Milt Sublette jist askt 'er first is all, though what with an old knife wound festerin' and needin' a wound dresser to keep from lockjaw and blood p'ison and going out of his mind he was hurt so bad nothing Mountain Lamb could do to save him, nor any Shoshone medicine man neither, so at last he went east one day to St. Looie before he lost his leg, or his life. One morning he was jist gone, and me and Mountain Lamb took up with each other—no bride price, no runaway marriage on horseback.

Some time later we were riding south together with my party of trappers hunting buffalo on the Powder, me killin' and follaring that herd, she stopping to butcher out cows. I heard whoops and rode back over hill to find her surrounded by twelve Crows painted for war. I spurred on my pony and galloped into that circle of warriors, hollarin' my lungs out. The Crows were so surprised they sat agog on their paints till my men caught up with me and commenct firin' so many rifle shots the Crows they skidaddled.

Wal, says Sam Deon, that was mighty brave. Aw shucks, says Joe Meek, I jist couldn't hold my horse is all.

Everybody laughed, and that was just as well, for every man in that smoky small room had a story something like Joe Meek's about how he come to be married to an Indian gal, and there wouldn't have been room to breathe for all them whiskied sighs from bewhiskered old sots overwhelmed by their soggy sentiments, all except Sam, who had always lived alone.

Sam ran a gaming table in his front room, scuttling under a leathern apron with drinks, buffalo tongue, sweating not from work but fear that one Jack Slade would lean over to grab a jug and bolt while his back was turned. If I saw Jack stoop through the doorway of Sam's cabin, I gave Sam a secret signal by sawing on my fiddle a little tune in French,

> *Je suis parti-z-au ancien Laporte*
> *Avec la jogue au plombeau*
> *Les ferrailes à la poche*
> *Et le jeu de cerates dans la main*
> *Et je cherche qu'à malfaire*

which I might roughly interpret as,

> *I've left for old Laporte*
> *with my jug on my saddlehorn.*
> *With a deck of cards in my hand*
> *and with brass knuckles in my poke*
> *I'm looking for a brawl*

which might pretty well describe Jack Slade and his disposition.

Drunk past insanity, Jack would stumble down to the crossroads in Laporte where Ab Stover kept his store and start another row where he'd pour flour on the floor, then molasses, then salt and vinegar, claiming magic powers would combust out of the heap at his command, slapping people around, lassoing the storekeeper before he could find his pistol, disappearing on his own stage, cackling like a happy undertaker at the reins, dumping poor Abner in dry sagebrush up Cherokee Park way.

Slade was an old desperado of the first water. What law there was was just we members of the Claim Club. Had no sheriff those days, though years later Henry Arrison got elected. Right then it was the golden rule. No one locked his doors. Who would steal if Laporte was filled with Colorado's best trackers?

First Elk Woman and I lived on the north bank of the Poudre a quarter mile upriver from where the Overland stage swing station stood, tending their horses, grazing them in the big grassy meadows on our land, backing them all harnassed as teams into their traces and strapping them in for long hauls up to Virginia Dale and west carrying mail pouches, passengers, and sometimes gold.

Talk about the fox in charge of the hen house! Jack Slade ran the main station at Virginia Dale. He knew two things—when the stage was carrying gold and what the back trails were. He'd hide his face behind a red bandana, rob the stage, and gallop off down the back way to Virginia Dale where he'd greet the stage and cluck like some mad mother hen over this shocking news of another robbery in his neighborhood. He never did me harm, though I never had dealings with him except once when I found myself at his wife's dinner table and heard him rant on in his cups, What is this country but a nation of high-toned thieves! It's getting so you can't trust Republicans anymore'n Democrats! He fancied himself a wit.

I kept my lookout to myself, though he turned to me and asked, Where do you think money comes from out here but stealing indian lands? I consider it my bounden duty to steal from thieves, Antoine. Robin Hood was right, don'tcha think, he says, slapping his knee and laughing at his own joke. Why don't you throw in with me, he says. I hear from Jim Bourdeaux you're handy with a gun.

Mr. Slade, I says, I'm nowhere near angry or crazy enough to suit you. I excused myself with many a compliment to his Missus.

It was always in August, the thunder moon, that First Elk Woman got ideas and would lead me down to the love spot, as she called it, this small sandy beach among willow reeds, like an island in the Poudre, and I suppose that's why so many of our children had their borning during the June rise.

Once, though, I remember that as we lay there, our arms around each other, our daughter Louise stumbled over to us, sleepwalking in her nightshirt, carrying her little leather pouch in her arm like a doll. What are you doing out here, I whispered to her trying to get her to talk to me without waking her. Why aren't you in bed? She answered with her eyes closed, I hear the trees talking, she said.

After we carried her back and put her to bed, First Elk Woman and I walked again under the full moon. The girl doesn't feel natural living in the cabin, she said.

After all the work I put in raising it, I'd sure like to know the reason why.

It's square. It makes her soul restless. She wants the tipi circle she knew before her ears were pierced. She needs something to remember the circle by.

Next day, I sat down with Louise and asked her to show me what was in her leather pouch. It was some things she was collecting—thrown horseshoe nails, the tail feathers of a red hawk, a chip of alabaster I gave her that I'd found up Box Elder canyon, a tattered ghost of DeSmet's scapular with its cord lacing and its black piping around that Sacred Heart picture, old and shredded like a ragdoll, the angel of her sleepwalking, keeping her from harm.

Come with me, I says, and took her to the blacksmith's at the Overland stage station and had Provost make a chain ring on an old bent horseshoe to hold all her keepsakes on. We'll go to your favorite tree that talks to you at night, I says, and the thrown horseshoe nails will clink on the ring and stars will wink in the same measure.

I hoped that through that ring she'd find her

way back to the circle and something inside her would become the tinkling music of those stirrings that'd rock her to sleep in the night.

That seemed to be the charm, at least until Louise was grown to young womanhood and spent altogether too much time alone by the river brooding about what I never really knew, for she never would say, though I half suspicioned it was this cross she bore in her blood. Was God white or Oglala? And who was she? To judge from what she wrote in her diary that I found two days after she hanged herself, I guess she never answered those questions.

Let me leap ahead several years, Mr. Watrous, to that one morning when we set hotcakes on the breakfast table and noticed Louise was missing.

She's probably down along the Poudre thinking her thoughts, I said to First Elk Woman. So I walked upstream, calling her name, until I came to the talking tree, and there she was, hanging from a horsehair noose like a rag doll of herself, swaying in the same breeze that made her charmring tinkle as it had since she was a girl.

We buried her up Bingham Hill cemetery, as I said, years later, though the circuit priest would say no word above her grave. I placed her secret diary on her white shroud before we shoveled the earth back in. I read her words, though I was never able to make sense of them. Mostly, I think, it was a prayer, for often, as in some refrain, she would write, *O, God, what am I going to do?*

Among other words I saw repeated were, *The world goes away.*

I remember a passage where she said she had tried planting some potatos in the flower garden near the wheel-rut road leading up to our house. She wrote, *I am those purple flowers along the roadside crushed by wagon wheels. Today my fate is more than I can bear.*

She confided to her diary that some young man had said, *What, do you think I married you for your looks?* Then the refrain again, *The world goes away. As if he stood in white space. No sky. No white gray clouds drifting east across the plains. I can't sleep. I get so tired I can't think. The world goes away. I know what I should do, I know what my heart tells me. I should leave him. But what of the children?*

I have pondered those strange entries long, Mr. Watrous, and never once has a word of them made sense. What was all this about her cruel husband? She was never married, nor had she ever borne a child.

I found it hard to console myself with such a mysterious death to wonder about. It was as if the words she used in her secret writings, *The world goes away*, had somehow taken root in my mind and repeated themselves until my life went all blurred and day followed into day and all I had left was work.

You could say that's the virtue of having a big family. I'd have been more taken up with how the world had grown so dark since my darling Louise had put an end to her very young life. Yet things must be got on with. I had other sons and daughters that needed me too. And that is what I told First Elk Woman, too. She of course was wrecked and ruined by her grief over Louise's death. To lose her child so young, and in that way. She began to cry and sing Louise's death song, and I knew she would do something like she had done when her father died, like cut another finger off. What could I say? Could I tell her, You can't afford to lose another finger? Could I offer to cut one of mine off instead? She would tell me that it doesn't work that way, that grief is entirely personal, that one person's gesture of grief cannot stand in for another's. It was a full year, as was her custom, that First Elk Woman talked to Louise at all hours of day or night before she had me put up a pine post and drape a buffalo hide on it, and we all hugged Louise goodbye.

But, to return to my present story: what days then were is what I chiefly recall, summers when a bright morning on the foothills would give way to an afternoon when black clouds would mass, then launch themselves across the plains. Lightning forked down across wide prairies out east, the Thunder Beings First Elk Woman prayed to, crashing down their word with power that split cottonwoods, or winter nights when we heard a roaring in the bare trees and stepped outside to feel this hot chinook wind on our faces eating snow, astonished to wake to a January thaw that lasted for weeks of shirt-sleeve weather.

It was such a day when a big burly man in a plain black suit tied up his wagon at my door and introduced himself as Rev. John Chivington, Methodist preacher, late of Ohio, Illinois, Missouri, Kanasas, Nebraska, now presiding elder of the Denver First.

I have been told you are the whitest man in these parts, he said, lighting down with groans from his buckboard's springs.

Well, I'm sure you must've heard wrong. Are you trying to give me a compliment? I asked.

Why, yes! he says. And for that reason I've come to offer you a chance to do God's great work. I have come to minister the holy Gospel among the mining camps west of here, and what would aid me most is to exchange my played out horses for fresh ones before I head up Poudre canyon.

What would God be willing to pay to get his work done, I asks.

Pay? he says.

You weren't expecting me to *give* you use of my horses free, were you, Reverend?

Not give *me*, he says, give *God*, so I may do
his great work of saving drunken souls and bringing Christ's gentle yoke to the heathen Indians,
for if the red men sow not neither shall they reap,
and if they do not become masters of the plow
then they shall be plowed under. No middle
course presents itself, he went on, building a head
of pious steam. The crusade begun from Plymouth
rock to this western river has marked its trail with
the rifle and the torch. We cannot halt at the
Poudre and declare all west and north of it to go
unimproved under the rule of savages who will
neither toil nor spin and whose destiny requires
no watery lens of prophecy to foretell.

I was trying to frame some simple words to
tell this man to get off my land when First Elk
Woman steps out of the cabin dressed in gingham
though with her braids hung about her shoulders
Oglala style. She was carrying a pot of hot coffee
and a basket of rolls, and preacher John Chivington was at first fooled by the gingham, and then
he blanched when he spotted her braids. Then
Pete and Willie come round the corner from our
corrals, all buckskin and feathers. I could almost
hear wheels turning in his anvil-shaped head.
These boys were to him not only half-breeds but
bastard offspring of a sinner and his savage
Delilah. He placed his finger acrosst his lip as if to
say no such satanic brew would pass and mounted
his wagon with not a further word, his scowl so
black I pitied the man who forgot to tell him I
was a squawman and not to waste his brimstone
breath on me, for he was all of six feet four and so
muscled about his shoulders I had no doubt he
could thrash any trapper living in Laporte those
days.

From time to time the awful thought has
plagued my mind that his failure to turn me and
who knows how many of the old free trappers to

his tithe prompted him to quit Chivington the
fiery reverend and be reborn Lt. Colonel Chivington of the First Colorado Volunteers, would be
Indian fighter, would be hero, would be governor,
would be millionaire, as if there must be as many
deaths as days in this account, from what later
slaughter Chivington led of Cheyennes and
Arapahos under Black Kettle's flag at Sand Creek.
As time has passed it has come to me that I never
seriously entertained such an idea.

Nick and I put notice in the Rocky Mountain
News that we were hiring out as guides to gold
prospectors, with a quote from Kit Carson saying,
"They are the most celebrated mountaineers of
their times, and as courteous as they are intelli-
gent," which made us blush to think what we
were brought to—to make a big impression on
these greenhorns. We gave our parties two
choices—either a high flat fee or a lower with a
percentage of profits. There was gold up the
Poudre, we felt in our very bones, though it was
not in nuggets or dust panned from the stream in
sluices but ore that assayed out high enough to
tease greenhorns yet not high enough to start
companies with capital enough for huge rock-
crushing machines that might yield six hundred to
a thousand dollars per ton. Way up Cherokee
Park there once had been geysers, little volcanos
the size of prairie dog hills, venting minerals in
circles. If we could find arcs of those circles we'd
find whole rings of gold.

Skies were filled with signs those early years.
Off south, smoke turned our foothills black from
fires set by stampeders who only perished in the
flames they kindled to burn off all the brush and
expose bare rock for mining. And one night I
called First Elk Woman to view the northern
lights. She said it was the gods dancing at some
feast. We stood with our arms up, beholding.

Maybe that aurora flared to foretell gold strikes in Poudre canyon like everyone hoped. Men like Sam Deon would get rich owning land right on the squat crossroads of Colorado's biggest town or whatever these lands might be called, late the western tailings of Nebraska territory, there on Overland stage lines between Denver and Cheyenne, or from there northwest to Virginia Dale, Laramie City, Green River and beyond—valley after valley surrounded by spruce forests up past the Medicine Bows where Arapahos and Lakota went to find ash saplings to make the strongest bows.

I'd got my wish to live in a vast place and feel my chest expand to fill its distances. When I knelt along the Poudre's banks to part the tall wheatgrass and dip my hand in the cool water to splash my face and neck I felt the glacier far above me hanging on the mountainside and took a small portion of the flow of the river that starts with the snowmelt of the June rise that is part of the endless waterwheel's turning.

I heard the engines of a million bees in my head. Only when my mind turned to thoughts of money did I feel I touched cold lead, yet it was hard to know how that felt as it was more numbness than feeling. I was accounted a rich man from all my trading and the value of my landholdings, though that was all on spec, awaiting news of that first great gold strike.

Provost was already getting rich charging top dollar for meals and lodging by the bridge across the Poudre river on the Overland stage line. I was always off up Poudre canyon guiding another gold prospecting party after I'd taught my oldest boy, Antoine, how to work with horses and to size up the cut of their hindquarters for what their suited work might be, such as being a cutting horse or a hauling horse.

Watch out how you call what you do, I told him. If you call it "breaking a horse" like some folks do, that's what it'll be, scaring horses into a barbwire fence until they don't anymore trust their own senses, what with all the bloody slashes acrosst their knees.

Ever notice how a wild horse gets spooked by your mother's clotheline, all flapping shirts like tongues of ghosts? You can talk a wild horse through, soothing it, keeping it safe from spirits. Call it "sweet-talking a horse," if you like. Stand up next to its left ear, I told him. Whisper to that horse just what you're fixin' to do. Say, Alright now my fine dun brave, we're going to fit you with this here hackamore which will fit in the slot of your back teeth like a sword in the hand of a buccaneer. Then we're goin' to take ten minutes to rub you down with this here burlap sack until your coat is sleek and shiny like a new penny. Then we're goin' to slip a blanket on your back, and then a saddle, and I'm goin' to rock it back and forth until it fits your shapely spine just right before I reach under and slip this here cinch strap through the double rings and tighten up a bit. You can go on and on like that, Antoine, I said, to a point some folks'll say you're spoiling that bronc. But it'll make a good riding horse that trusts people and people can trust.

It was Antoine who took to my fathering best. Call it the power that lives in a name, but from boyhood up it was him who camped with me, listened, learned all my stories and took up my habits, studying my dress, and preferring my ways of doing things, which was some mix of St. Charles and Oglala, silence, love of the forest wilderness, my natural choice to travel invisible, my belief that human beings have to act as if life's treasure lies right before them in their gold pan or they won't give things the delicate hand they need to uncover themselves to us, and my willingness to go out of my way to avoid a fight.

It come clear by 1862 that Denver was to be the capital of Colorado, and the grand scheme for Colona wasn't going to pan out. The land office would not honor our claim on all former Cheyenne, Arapaho, and Oglala lands as ceded to us by their chiefs in 1858. Each of us would get only one hundred sixty acres, the same as any got from the Homestead Act.

I filed and told the tribes they were always welcome on what land I held title to. One hundred and fifty tipis camped on my land that summer. It had been their council grounds, where I had first spoken to them in 1844 when my father gave me to them and sealed my fate.

The big news came when Capt. Hanna located a troop of the 11th Ohio cavalry right there on my land, not a quarter mile from Provost's bridge across the Poudre.

Once all the hoopla died down, I went up into Poudre canyon with Swift Hawk carrying the remains of his son's body on a pack animal for sky burial. What happened was a Pawnee claimed Swift Hawk was a squaw woman with no heart to fight white men for the land. Not even Red Cloud made such a charge against Swift Hawk to wrest the chief's place from him. Swift Hawk's son shot that Pawnee fool dead, then lit out north with his wives until things cooled down. But when he thought the storm had blown itself out on the high plains, he came back, only to be killed by the Pawnee's kin, his body torn to pieces, his head stuck on a pole.

Early snow fell through a dark light as we made our way up canyon. *How many winters have these mountains rinsed men's sorrows with their rains and snows?* Swift Bird sang, as we saw a nighthawk's white underwing chevron fly above us.

Balm for his grief over his son's death did not
come until next June when I askt him to come
east to teach Willie and Pete to hunt in northwest
Kansas in Republican river country where buffalo
still came to feed on the lush, green prairie grasses.
The boys wanted this buffalo hunt to be with bow
and arrow from horseback as in the old days. As
they had not reached their full growth, I hesitated,
but they pleaded like two puppy dogs until I
couldn't anymore say no.

Swift Hawk took the boys and me up Round
Butte to sing and lament for a vision that night
before we left. I watched him do his magic with
Pete and Willie in strange weather that began in a
warm drizzle and turned clear, so that the stars
sparked like silver flints. Almost without words he
gave us his meanings from his gestures toward
features of the land. Look, he seemed to say, the
top of Round Butte is separated into two spots,
the upper for signal fires, the lower for dancing.
We could see from that vantage along almost the
whole of the front range down south to the blunt
skull of Pike's Peak silhouetted by what little
remained of dusk. And above, the stars covered
us, from the Lion in the south to the Swan in the
east to the Bear in the north. We lay on our backs
and stared until we became very small.

Swift Hawk took out facepaint from his
medicine bag and sat them down to make arrows
of the Thunder Beings flash across their cheeks.
What I could teach—tracking, the order of days,
cooking, cleaning, repair—what my father had
taught me—was not what my sons needed. I
squatted in the light rain under my poncho and
watched him paint my boys' faces, and I loved
him.

Swift Hawk gave them a buffalo song. While
they sang and danced on the dancing rock, he

disappeared. Then as they sang and sang looming out of the darkness we saw one buffalo bull who strayed off by himself and climbed to the top of Round Butte. At first in the flickering light of our campfire we saw the buffalo like this spirit come to warn us to be good to our women or we would be like the man who first saw White Buffalo Calf Woman with so much lust in his heart that his chest leaked smoke that covered both of them like a cloud. She walked out of that cloud and stood there in all her beauty, but when the cloud blew off, the man was nothing but a skeleton with worms eating on it.

Swift Hawk spun out from under his buffalo horn hide, and I found myself dancing as I had not had to before because my oldest, Antoine, hadn't askt me to. He was content to know what I could teach him. I wondered though about the Cheyenne way, for never had my shadow-brother Two Bears left my thoughts.

As the four of us passed in the days that followed from Round Butte to Pawnee Butte east to the Kansas plains, ground I'd passed when still a boy with my father opened itself to me like pages of dreadful scripture I read from so often I must have seemed distracted to Willie and Pete. I felt naked and helpless like a child wandering from one day's sage prairie to another, begging creekbeds with their budding curves of cottonwood and willow and box elder, dry washes, piles of red rock, and my father gone into the sky for a vision. I was without any idea how to save Willie and Pete from harm in Camp Collins where there were many like Chivington who despised their half-breed wildness. No more than I'd had any idea of how to save Louise, or even that she needed saving. Many was the time they'd come home bloodied from scrapes in town with some spooked newcomers who saw their braids and couldn't tell them from full-bloods in a war party, which is just how the boys wanted it anyways.

No sooner had Swift Hawk taught them to hear buffalo hooves by putting ear to ground than they went galloping over the hills in search of that herd, and nothing I or Swift Hawk could say held them. So we men found ourselves following after the boys at a clip around the base of a low hill smack into a small herd they began to stampede south toward the bank of the river by waving their blankets over their heads and shouting so the herd would be rimrocked and have to turn back toward their arrow points.

They raced alongside a large bull, and then my older boy, Pete, drew back his arrow. His aim was true, striking the bull just below his shoulder, where the arrow lodged. But he wasn't strong enough to drive it straight through into the bull's heart, so the wounded beast gathered himself up and charged. Pete's horse went down from being gored in the belly, and Pete's left leg was pinned under. The bull mauled the horse for a long minute, then turned to look at Pete. He was going to charge. Pete would be trampled and ripped.

I pulled my Sharp's and would have laid a round between that bull's horns so he'd fall where he stood. But Swift Hawk drew my arms down when I put rifle to shoulder. Wait, he seemed to say.

I have to try to save him, I said.

You can't, Swift Hawk whispered. Pete has to know if he has *wakan*.

It was as if my ears were filled with some river's roar, as if I could hear my father tell me yet again to just let myself go down a sinkhole.

As I was trying to understand Swift Hawk, Willie sped up to Pete, leapt off his horse, and dragged him out from under. That buffalo just stood there baffled. Pete and Willie forked their horse and galloped off far enough for Pete to get up on another horse with a fresh bow and arrows and charge the bull again, only this time striking him deep enough so its legs buckled.

Willie had saved Pete's life, and he was all the *wakan* Pete would ever ask for, a right-hand man, someone to cover his flank. Pete and Willie didn't stop to skin their prize. They kicked their ponies' ribs and started to race off westward toward home.

Ho! Swift Hawk cried. Where are you two going?

To tell our mother, they said, almost in one voice.

Do you think your mother will be proud when she asks you what prayer you said over *Tatanka,* and you tell her you forgot? Off your horses. Come, let's kneel down beside your brother who has given you this day. Your mother wants that meat, that hide, those hooves, those cords that held his muscles to his bones so he could run.

It's a funny thing about *wakan.* Pete thought it was like the end of a fairy tale where it says "and they lived happily ever after." Once you've got it, you've got it for life. To me it's more like playing the fiddle. Some nights when the whiskey burns in your blood and won't stop, you take bow to strings and fire springs up like when you strike a lucifer. Everything and everyone you've ever loved comes welling up through the music and you know you need more lives and all the whys and wherefores fall, each to their own measure, and everyone who struggled is blessed and all their *travaille* finds its reward. And sometimes, as my father would say, the music she is not with you, and you might as well keep your instrument in its case.

As I look back on it now, I remember riding that day back to First Elk Woman to tell her I stopped myself from trying to save our son at the same time Swift Hawk helped me see I could not save him in any way that meant anything to him, for he'd rather have died than lived without *wakan*. This hunt wasn't only about Pete and Willie. Swift Hawk showed me that my shot—anyone's shot, missionary's or government agent's, no matter how well intended—would only have spoilt the mystery.

December 9, 1884
Pine Ridge Agency

"Washed Out"

I like to sit outside in the cold on late mornings here at Pine Ridge where clouds cover the sky to all points with not enough moisture in them to snow. To while away the time I sometimes haul my fiddle out and sing some tune I heard back in my youth on the Missouri that had come on a stern-wheeler up the Mississippi from Louisiana.

> *Le soleil est proche couché*
> *Et mon cheval, il est proche las*
> *Et j'ai faim et j'ai soif*
> *Et je suis loin de ma famille.*
>
> *Bye-bye jolie brune et*
> *Bye-bye jolie blonde*
> *Mais ça c'est tout pour la brune*
> *Et pas rien pour la blonde.*

And I think about those golden-haired girls and dark-haired girls. In the sky a silver sun makes small rainbows around itself, two sundogs.

Even to stand at the doorway of this light is to touch the whole of it. Such was the light in Billy Provost's eyes for Little Bird, Eagle Wing's first daughter.

I can still picture him knocking at my door, begging me to give him horse enough for bride price.

If I'd gone out to gaze at water for a spell I

might've seen what would happen and given young Billy what he needed. It's been different for the half-breed boys, specially the ones that came to Pine Ridge with their mothers. They've a bad need to love, it seems, to win some young girl of their mother's tribe.

Billy asked Crooked Foot Little Owl for three horses, and the man I'd knocked senseless at Horse Creek in 1851 gave Billy three horses— only they weren't his to give, they were Clement Bernard's, Billy's chief rival for Little Bird's hand.

Billy and Little Bird were standing up for their wedding when Bernard rode up with his *vaqueros*, discharging pistols to shock the vows to a stop. He asked Eagle Wing to check for his brand there beneath the horses' bellies.

Eagle Wing was so put out with what he found there, he threw Billy out of camp. Billy later that day took a pistol and blew his brains out on the ground. When his brother Johnny learnt of Billy's death he found Crooked Foot Little Owl and Bernard at the agent's office and shot them both, killing Bernard and wounding Crooked Foot.

And now, from Johnny, who went to live in Michigan after he was acquitted on a charge of murdering Bernard, I get word by post that Joe Mason has died mysteriously. Did he die as was reported in the *Chronicle* by being head kicked by some bronc in his stable, or as it was rumored around by "accidental gunshot," which everyone knew to be sweet talk for suicide?

Please answer. He was my friend, at least for a while until he showed me his true stripe. We shared this dream of our township at Laporte for a few years. He was what me and Sam Deon and John Provost knew Laporte needed, a real money man with a lawyer's mind, someone who knew how to get things done in high places.

All the while the federal surveyors went through Poudre valley with their instruments on tripods making their notes on their maps, he served on Laporte's town council, waiting, as most of us were, for that day when word of a gold strike up Poudre canyon would suddenly make everyone's land holdings shoot up in value. We thought then a man could get so rich no one and nothing could ever touch him, and that was part of the dream, for what was wealth but a hedge against your dream of good communities where people—both white and indian—can live and let live being buried with your bones?

He shone in my eyes. He wanted to get himself a Sioux wife, as he saw that's what all us old free trappers had done, and he got one, not by giving horses or running off with Mary Polzel, but in a gun duel with the blacksmith Robidoux on Cherry Creek. All Denver rang with the news through street after street of frame brick hotels and houses, and in full view of at least a hundred witnesses he won by default when the muleshoer's knees buckled as his seconds primed the pistol caps. People allowed as how the city might yet become as civilized as New Orleans if such killings became Denver's everyday rule. I imagine Joe's knees never buckled until the last.

There was something between us that got swept off that June rise of 1864. No one had ever seen the likes of such heavy snows up in Poudre canyon and the Seven Utes country. On any given winter there might be twelve foot. But this year word kept trickling in from prospectors half froze from wintering in cabins colder than the outside air that there might've been near twice that amount, with a cold Spring that lasted till June. And then it began to rain, day after day, until a flood blew out the mouth of Poudre canyon with a roar like Noah must've heard. It wasn't only the

Poudre, the Big Thompson and Cherry Creek all
blew that day, so that people said they heard the
rivers explode all up and down the front range
from Laporte to Denver.

The Poudre river soon topped its banks and
swirled at my doorsill, and First Elk Woman and
the kids and me we made our sodden way to
higher ground, salvaging every household thing
we could carry on our backs and the babes in
arms. Then we went back and took the horses
from their corrals.

In the days after the flood, Joe talked Capt.
Hanna into moving the 11th Ohio Cavalry
downriver since the wall of water tore from its
picket pins their tent encampment that was on the
floodplain between my cabin and Provost's Overland stage station and restaurant and left their
canvas high on the south banks at Joe's land, right
there near the north end of what is now Linden.

As I look back on it now, I wonder why I
never expected Joe would do that. When I rode
down there to ask him, he says, My land's on
higher ground, giving a better view of the plains,
but you're blind to the facts. You're just like all
the old trappers. You got yours and don't like
seeing the next man get his. You cut trees enough
to build fifty houses in Laporte, then complain
when I take enough to build five hundred. Why?
Is it that you're not getting a cut? Well, that's not
the way we do business in this country.

I respect you, he said, but not enough to let
you lord it over the whole Poudre valley, you and
Provost, and people like you. This flood has swept
all that away, Antoine. It's time for a new deal.
You had sense enough when you saw that the
beaver trade went belly-up to turn the skill you
learnt trapping into a living as a scout and trader
at Fort Laramie. But time has come for you to
change again if you're to keep up.

There's going to be a real town here, where my land is, at what is to be called Camp Collins along the south bank of Poudre river with a rail stop along the line between Denver and Cheyenne, with lumber yards and hired men working at grain mills and elevators and stores and banks with money to loan to well-off farmers to buy better equipment for bringing in bumper crops of grain. Trouble with you is you're this big dreamer with crazy ideas about whites and Indians living together in peace. Can't you wake up enough to see that that can't ever be? You can throw in with me and Auntie Stone or get plowed under, Antoine. Which is it to be?

I give up! I was thinking. Why is it that no one can get through life without the need to adapt and the need to preserve what you've built, what you believe in, what's come to be important for you? You try not to be some braying ass claiming the airs of a lord, and damn if that isn't just what gets thrown in your face.

For such a smart man, I asked, why can't you see the land hereabouts is like bank principal you don't spend if you want to avoid ruin? At least the Oglalas are smart enough to know that. If you won't live from this land's excess, you'll only build something unnatural that will collapse of its own weight. Look what's happening hereabouts these days. Some local men with English money show up with two thousand head of longhorn cattle that spread out all over these prairies, except it isn't the open prairie like when buffalo grazed here only fifteen years ago, it's farmland now, and farmers start hauling into town with their wagon teams to buy big spools of barbed wire for making fence to keep the cows out of their corn. Next thing you know you got cowhands tearing down barbed-wire fence. One thing leads to another, Joe. Pretty soon there's a range war right here out in Larimer county with farmers and ranchers killing each other, and for what?

It's *competition*, Joe said, looking at me as if I was a fool with no brains to comprehend that a noble struggle was taking place before my very eyes.

That's the new fact of life, Antoine, something you old free trappers never knew because you were the only ones out here when you first began.

And what's it for, I asked, but to narrow everything down to the one thing that makes the most money? But the law of life is difference, Joe. Over the long haul of years, we will regret everything we've disposed of.

You may think it strange after such words between us, but it was Joe Mason who got my son Antoine the job as scout with Capt. Hanna. I meant to ask him to look after First Elk Woman if I should kick before her. She knows nothing of deeds or accounts. I could count dollars and cents, though I was not the money man Joe was—I was strictly small time. Joe understood interest and could charm a banker out of his gold stickpin if it would help build the grain and saw mills to make them all richer.

Joe Mason told me I was wasting my life with dreams of making time stop so I could go on feeling how the forest always took me in and let me be, the way First Elk Woman did, with her skin as warm as buffalo hide that softens as you enter sleep to take your earthly shape while your sky soul flies in dreams. I guessed he was right about the future, and that moment I felt tiny cracks inside my body begin to leak my soul's blood. I could not stanch it.

February 26, 1885
Pine Ridge Agency

"Mocassin Posse"

To have fought the river all night,
lantern in one hand, the other free to slip ropes on
drenched horses, panic flashing from their black
eyes, my sons Pete and Willie walking geldings
north to high ground to calm the spooked colts
until all forty head were safe from drowning, and
to wake two mornings later only to find my herd
gone from the corrals—that was enough to find
me slamming mud under my heels in a sharp
damn!

The thing about living in town is the lull of its
shifts, the way you come to expect the blacksmith's anvil will stop ringing at sundown. It
soothes you, puts you off your guard. But up in
the mountains, no one could untether my horses
no matter how moonless the night. I would sleep
with their reins tied around my waist.

Plain fact was there in mud pocked with fresh
hoofprints, in unbarred lodgepole fence gates, in a
corral enclosing a nothing that sank its defeat in
my belly like a sickness from bad water. The
whole river bottom was wrecked still, wracked
canyon pines littered with dead sage over
blanched stones, the flood plain widened to past
my very threshhold, the sky strange with cross-
hatch, the cavalry camp tents blown down river,
soon to be removed to Joe Mason's land southeast
of Laporte.

Night's warm skin in a wooden house that muffles all sound but the cry of hoot owls was the trouble. Owls make easy cover for even the least clever thieves. So there I was, still exhausted from battling floods, on my knees reading sign in mellowed earth. No bootprints: one set of tracks with a crooked right foot twisted inward, the rest with that back stitch that says *Sihasapa,* Blackfoot, Blackfoot, the ones that killed your father.

Now they'd raided south hundreds of miles to my place on the Poudre, led no doubt by Crooked Foot Little Owl. Was I cursed? Little Owl had bushwhacked me. Was I to be prisoner in my own house? Or was I just fat and stupid enough to make an easy target? Eight, maybe ten unshod ponies among my herd of two score, headed north with their plunder up Box Elder canyon and up through Horse Thief pass.

Pete and Willie wanted to make up some mocassin posse to take out after them on foot. They were Oglala bloods with a big strut in every step, hearts pounding with this chance to show the *wakan* that had come to them when they hunted buffalo herds up on the Republican river the year before.

For the first time I felt my age. Not that my body was tired but that some fire in my heart had never burnt keenly for fights and was sputtering out. Now that I think on it, it's as if I knew at last that I would need to hate to kill, and I couldn't bring myself to hate, recalling all those good years First Elk Woman and our boys and girls lived with us in the Poudre cabin. I held her in my arms, and she held me in her Oglala family. Call it love and politics, Mr. Watrous. And I felt close enough to Swift Hawk's band to know bonds solid as an iron tripod.

We hadn't good horseflesh enough to keep it a family matter, so I went from cabin to cabin borrowing a horse from Provost, from Deon, from Stover, one for me, for young Antoine, one each for Pete and Willie who wanted to light out on instant over Cheyenne Rim hot on the trail of Blackfoot thieves. While First Elk Woman stuffed pemmican in mocassins so as we emptied them of food they'd make us new footgear, I sat Pete and Willie down, though they were fidgeting, wanting to go off half-cocked, and I tried my best to tell them one of the many Cheyenne stories my father told me when I was their age. He would begin by saying, Come to rest in the quiet place in your waters, stare down into the underwater world, the place where when you were a boy you sat beside the Missouri and looked at the shadows of wild rice stalks shimmer in the ripples. But I just began saying, Once there were two poor boys, brothers, who had no family, no one to look after them, so they had only rags of skins to wear.

Their people traveled hard and long, crossing rivers and streams, following a herd of buffalo, so no one had time to care for an old camp dog with a litter of puppies.

The two boys were hungry and tired after crossing a wide river, and when they laid down to sleep the old camp dog came to them in their dreams, saying, *Take pity on my children, carry them across the river tomorrow. Then she sang them a song in a young woman's voice, I know you are poor boys with no home. If you take my children safely across the river, I will take pity on you both. You shall have a name, and many friends, but only if you do as I ask. When you reach camp you will find that men are going to steal horses from the Crow. You must wait three days before you go after them and join them in the raid.*

The two boys did as the old camp dog told them in the dream. They were patient, they waited three days, and when they joined the war party and came at night to the Crows' camp they found that they could see as well at night as during the day.

With this power they took many fine horses and soon were among the richest young men in their band. Men offered their most beautiful daughters in marriage to them, and they lived long and were honored among the councils of the tribe. Everything the old dog told them came true, I said, as I saw in my mind the figure of Two Bears who surely must've heard this tale.

Pete and Willie all the while shifted from haunch to haunch with a terrible longing to be on their way. Can't you heed your father's words for once? I askt.

You're not supposed to tell that story in the daylight, Pete said.

You could be turned into a hunchback, Willie said, not loud, not with the blood of an Itesica hothead, but almost whispering.

I gave them their bridles and sent them out ahead of me and Antoine. Go to Fort Laramie, I told them. Get word to Capt. Willson what has happened here, but on no account are you to try getting the horses by yourselves. Wait for me and Antoine and the soldiers.

Yes, father, they said, as they kicked their horses' ribs and galloped north with many war cries shrieking over the hill and gone.

Antoine and I lit out after them at midday, 11th June, keeping a good pace on their trail. Forty head and eight drovers leave a mighty wake. We did not ride so swift as to overtake them, though. I didn't want to see arrows in my boys. Trouble comes, they say, in threes, and I'd sooner it not be flood, stolen horses, and dead sons, thank you.

The Blackfoot rode for dawn up Laramie plain, past Steamboat Rock, past Virginia Dale,

Red Mountain, north and west until they reached
Morton's Pass and turned due east before they
broke out onto the plains of the Moonshell.
There, two days later, Capt. Willson shot it out
with them, killing three. My herd was a little
starved, but I could fatten them up on spring grass
after me and the boys hazed the horses home.
They weren't my fortune—my family was, First
Elk Woman, the boys and girls, so bitten, some of
them, Louise, I think, specially, by being called
"halfbreed" they were scarred, and some the
stronger for it.

Yet I felt it high time to sharpen my senses so
I could tell an owl from an Indian and ready
myself for this long fight with the drag of the
earth on my body, lulling me with its openings
and closings, its lights and darks, its silences and
songs, asking me, *Why not just lie down right here,
where it's soft?*

But before I could disappear into some bright
dawn somewhere west of axe and plow, somewhere north or south of Union Pacific railroad's
iron teeth, that summer of the flood became the
summer that the Fourth World began to end.

Bold Wolf and his band arrived at my place
on the Poudre a week into December or so,
hauling his daughter, my father's Cheyenne wife,
on a travois. Among them was Georgie Bent
wearing mocassins, leggings, and some cavalryman's dark blue tunic. Everyone looked gaunt and
hurt. They needed time to dress their wounds. I
butchered out a goat, made a pit of coals, and
First Elk Woman and I roasted it. That night
Bright Star told us what happened.

We were camped along Sand Creek, she said,
down among the cottonwoods along the dry bed
at the foot of the sand banks. Two Bears didn't
want to join Black Kettle and his Cheyenne bands
when Governor Evans sent word that all who

didn't want to be considered hostile should go to Major Wynkoop at Fort Lyons. He would give us food and supplies. But when I went, Two Bears came along to keep me safe.

Georgie Bent cut in bitterly. Evans knows Colorado will never be a state unless we and the Oglalas are driven off somehow. But rumor has it the First Colorado Cavalry got their orders from Washington to go into this war between the whites, and none of them, not men nor officers nor Governor Evans, wanted that. More political offices would go to soldiers who fought Indians instead of the gray men. So Chivington was hell bent to make his fortune that morning he led his troops into Black Kettle's camp.

Bright Star resumed. With some other women, I was digging in the dry creekbed and scooping bladders of pooled water out when these soldiers came charging down that furthest cut-bank. We picked ourselves up and ran to gather with Black Kettle and his family under this big U.S. flag that waved from his topmost tipi pole that had been given to him by the great father in Washington as a sign of peace.

Chivington's cavalrymen came roaring down the nearest bank. He himself leaned back in the saddle. He is such a big man he could kill a horse riding hard down sand banks. Shooting started, but I couldn't take my eyes away from his horse's hooves digging so deep into the loose, crumbling sand up to its fetlocks. His men rode right through us, shooting with pistols, hacking heads with drawn sabres, scalping as the women begged mercy for their children.

I ran alongside the women I'd been gathering water with to some scooped-out caves in the sandbanks. Two Bears covered our escape by firing on Chivington himself with an old flintlock.

He missed. Chivington's men turned their horses toward Two Bears and rushed toward him. He threw down the rifle and tried to run, but they rode up behind him and slashed him with their long knives. I saw it as I turned to run. He took many cuts. He fell, and got up again. Three soldiers jumped down off their horses and knocked him to the ground with their long knives. He got up again, and they cut him again, shouting *stay down, stay down,* until he bled so much he moved no more.

I know, I said, quietly.

How could *you* know? You weren't there, Bright Star charged, with anger and sorrow.

I saw it in a dream, some five years ago, I said, remembering my strange vision of that cavalry charge roaring out of Two Bears' mouth when I nearly froze to death on the horse raid.

Well, she said, respecting the power of anyone's dreams, there were other things that happened strange as dreams. We drew some dead sage branches over the mouth of the little cave and stayed there until dark. Then we slipped away north on foot carrying our wounded. Days and days we walked back here to Poudre valley. We had no food, and soon the children were crying from empty bellies. I had no time to grieve my lost son.

Just when things seemed worst, one night here comes this she wolf with a rabbit in her mouth up to our ring all huddled together to survive another winter night. Before we even cut that rabbit up, the she wolf come with another and another until there was enough meat for each one in our band to get a mouthful. And each day we walked further northwest across the plains, she followed us and gave us food until at last we ran into a part of Dull Knife's band, and they gave us the one

horse to make it back here where we could rest
and sing our thanks to the she wolf and decide
what to do next.

That night as I lay abed awake talking with
First Elk Woman I knew this massacre at Sand
Creek would change everything. Even Swift Bird
who was known to love the whites said, We might
as well fight. Is Governor Evans's word worth the
powder to blow him to hell?

Swift Hawk asked First Elk Woman to come
north with him to the Powder River country, and
I went with her, come late October of 1865, as
my way to deal with the news from the Little
Arkansas treaty council. Seems Black Kettle signed
over to the U.S. government all lands ceded to
him in the Treaty of 1851, from where the north
and south Platte rivers split out in Nebraska west
to the foothills, including those lands that were
the claim for Laporte, from Box Elder creek south
to the Poudre. I suspected that the government
would never let me claim that much land. What
else could I do but comfort myself by saying to
myself, Nothing ventured? Still, it was like a grief
that I bore when I knew for certain that the
Laporte dream would never quite come true.

My family now was all split up, and I was like
a rolling stone across the plains returning south-
ward to Laporte to tend our horses. I got a jug at
Fort Laramie and decided to get so drunk no one
would recognize me.

West of Chugwater Creek from one little bluff
in an early snow I came upon a fog that as I saw it
first in that valley called to mind Jackson's Hole
where geysers vent and all's touched with icy lace.
I stared down into that white valley until the
whiskey made it seem one giant lake where lay the
half-dead carcass of some huge black land whale.

As I rode closer I saw it was a locomotive still
huffing, steaming, though with its engine cracked.

The engineer leaned down like a cheerful, buck-tooth beaver from his tinder box to say a brake-man was already sent east to telegraph for tow trains to haul its steel bones off. I fell off my horse, dead drunk.

The engineer jumped down to see if I'd broke my neck. As he knelt down beside me, I raved, *Loco-motive, loco-motive!* The Sioux word for white man's machines, Mr. Watrous, means "it-won't-go-away."

The buffalo were now split into a northern and a southern herd as they smelt the iron and would not cross that railroad. The Sioux believed what had always been would always be. They beat the drum and danced to help the south wind blow and with it came warmth, rain, new grass, and buffalo herds. But the southern buffalo herds smelled, snorted, stamped, pawed dust, and would not cross. So began the ending of what Swift Hawk had told me so many years ago was the Fourth World. What new trickster waited in what unseen quarter I did not know. I'm getting on in years, and still I have not seen how long it takes for an age to end.

March 1, 1885
Pine Ridge Agency

LETTER XIV

"Denizens of the Wilderness"

Maybe Joe Mason was right. Maybe I was a man against the times I lived in. You ask why I never spent much time back in Laporte and Camp Collins after 1865.

Well, it was hard living in Colorado those days for a squawman and his family. In Denver there were torchlight mobs marching to pledge five thousand dollars in bounties, $25 each for Sioux scalps ... with ears still attached! Imagine finding a ledger in your historical research with those transactions written in them, Mr. Watrous.

When most have split into two armed tribes, white and indian, then the loneliest, most danger-ous place for an individual who ain't prompted in every thought by clashing interests is in the middle—which is why there aren't that many individuals.

My spirits went into what you might call a decline. It was as if some part of me, like my Cheyenne half-brother, had come into my life and passed away out of it, and that seemed peculiar enough to spin my brain, so I busied myself with my horse ranching business. I had to believe that if I kept my eyes fixed on where my own stick floated such as my horses' feeding and grooming somehow that would pull me through this shaky time, as if in cleaning their stables I would find the gold I sought as a younger man.

Though young Antoine saw Capt. Hanna succeeded by Capt. Evans when orders came that sent the 11th Ohio Cavalry eastward into the last big push of the Civil War, Laporte was not a safe place for half-breeds or full bloods. As I said, First Elk Woman and our remaining children traveled north to be with Swift Hawk's band as they rejoined Red Cloud's Bad Faces somewhere on the Powder. Sand Creek had joined the Oglala that had been split apart by family politics, and I was living a lone bull's life that early spring while Cheyenne, Arapaho, and Oglala took their revenge for the deaths at Sand Creek by burning all Overland stage line stations but one between Denver and Fort Kearny.

Denver itself was cut off. People there were like to starve unless roads east could be reopened. Capt. Evans stopped by Laporte one morning with a poster carrying Colonel Moonlight's call for men age 18 to 50 to gather at Camp Collins to enlist them as reserve militia. Young Antoine and I stood on one of those early February mornings when the sun's a silver disk behind rising fogs. Col. Moonlight hopped up onto a whiskey barrel beneath the flagpole near the south end of the Laporte road.

Denizens of the wilderness! he shouted, though at some distance so his words echoed off the brick walls of the few shops that lined Linden street. *Do you see that flag waving in the breeze? In the name of the stars and stripes of that grand old banner I hereby proclaim martial law. War is breaking out all around us. Julesburg's been torched to the ground and raided. Therefore I call you to arms. I will promise you only one thing: Any man who will not obey my commands, I will make wolf's bait of his carcass!*

I didn't fancy being drafted under command of such a vulgar man and lit out north to find

First Elk Woman and our many children who were living somewhere between the Powder, Tongue, and Yellowstone rivers. Moonlight may as well have said, Darkness surrounds us! Let us therefore race up and down the country like snowblind stage drivers in a blizzard until we die or new days dawn! We called it "the bloody year on the plains," that year, 1865, the year Colonel Moonlight issued the order that no Cheyenne would be allowed within Camp Collins, in the belief that Swift Hawk's band who'd been camped on my land since Sand Creek would steal everything not too big to carry off as if they were more thieves than private soldiers hereabouts who stole cattle from one farmer and sold it to another with no little hints that barns could burn. That's how they added to their meagre wages. I'd thought 1858 was to be the craziest year I'd ever see, but things that summer of 1865 were crazier still, as if craziness nowadays was building like huge clouds from the dead souls of Sand Creek that darkened the whole vast sky.

After I arranged to have Garbutt look after my horse ranch in Laporte, I pointed my pony's nose north to the Powder River country, looking for sign along the way—small fires still asmoke, yellowed and beaten down grass of tipi circles, groves of cottonwood and box elder gnawed at by indian paints, wrapped bodies on scaffolds tied into tree branches, until at last I found my Oglalas. First Elk Woman was with Red Cloud, Young Man Afraid of His Horses, Crazy Horse, and all their bands with a thousand horses camped along the Yellowstone river that summer from which they sortied out small scouting parties south and west, looking for General Connor's columns.

I went out looking for General Connor's camp to find my brother Nick who was scouting

for the Army, along with old Blanket Jim Bridger.
I found him in camp on the second night out
beside Wolf Creek.

It's been a comedy from the start, he said,
staring into the fire the way our father used to.
Colonel Walker's command would not obey his
orders to mount. They were mostly what Red
Cloud calls "gray men," Galvanized Yankees and
Union short-timers who said they hadn't lost no
red men and didn't aim to hunt for none.

Connor had to threaten them with cannon
before they'd head out. But even so we made but
poor progress north as Connor's officers rode off
each morning to hunt elk and just get lost for days
sometimes, and the troopers, sent west after the
Civil War and still green, set fire to dry prairies
from sheer ignorance. We did have somewhat of a
fight with Black Bear's Arapaho band where we
burnt up their tipis and parfleches of meat not a
week ago, which started very unpromising. Jim
told General Connor he could see smoke from the
Arapaho camp, but none of Connor's officers
believed him.

Why that horizon is a good fifty mile off,
Connor said. You aren't pulling our legs again, are
you, Jim? Connor was not used to being kidded,
and Jim had told him once while they were laying
their plans in Fort Laramie's camp commander
quarters that he would take Connor up Yellowstone way where there were "peetrified trees" and
in them trees were "peetrified birds who sung
peetrified songs." Connor was cautious from then
on not to be taken again for some greenhorn fool
by Bridger's wit, so he took everything Jim said
afterwards with a whole handfull of salt. Thing is,
after a near two days' ride Connor's column did
come upon Black Bear's camp, and all the officers
began grumbling with an embittered awe that it

seemed Jim Bridger could indeed see smoke
curling above a horizon fifty miles distant.

But since then everything's turned spooky.
You been hearing the wolves at night, Antoine? I
swear there must be at least one thousand wolves
calling from Wolf mountain's foothills. Jim and
me, we got shaken from sleep the same moment
by howls. We looked at each other in the last light
of our campfire and said "Medicine wolf" both in
the same breath.

We tried to warn Connor, but he would have
none of it. Is this some new *intelligence* you've
brought me, Bridger? says he. What do you mean
by a "medicine wolf"? How is it different from an
ordinary wolf? Well, says Jim, you can tell a medicine wolf call from either ordinary wolves or
indians using wolf calls as signals by the fact that
it leaves no echo. When medicine wolves call,
thar's only one thing left to do, and that's to make
tracks.

Superstition! General Connor shouts. Why he
won't listen to the man he hired to guide him has
me stumped.

Well, I says to Nick, why is he out here but to
dominate the Sioux? He has to bull his way
through with one fixed idea, that there's nothing
Bridger can teach him he'd want to know. Old
Jim learned most of his tricks from the Sioux.
Think about it: if Connor let himself know what
might could happen to him and his men out here,
if one sliver of fear entered his little finger, he'd be
open to death. If he was open to his own death it
might touch his soul. If his soul was touched,
well, it might get between him and his West Point
training and his military orders.

A Sioux or a Cheyenne might know there's a
water spirit called a *nihm* that lives on some sandbar in a river and eats human souls and casts their
drowned bodies downriver on further shores.

There's no way to reason or treaty with it; it's a god, it's *wakan,* it does what it wants. He might stand in the water and offer to smoke with the spirit, or sing songs to it, or dream dreams of the water spirit that might appease it. Maybe the spirit might relent from eating his soul, but he's entirely at that spirit's mercy.

There's no Sioux word for what that is among humans. Say the spirit looks like an iron mouth that spits a killing tongue that curls around a man's waist and draws his soul down its black throat. What medicine will the water spirit accept he does not yet know. But this one, this General Connor *wakan* might eat all their souls before they found the right prayers to sing to it. A man is always ready to face death. The Oglala say only the earth lives forever.

Maybe a long time ago General Connor's Irish ancestors believed a small pond outside their village was a spirit. They might have gone there on midsummer nights and sang with flowers in their hair along its murky shore. But Connor's people are in the Church now and don't anymore believe in misty pools shining in the moonlight. Perhaps in Connor's dream, songs rise from the faun drinking at the meer, but in the light of day only cannon speak, while for Lakota Sioux there are medicine wolves to listen to as they foretell storms that cover General Connor and his men with ice until at last there comes a general with a will to follow orders as hard and unappeasable as a water spirit's.

Since the hour the medicine wolf called, one disaster after another has plagued us, Nick said. At last, Cole's and Walker's troops showed up at Wolf Mountain—though Connor's battle plan said they were supposed to meet us up on the Rosebud—a beaten line of frozen stragglers more like ghosts than men.

They shot six hundred horses and mules where they stood on picket lines, covered with thick sheets of ice from a big sleet storm that started to fall that next morning after the medicine wolf howled. I tell you it's been a comedy, with the army split and wandering around despite all Jim Bridger's done to keep his promise to General Dodge not to let old Connor set his foot in a trap up here.

Red Cloud, Crazy Horse, and these other Sioux leaders know they can't really deal the U.S. Army a bad hurt, for now they seen the whites truly were as endless as a plague of locusts eating everything right down to the ground and below into the roots, so that not the Oglalas' bravery, their numbers, nor their massed charges will ever mean a thing if their braves are armed only with bows, lances, clubs, and the few old flintlocks they've had since fur trapper days. Best they can do is watch this army of 2500 soldiers get lost, run out of food and supplies, and start shooting each other.

April 2, 1885
Pine Ridge Agency

LETTER XV

"The Circus Comes to Town"

For almost three years from that night
along Wolf Creek with my brother I made my
way between the Oglalas and Nick, who scouted
for the Army, first for Connor, then, after Connor
was stript of his command by General Dodge for
admitting he'd made mistakes, for Harney,
Sanborn, Carrington, and even the hapless
Fetterman whose command was wiped out by
Sioux and Cheyenne. My family also moved
between our place in Laporte and Young Man
Afraid of His Horses' camp along the north Platte
in Nebraska.

The summer of 1867 we lived in our Laporte
cabin. I remember the big doings was that
Robinson's Circus came to town. A big yellow
banner across Overland Trail strung from roof to
roof said, "It's A World Full of Wonders!"
There'd be a mule and horse show, trick riders,
and a clown. Everyone, even Bright Star wanted
to go, but First Elk Woman was reluctant.

People will wag their tongues, First Elk
Woman said. If we're seen with Bright Star, that
crazy story that Pete and Willie are Cheyenne will
come buzzing around like some horsefly with
green eyes and a nasty bite.

I knew better than to ask her why it should
matter what people say. To her it wasn't just
gossip, it was her honor, it was her standing

among the Oglalas. She stood for Young Man
Afraid of His Horses, and though she said she
didn't stand *against* Red Cloud it amounted to
the same thing. It seemed by that time that Swift
Bird was never going to mount a real campaign
for peace chief of the Itesica Oglalas. Young Man
Afraid was her best hope to bring back the old
days and old ways of leadership, and I as usual was
along for the ride.

Yet First Elk Woman decided finally she could
be better served by being in public where she
could at least have a little control, and we all went
to the circus one July night, First Elk Woman and
Bright Star and Pete and Willie and Louise and
me. Pete and Willie were like the Cheyenne in
claiming the right to make a marriage for Louise.
Louise wanted no part of their interference, but
every time a young man came calling on her they
took the fellow aside and told him they had better
plans for their sister than him.

First Elk Woman was right. We heard men in
the crowd buzzing about what a spectacle we all
cut, but we wouldn't pay them no never mind
and just kept ambling along down the midway
through the booths with games of chance for
fools, a wooden croquet ball hung by piano wire
from a little gallows that could knock a ten pin
over if it was set on the spot exactly over the
crosshairs, which it never was, so Pete and Willie
stood there swinging the ball at a half-penny a try
until their pockets were empty, and for what?
some geegaw made of feather and sequin.

So what if they couldn't see to choose between
junk and jewel? Night was coming on slow, a few
fair weather clouds glowing orange gold in the air
above the Arapaho Range. There was music, one
cornet player sitting in a circus wagon sending out
one long stream of melody across lots where
lanterns wrapped in colored paper threw their

lights on booths that were set with bits of broken mirror around their cheap pine frames making oncoming prairie night into the gates of the land of dreams. I knew the tune from Fort Laramie where new troops from back east brought their music to the sutler's saloon, and they sang together in their cups their sudsy sentiments:

Darling, I am growing old,
Silver threads among the gold,
Shine upon my brow today;
Life is fading fast away.

It was like St. Charles had finally come to Colorado, though there was never anything back there quite so Santa Fe wild as the reds, yellows, and blues that the booths and wagons and tents were painted.

We paid our 35 cent admission to enter inside the canvas walls where the circus ring was set and took our seats among the crowd, families mostly —the Provosts, Joe Mason and his wife Mary, the Stovers, the Whedbees, the Loomises—all with their many children so that the little inner circus looked to be sold out. Also Capt. Evans of the 11th Ohio Cavalry was there with his officers, all in their dress blues and with their swords and pistols.

Before Professor Robinson began to call the crowd's attention to the show, in came, one at a time, first Young Man Afraid, and the soliders bristled, then Sword, and the soldiers slid their right hands up to their holsters, then He Dog and the soldiers licked their lips as if all of a sudden their mouths run dry, then Little Big Man and those soldiers popped the catches on their leather, then Yellow Bear and they thumbed the hammers of their sidearms, then Three Grizzly Bears and American Horse and all their wives in their best feather and finery. The ringmaster was clearly going to crack his whip, but anyone could see from the expression on his face that he thought the better of it for the whip's report would sound too much like a gunshot. He stood silent, not knowing what to do.

The Army officers could not contain themselves. They sat in the grandstands, nervous and clutching at their waists for their Colts and swords at the sight of those very men who only yesterday they were shooting it out with at these sandstone rocks between Cheyenne and Camp Collins. And when the Oglala warriors saw the officers bridle and pop their feet nervous on plank stands, they too glared back across the little sawdust ring.

Ladies and gentlemen of all persuasions! Welcome to the bigtop! Professor Robinson cried out. It's a world full of wonders! A world about to be transformed by miracles of science! Evidence beyond dispute of man's dominion over nature!

Capt. Evans with a mild cough drew his officers' attention with a quick move of his hand and bid them contain themselves as if for this one night on the high plains of Colorado what was being called Red Cloud's War was at truce.

Then the cornet player sounded his *Ta-ta!* into the closed circle and a chute opened and out came the two strangest mules I had ever seen. They were covered with white stripes from muzzle to haunch, mules with dandy red plumes sticking up out of their leather halters.

Observe the strange markings on these beasts! he shouted. They are the barren offspring of horse and zebra, brought at great personal expense from the dark continent of Africa, ladies and gentlemen! Fanciers of horseflesh, ponder the points of these low powerful frames that hug the ground and change every prairie you come across. The plumes, inspired by ancient Egyptian tomb decorations, come with them and are entirely yours to bequeath as you wish should you purchase them at the close of this evening's entertainments.

How, you might ask, can a mere set of mules be taught the secrets of higher mathematics that have been hid from the understanding of ordinary men since the sealing of the Pyramids? I wave my wand of command over my head and up! These half zebras, half mules rise on their hind legs as if they were mortal humans! Everyone in the crowd shook their heads and clapped long and loud for the Professor.

What is two and two, I ask them. And down they come, and now with right front hoofs they mark it. Count along everybody—one, two, three, four!

And everybody clapped their hands like they had just seen Lazarus rise from the dead, and leading them in loud clapping and whistling and stamping their feet is this Clown with painted white face and no hair on top of his hightopped head and big red lips dressed in a polka dot suit and huge floppy shoes.

Come here with that bucket of water, Clown! shouts the Professor from across center ring. I'm thirsty, and I need a drink.

Especially the Oglala warriors and their families watched the Clown, for in their tribes there was no telling the difference between a fool and a holy man and a prophet.

The Clown came over real quick with this pail of water splashing on the sawdust, acting happy to be of service, only he trips on the low wooden blocks that make the ring, and whoops! there it is, water all over the Professor who begins howling and making a fuss, shouting, You are dumber than an animal! I can't teach you anything! You just make a mess!

And taking his buggy whip, the ringmaster begun beating on the Clown for his clumsiness, and the Clown he starts running across that ring, flinging himself down in the sawdust like a fish flopping on a dock, punching himself with his white gloved hands, until the crowd roars each time he kicks up his feet and falls on his back—Capt. Evans and Young Man Afraid of His Horse alike all laughing until tears came to their eyes—when the Clown reached inside his tunic and pulled out something inside his two cupped hands that he made pulse like a beating heart, his hands working together slower and slower until the crowd went silent and saw a red glow inside his hands go bright then go out as if it were a shooting star.

Everyone was silent for a full measure, then the Clown he hooked his thumbs and made his eight fingers the harmony of two wings beating together and fluttering higher above his shoulders until he's on his tiptoes and lets go of his hooked thumbs and the wings disappeared upward into Heaven, and everyone let out an Oh! as if it was the Fourth of July and they were watching fireworks go pink and silver in the sky.

Once the festivities were over, I headed back north into the Powder river country by myself. My father had taught me to pass without notice, to use steady bird calls for blotting out my footfall, to walk with my horse's gait, my legs cloaked behind hers, to cast myself like question marks into shadow and travel as invisible as Cheyennes across these plains, born it seems to lead a double life, to carry messages from one part of the mystery to another, between my brother and me, for we had often used knowing the whereabouts of the Oglala to keep the two armies apart until that treaty got signed.

If Red Cloud's horsemen could be kept from fighting—and possibly losing—another battle with the cavalry, he could parley with the Peace

Commissioners from strength. I read the eastern newspapers aloud to him in his tipi some nights when he'd have First Elk Woman and I join him and his family for a meal. It was there one night we read an article about the Indian Peace Party, mostly Quakers who wanted the government to sue Red Cloud for peace so they could send their missionaries out west to bring their "inner light" to the Sioux. Ever since Red Cloud had led both Sioux and Cheyenne against Fort Phil Kearny and won, his name was magic.

I lived those days alone and traveled by moonlight, and always with a pack mule and jugs of whiskey big enough to last me a month of headaches and otherwise just worn by the cark and care of my task, so much so that one night, saddlesore and hungry I lost sense enough to feel watched, no, stalked. That's the promise of and the problem with whiskey. It dulls your senses, which is just what you want it to do. Which invites the reaper.

I turned my pony's head into shadows of gullies that streak that whole plain east of the Big Horns. I stopped, long, to listen for any footfall, a shambling horse's neigh or snuffle in the small breeze. Nothing. Not owl, nor coyote, nor even wind. I then begun to worry in earnest if I was to be dry-gulched by some bad gang of whatever stripe. I sat ahorse it seemed for hours sleepless in the moonlight, wondering about this life of ours, wondering about the words we use to think about life, so that I no longer knew for sure about our successes, our failures, and those strange times between when we're most awake and most in doubt on the soul's long night watches, taking swigs from the jug each time I convinced myself the sounds I heard was nothing, so long I may have dropped asleep awhile, for it must've been in a dream I joined this column of riders slowly

walking their horses westward into a pass through
the Big Horn mountains, disappearing into a
canyon moon shadow, and then, spurring up a
dry gulch, that very moon showing me in silhouette the men and horses I had been singing a slow
waltz in caravan with were skeletons.

La lune qui rayonne
éclairera la nuit.
Il faut qu'avant l'aurore
nous soyons de retour.

Next minute, I was on the ground, knocked off
my horse by the leap of two men from the lip of
the gulch above me. I wrestled, trying to unholster
my side-arm, only to find myself pinned, dragged
into the moonlight where I saw the grinning faces
of Pete and Willie. How they laughed! And how
proud they were to have bested their father at this
game.

It doesn't take the greatest skill to sneak up on
a sleeping man, I said, trying to put them off
balance and save a little face.

We've found we can see as well as night as in
the day, father, Willie said in a fake deep voice of
utmost seriousness.

Yes, you make big medicine with your Cheyenne stories, Pete said.

Mock not lest ye be mocked, I said in my own
fake deep voice of utmost seriousness. You're
looking at a drunken sot who sees everything
double and isn't sure if men or beasts ain't some
awful dream of skeleton caravans winding their
way west into the Big Horns.

They'd been fighting in Red Cloud's army
alongside other breeds like Johnny Reeshaw, Jr.—
mostly skirmishes here and there with different
war parties, sometimes with Crazy Horse's band,
sometimes with Dull Knife's Cheyenne. They
filled me in on their doings as dawn's first light
began to blot the last stars.

We've seen great medicine, Pete said. Just before the fight with Fetterman's command we followed this half-man on horseback as he wandered through the hills lamenting for his vision. He zigzagged across hill and dale, often falling off his horse and rolling on the ground as if he'd gotten hold of wriggling snakes or fishes that walk the earth, singing, making strange noises, throwing dust in his own face as if he were in mourning for a lost loved one. He came back to lie before the feet of Red Cloud, saying, "I have the souls of ten white men in my spirit catcher." "Not enough," Red Cloud shouted. "Not nearly enough." So this *bardache* began to sing again, mounting his horse, crossing and re-crossing the hills again, falling on the ground, wrestling with more invisible things until at last he fell at the feet of Red Cloud a second time with ten more white men's souls. "Not enough," shouted Red Cloud, and the half-man, half-woman *hemaneh* climbed on his horse and again went singing into the hills all day, all day until at last as the sun was setting he fell upon hard ground at Red Cloud's feet and said he had one hundred souls in his hands, and Red Cloud at last said, It is enough.

You would have been proud of us, papa, Pete said.

Don't be vain, Willie said. That has been the hardest thing. Waiting. This one, he often can't hold his horses. Instead of waiting for Crazy Horse to spring his trap the way Roman Nose taught us—riding with a small party as decoys to get the soldiers out of their fort and chasing them until they came into places where our main war parties lie in wait—he charges ahead wanting to be the one who counts first coup. But against Fetterman we held our horses, and when Crazy Horse and his men came rushing past us we sprung the jaw of the trap and caught them in the open, killing as our *hemaneh's* medicine had said one hundred soldiers that day. And we have scalps to prove it! Pete shook a tiny piece of hair in my face until I brushed it aside with a wave of my arm in disgust.

They had heard from Nick that I was heading north to find Red Cloud's band and bring him star chief Carrington's message to come to Fort Laramie that June at last for peace talks, and they thought it a fine idea to hunt me up. I was so shook to be snuck up on like that I told them I thought it about time to sober up. It had taken me years to get over the Sand Creek massacre and what I saw coming in it that seized me up so bad I'd rather be blind drunk than look at it.

At last in 1868 Nick and I got called to Fort Laramie to help with interpreting Sioux at treaty talks. I told Red Cloud he should not touch the pen to any paper until all the so-called Peace Commissioners came up with a treaty, granting almost the whole of Dakota territory, including the Black Hills together with the lands west to the Big Horns, to the Sioux nation as "unceded lands."

I believe somewhere there's a photograph of me and Nick sitting crosslegged between that row of chair-seated generals under two wide open tipis and Spotted Tail and most of the Sioux chiefs of the seven bands, except for Red Cloud. You can only make out the backs of our heads, though it does show we never had parted with our hair.

To celebrate the signing of the treaty, Nick decided he would be the trail cook and prepare a feast for the generals—Harney and Sandborn— and the rest of the Peace Commissioners at the well-appointed home of Colonel Carrington, the camp commander. Everyone was red-faced and laughing from generous cups of whiskey and many toasts to America and the flag and the President and God and everyone's mother when

Nick carried our meal in course by course—cooked corn, boiled prairie turnips, and a toothsome meat stew in gravy served up on a bed of wild rice.

It was Harney who demanded that Nick write out the recipes for all the dishes Nick set before them. It was Nick who told the assembled that the main course was puppy dog.

Knock them puppies on the head, he said, and throw 'em on a campfire till you got all their hair singed off. Then gut 'em out, cut 'em up from joint to joint, and fry 'em up in a big pan to render out 'nough fat to make the gravvy for stew. Then boil them doggies till they tender, stirrin' in flour and dog renderin's so's that whole thing gets nice 'n thick.

General Sanborn, on hearing that camp dogs supplied the meat course, gagged and had to run outside. Harney just laughed and declared, I can not tell you with what relish I shall tell this tale along the old Potomac.

I had another reason to keep to shadows in those years. I wanted to stay alive. It was that simple. You have no doubt heard the old saying about killing the messenger who bears bad tidings. That was me, as dusty an angel as ever strode across the hills of Judea, parched enough for whiskey to risk a .45 slug in the liver from some Galvinized Yankee busting out of his britches to head out looking for gold in Red Cloud's Black Hills. If he could put my face and name together, he'd as soon shoot me dead in some dusty Cheyenne street as look at me.

As I sat quietly drinking shots in this dark corner of the Long Goodbye saloon, watching where my own stick floats, I heard them talking.

Ever hear of a feller the name of Antoine Janeece, says one ex-Confederate still half dresst in his Rebel grays.

Ain't he and his brother the ones been helping Red Cloud?

Yep. Goddam race traitors is what them two are, says the first man.

I got up and pulled my hat on real casual, with the intent of making my exit quietly through the front door, except I made the mistake of uttering one word when one of them turned from the bar and askt me who I was.

You Jim Bridger?

No, I says.

You look like 'im, or some feller from up in the mountains. An injun fighter, er ya?

No, I says.

Ain't much for talkin', er ya?

No, I says.

You one of them 'air half-breeds?

Who give you the right to stand there and pry into a man's personal business? I askt him back.

A man's got a right to know where his neighbors stand, for 'im or aginst him, bub.

I ain't your neighbor, I says.

You ain't much of anything at all.

I could see it in his eyes he was starting to wonder if he could take me in a fight. He began to lick his lips as if the thought of shooting me had already begun drying up his spit. He had a pistol wedged in his pants beneath his coat. I knew how he felt. It had been a lifetime since I took a blade to a man's ribs.

The time for talk was done, that much I knew. My blood begun to pound in my ears as if I was some greenhorn kid. In that rhythm I heard my father saying, *You have to let yourself go down ...*

I reached behind me and grabbed ahold of the whiskey bottle I'd been drinking from and swung it side-arm across this gray man's teeth, and he went down with his mouth bloody. Then I drew my pistol on his partner and without so much as a word I backed out of that place, sweating so bad I began to stink even to my own self.

There were lots of men with nasty tempers living in Cheyenne those days. I thought it wisest to climb up on my roan mare and disappear into the sage and never show my face more in that town. It got so I didn't want anyone around me, especially my friend, Swift Bird. More than once I had this dream. It was a godawful rain that made the air black as night, a rain that would drown a man who looked up into the clouds and opened his mouth. These gray men come out of that black rain and catch me at my house in Laporte. They kick in my door and come rushing in, and quick as a blink I'm hogtied and hauled out into this rain to be hanged on the same tree where Louise's trinket ring is droning like an aeolian harp in the wind, and I wake strangling at the end of a hemp rope for the simple crime of frustrating their dream of becoming millionaires.

I figured the government was far in debt for the War of Rebellion and needed gold to settle up. I heard it rumored about that Grant in Washington thought it best always to keep some malcontent herd about Cheyenne to stir up noise about the new gold fields.

Can I make it any plainer, Mr. Watrous? Can you guess the cause of my first reluctance to answer your request for all the particulars? Nor do I forget that there's still men in these parts who hate my name. First Elk Woman had impressed me years before that to her lookout it was best to go invisible across these plains and salvation was to be found in going nameless to the spirit world.

Nick's name and mine are all over that treaty as interpreters for the Sioux nation, though I defy you to find my name attached to the letter Nick drafted to represent the old free trappers, heads of Sioux families, petitioning the government for half sections on what is now Pine Ridge land, under the belief that the Sioux would the sooner be led to farming and be made civilized if the white men married to their women showed them how. That's why, when Henry Arrison rode up with writs from the government stating that I might legally either keep my land in Laporte and divorce First Elk Woman or stay married to her and share her fate at Pine Ridge I was stunned.

April 12, 1885
Pine Ridge Agency

LETTER XVI

"Un Regard Foudroyant"

Lots of squawmen in Laporte and Camp Collins and thereabouts got notice from Henry Arrison those days that they must quit their lands along the Poudre river to get other lands in Dakota territory as part of their Sioux wives' reservation settlement along the White Earth river, among them Joe Mason, who got shut of his Mary in short order.

What if he did get a half section in Dakota for his quarter section here? Land here was lovely, green, sheltered from winter's brunt, its foothills covered with yellowed grasses like soft buckskin curves that feel kind, not cruel like Dakota where I've heard that white women have gone mad with the wind blowing forever across the clay hills.

Joe Mason owned a large portion of what had come to be called "Fort" Collins, though there never was a walled fort like Bent's or Fort William there, only an encampment of tents, only a log cabin post with a few supply sheds, only rows of barracks somewhat like the new barracks at Fort Laramie is all, though Joe foresaw it would soon become a large thriving town. I heard he rigged the election which proclaimed it the new county seat where all must come to pay their taxes and buy their supplies. There was even talk of building an agricultural college about a mile south of Linden.

Yet something broke inside me that New Year's day 1873 when I got word in Laporte that my Pete and Willie got murdered at Nick's ranch, so that I did not have the heart to fight against the government. Sometimes a fire in the heart will go out.

That wagon ride east from Fort Laramie out along the North Platte with Nick's daughter Emily beside me stone silent as we headed toward the Niobara country was the hardest of my life. She had married John Reeshaw's son, John Jr., only two years before and was already a widow. When Emily finally broke silence her words were fists of lead that struck my ears with dull thuds.

Can't say I'm sorry to see Peter dead, uncle Antoine. If it weren't for him, my Johnny would be alive today. Billy Garnett swore an oath that would blacken your tongue that all I'm telling you now is gospel.

Pete and Willie and Johnny and Louie Shangrau went down the Platte river in a big rowboat to the Sod Agency to pick up eighty horses with Billy Garnett and drive them north back to Fort Laramie for General Smith. They got in and started rowing and drifting for miles downriver past an Arapaho camp, and five miles farther they floated past Young Man Afraid of His Horses' camp. Once they got about where we are now and were half in the bag Pete started taunting Johnny.

Pete spots Yellow Bear's camp, and he says, Let's us cross the river to pay Yellow Bear's camp a visit. Ain't you paid bride price for two of his daughters, Johnny? You should collect those two young women.

Johnny says, I given bride price for them before I even laid an eye on your cousin Emily. Now I got her, what I want with them two Yellow Bear hags?

Pete said, Why let that stop you? Your father

and my father, who knows how many wives they
had, and they were giants! Are you any the less?

Johnny never could blow off a challenge to his
idea of himself. That was part of what I loved
about him. So he went to Yellow Bear's lodge to
ask for his women. Yellow Bear was seated on a
buffalo robe and claimed the women were miles
away at a scalp dance. Johnny didn't believe one
word Yellow Bear told him. Well, then, Johnny
said just to tease him, since I've given you them
horses that're tethered outside your lodge, I think
I'll shoot them.

Yellow Bear looked up at his pistol hanging
from a line, but it was too far away from him to
go for it and hope to shoot Johnny who sat by the
fire with his Winchester across his lap watching
the chief's every move.

You may do as you wish with the horses you
gave me, Yellow Bear said, trying not to show
how afraid he was when he heard the click of
Johnny's hammer cocked back.

Johnny got up as if to go outside and vent his
anger on them horses, but almost as an after-
thought he reached back into the tipi with his rifle
and pulled the trigger. Yellow Bear was shot in his
chest. He tried to hoist himself up, but he fell
over dead.

Some score of Yellow Bear's Brulé followers
jumped Johnny in that crowded tipi. His rifle was
too long for close quarters, so he pulled his six-
gun, but Yellow Bear's brother Slow Bear grabbed
and held his right arm up, and Johnny began
firing into the air above his head up through the
tipi smoke hole. One of them Brulé buried a knife
in Johnny's chest, and Slow Bear put the pistol to
Johnny's head and fired.

It was my turn then to ride out there alone for
Johnny's body, all shot full of holes, where Yellow
Bear's people counted coup before they hightailed

it north to escape the Army in such haste they left
Yellow Bear's body in his tipi. I dragged it outside
and stared at it so long all I could see was my best
hopes in the dust along with his corpse and went
so mad I cut his heart out with an axe and covered
him with dry wood stacked inside the tipi and set
his dead body afire before I packed Johnny's
remains on the wagon to bury him and all my
dreams.

We were meant for man and wife, that much
was sure. He killed anyone who messed with him,
just like his father. I was proud that Red Cloud
pleaded for Johnny's pardon to President Grant
after Johnny shot Corporal Conrad at Fort Fetterman. This was the man who was in love with me.
His life seemed charmed. I loved the wildness in
him, and now he's gone, like Pete and Willie.

When we reached Nick's place I saw my sons
on the hill behind the bunkhouse with huge crows
already picking at their bodies covered by buffalo
robes on rickety poles holding their platforms up
in the sky burials their murderers, the Reeshaw
boys, Charley and Joe, gave them. What did it
matter to me how they died and were buried?
Later, when we laid their bodies out to wash them
for burial in the Fort Laramie cemetery I would
read their wounds. The story of their deaths
would then unfold, the days of drinking at Fort
Laramie celebrating Christmas, the near fight in
the sutler's bar with some new Army recruits that
got them kicked out so they got the idea of going
on out to Nick's ranch to keep on drinking, the
fighting words from young Charlie's mouth
accusing Pete of Johnny's death like Emily had
just done.

Emily told it slow and hard, the way she did
everything.

There was a hard wind all those three days,
and after we all got to Nick's ranch we kept

having to close the bunkhouse door as it kept blowing open, and I was feeling more and more strange as if it were Johnny's angry ghost that kept banging at our front door.

I don't know when the idea came into their minds, the Reeshaw boys', I mean. There weren't no mean looks passing between the Janis boys and the Reeshaws. They were playing poker, and Peter was dealing stud, and he kept saying, No help there! and laughing, and everybody was laughing. Nobody accused anybody of cheating. But I noticed Charlie kept trying to pull Willie off to one side, and get him talking and swigging from a jug.

I walked up to Willie, I says, Don't you get too much distance between you and Pete. Can't you see Charlie here's trying to separate you off from Pete? Just then, Charley pulls his six-shooter and whips me a good lick up alongside the head. I went down on the bunkhouse floor, dazed and bleeding, though not out cold.

Once Charlie hit me he must've just decided to go through with the whole thing and shot at Willie, who put his head down like a bull and charged through the door splintering its planks, with Charlie charging after him firing until he hit him square in the back of his head.

Pete jumped up and started to wrestle his two six-guns out of his holsters as he ran outside, but Willie was already dead. Pete had both guns out and might have tried to make Charlie eat the same bread as Charlie'd served to Willie, but something stopped him. A look came over his face that showed that for the first time in a long time Pete was alone and scared. Joe just walked right up to Pete who was standing there aghast and jammed his pistol into Pete's chest and fired.

Willie was Pete's *wakan*, I said, trying to hold myself up with my hands on the white table where the bodies lay as my knees had gone limpsy from Emily's story.

Then there come a loud knocking at Emily's door, her husband John Reeshaw Jr.'s house, the son of the very man I'd split with fifteen years before, that morning after the smoke from the Grattan massacre cleared. Emily was now a widow, as fierce a woman as I've ever seen, with a man's grit and great black eyes that stared anyone who crossed her with what my father would've called *un regard foudroyant.*

It was the poor crippled fool Baptiste, come to pay his respects. Emily asked him, Where are Charlie and Joe? Where have they run off to? Mr. Janis here wants to find them.

Over and over she asked the same questions, and Baptiste he had some impediment with his tongue, he just stood there, his whole body shaking, damned if he said anything, damned if he didn't, saying *Th-they they* until with the same fierce temper she had hacked Yellow Bear's body to pieces Emily pulled my six-shooter out of my holster that lay on a table in the hall and emptied all chambers into him.

What is there to say? A terrible wind blew up, driving dry snow across the plains in long drifts. And she lit out into those white winds and disappeared as so many have, her late husband John, Yellow Bear's people, north, to seek shelter among the wild Sioux still roaming in that old free life of hunters between Yellowstone, Tongue, and Powder.

Years later, she would return from time to time to Fort Laramie to visit Johnny's grave, her eyes as hard as ever, so much so I recall children at play outside the sutler's store stop to stare at her, and old Josey Hinton whittling a stick near the hitching post told them, You best stay clear of her, for she has done a killing once and mought again if you but cross her. I could see shivers of fear run up their spines and shake their trunks.

Many's the time since 1873 I stood before their graves and read their stone markers. Peter Janis, it says, Born July 15, 1850. Died Dec. 25, 1872. William Janis, Born Nov. 8, 1854. Died Dec. 25, 1872. This is what all my dreams had come to, narrow plots of ground.

My time I spent then and for two years writing letters to Robert Furnace, governor of Nebraska, to P.W. Hitchcock, U.S. Senator, to H.R. Clum, Commissioner of Indian Affairs, to have the murderers arrested and brought to justice, so much so I little cared to fight against the government to hold my land in Laporte. What was it for, after all, if not my children, Pete, Willie, and all the rest?

The Cheyenne *Daily Leader* summed up most people's feelings about the murders. "No regret at the fatal result of these Indian amusements is felt in this community. On the contrary, our people are disposed to consider these brawls blessings in disguise, as they free us from a set of hangers on to the Indian reservations who are and have been the cause of our Indian difficulties." I guess that was their idea of frontier justice. It was not mine.

What had I failed to teach my boys that they should come to such an early end? I taught them to love and honor the old way, the one-hearted way, but I could not teach them to be underwater men the way I did with young Antoine, who took to it natural. I knew from that day on the buffalo hunt beside the Republican river that I could not really save them from themselves without killing their souls, and from that moment on I thought I was prepared for what might happen to them. I was not.

It's a harder thing than I have words to say to be a father who outlives his children, who sees the future for which he worked gone to dust. I had lost Pete and Willie and Louise.

The Sioux and the government locked horns many times during those years. People back east claimed there was nothing personal in how they took possession of what the Treaty of 1868 said was "unceded lands." It was hard telling who was nailing who to which bloody stake. The government sent people out here that gave as bloody as they got, and how else should the Sioux take it but personal. Maybe it was having jobs Red Cloud hated above all. Having a job took all the free space out of your life. You could not then be a holy man and a husband and father and chief in the Lakota way.

My father had told me I'd only have one chance to name myself, that who I was would be shown by what or who I chose. Who I chose was the love of my life, First Elk Woman, and because of her I was with the Sioux.

May 1, 1885
Pine Ridge Agency

"Ghost Dance"

It's been a good while since last I took pen in hand. My age has begun to tell. The reservation doctor says kidney trouble. My skin has got sallow as candle wax. It's so much up-again, down-again for me I've askt to be set out-side these June mornings whether First Elk Woman will or no, though she calls the boys to carry me inside sooner than I'd like. I don't make no fuss. I write at the window then, sitting at table with her, listening to her hum as she stitches a line of bead down with fine threads of sinew along straight lines. Style's the first invention, isn't it, making the Winged god a grid in color and out-line of a Thunder Being ready to spring off east from foothills to the grasslands.

These gloves will fit your brother Nick two ways, she says. They are gloves for a proud man leading a large band.

When we were kids in school reading about the old days of knighthood in France, we'd have called them gauntlets, I say.

Gauntlets?

Yes, in the old days in the old world across the ocean. Gloves made of iron beaten thin that come way up over a man's wrists. Rich people's sons threw them to the ground to make the sign of war, of combats that killed so many farmboys.

You're right about my brother, I added. He's
always thought he would have made a good king.

That's one way, she says. The other way is
how his stubby fingers will slip right in to these
gloves. See? I have made them wide, like his
picture of himself.

If I go into detail, it's bound up with First
Elk Woman. She lives from the ground up
through these figures she plies her needle and her
good eyesight through, and I guess it's rubbed off
on me, some. I'm talking about this woman
sitting at the table with me, her head bent toward
her stitching.

She holds it up into the window's light,
making straight lines to grasp an eagle's form,
humming a tune that spirals and circles to touch
the cabin from beam to board.

When the weather's good I sit and watch the
sky, though my mind does drift back to days
when my friend Swift Hawk would come by my
tipi on the plain between the Laramie and north
Platte as I sat making myself a backrest of alder
saplings strung together with sinews threaded
through holes I bored with flint drills while I
roasted a rabbit to a fine turn.

And, strangely, there he is poking around for a
juicy leg joint, drooling out of his wide mouth
with the grin of someone who's five years old and
really hungry, knowing I could refuse him nothing.
Then I find myself bursting with wanting one
more rabbit to roast and Swift Hawk to visit me
these days, but he is long gone down the spirit
road.

Things went extra lonely for me since Dr.
MacGillacuddy, the agent, ordered Nick off Pine
Ridge reservation. Here is my lookout on how
that happened.

One late afternoon in the summer of 1882
MacGillacuddy came to my house. He sat at the

table and said, Talk is that He Dog and some others are going to jump the reservation and go down into Nebraska to fight some Poncas that have run off a dozen Oglala horses the other night. That means trouble.

Yes, I know, I said. But, to put an Oglala interpretation on it, as far as He Dog's concerned the treaties say that he must never fight the blue-coats. It says nothing about Poncas. To him it's two different things.

The whole idea is there's to be peace on the prairies, Dr. MacGillacuddy said. That means no fighting. I won't have it. It's bad business, and, if we can't prevent it, it will reflect badly on us all here at Pine Ridge with the federal government whom we all serve. That's why I'm here to ask you and your brother Nick to use your influence with the Oglalas to nip this raid in the bud. I want you and Nick to go down to He Dog's camp before dawn tomorrow and reason with them until they leave off their foolish plan to go seeking retribution among the Ponca.

I'll try, I told him, not realizing then what a big mistake that was.

Nick and I did go down to He Dog's crescent of tipis next morning before light and got there probably too late, for He Dog and his men were already on horseback when we rode up on our own mounts. I raised my hand in peace.

Don't go, I said to He Dog. You can't go off fighting the Poncas anytime you feel like it any-more. Things have changed. If you leave, Mac-Gillacuddy will take away your rations and your wives and children will go hungry.

We don't want to hurt you, Antoine. You neither, Nick, He Dog said. We are old friends and we've had some laughs together. Move aside.

I won't, I said.

He Dog and his men looked at me and Nick.

Light began to spill across the land. There was a slight chill in the air, as I recall. The horses were whinnying, as if to say, Let's go! We want to run hard to the south and deal them Poncas some hurt. I could see steam coming from their nostrils in long white jets.

Where is Red Cloud? I asked. Shouldn't he be leading this war party?

Who are you to take Red Cloud's name? He Dog snorted. Everybody knows you and First Elk Woman have crossed him in favor of Young Man Afraid many times.

He Dog spurred his pony forward, and his whole party of some score of warriors dressed out in paint and feather started to surge past Nick and me. I spun my horse about to get out ahead of them and face them again. Just then a war club smashed into my skull and my head was filled with bright bubbles, each of which shone with a hard silver fist of pain. I saw a man who was made out of picket fence floating in space with his wooden arm and a hand in a white glove that swung back and forth like a metronome. Down I went to the ground, blacked out. Nick got down off his horse to attend me and bring me home so First Elk Woman could nurse me. He Dog and his men went on that morning to track down and fight the horsethief Poncas.

It took a long time before I got my health back to where I wasn't seeing double. That was why, back in 1883, in my very first letter to you I begged off.

It was more than that, of course. It was my standing with MacGillacuddy, for afterward he blamed me for He Dog's raid on the Poncas. He fired me from the job as subagent at Pine Ridge and drove Nick off the reservation altogether, saying that I had neither influence enough with

XVII

215

the Oglalas nor was I anymore physically fit enough to carry out the job.

First Elk Woman said MacGillacuddy had worked it all out in his mind beforehand. He knew neither me nor Nick would be able to stop He Dog and his men from going off to take their satisfaction on the Poncas. It was one of their great joys in life, and they wouldn't surrender that to anyone, not even their good old friends.

I heard the good doctor brag about how he faced Nick down in the road between the storehouse and Pine Ridge Reservation office one evening when Nick was winding his way home to his wife, bluffing Nick with his index finger in his coat pocket.

MacGillacuddy has no idea. If Nick really wanted to kill any man, including him, that man would wake to find himself surprisingly dead.

And then, since Kicking Bear went west to the Pyramid Lake country to hear the Paiute Jesus speak, and since his return, Lakota families have been wearing the ghost shirt, dancing the ghost dance, singing ghost songs to bring all the dead back to life to help the earth turn upside-down and hurl the white men away and make this world new. They dance and dance, night and day. Agent MacGillacuddy worries that General Miles will take the dancing as an act of rebellion, not worship, forbid them to dance, forbid their songs, forbid the only words that give them hope, and have to send his troops in here to restore order.

Sometimes at night I'm wakened by their drums, and I lay in the dark with my mind drifting. Sometimes I find myself remembering my mother in her sunbonnet weeding the garden with her hoe, and there she is, not looking at me as I tell her I cannot enter the priesthood the way she wants. Nor could I live out her dream.

I think I began to back off from living her dream with my life that day I came home from the academy with my nose bloody from a fight with Frankie Desjardin. I can see that day almost better than I can see this day I'm writing in. Out front of Sacred Heart Academy there was long sloping lawns, and on a day in spring after Easter I saw Frankie beating my little friend Richie. So I stepped over to Frankie and said, Why not pick on someone your own size? And he says, Alright then, and he lands a roundhouse punch right on my nose. When I come home, my mother saw blood on my shirt and she said, What happened? And I said, I stood up for little Richie against Frankie Desjardin is what. And she said, Why don't you mind your own business? Then you wouldn't get hurt. I was stunned to silence. All my life she'd called me her little Sir Lancelot, and what after all was chivalry all about except to protect those who are helpless against the lawless black knights of the world? Seems she only meant me to protect her and not little Richie or my little brother Nick.

Her deepset eyes on me filled with such reproach and betrayal I was like to die. And dawn comes, and I'm standing by her side promising that though I couldn't be a priest like she askt, I'd grow up to be a good man. Perhaps if she knew my good man was not to be a Roman Catholic but a pagan underwater man she'd glare at me as she did that day before I left home with my father for a new life in the Rocky Mountains.

I hear drums at night and wake, I walk outside and hear the ghost dance song inside tipis, themselves stretched buffalo hides like drums, thin enough for light to turn them into lanterns glowing like human hearts inside these huge darknesses of the badlands, raked by constant winds though no less filled with spirits than the

Powder river country. I see their silhouettes against the tipi hides, I hear the singers calling back the spirits of their dead. I have been blessed, Mr. Watrous, to see them, whatever else may have been given to me, or taken away.

And I have heard drums at night and waked from a dream where I am a boy again, sitting at my desk in the school room at L'Academie in St. Charles, staring through the words in the book—*Omnia Gaulia est divisa in tres partes*—they say, and the voice of the Latin teacher, Sister Therese, drones on, and I am there, a boy standing in firelit night among women singing over the dead bodies of their husbands, brothers, sons within the swirling smoke of a burning village, a song to raise souls to their next lives, all the men pierced in the same place with the Roman short sword so the ribs on the right side look like they have a slit as wide as a mouth that speaks Roman magic, the shifting, changing shapes of legions on the battle-field, of how the soldiers hold their ranks, hold their blood as wild men in painted faces taunt them, call them out for battle, one on one, of Roman soldiers thrusting their swords always to the right under the raised sword arms of Frankish warriors, piercing the exposed ribs, of depending on the man to their left to do likewise to those warriors in front of them. Such a killing machine, those legions, the victory of Roman order over the disorder of lone tribal heroes. And now their widows keen above their dead bodies, and it goes on, their lament, their ghost song, sung from wounds like mouths blackened with dried blood, their crying into darkness that the hills have heard since human beings first rose from mud that swirled in tidal pools like fine blue clay swirled in a prospector's pan, like tea swirled in some Creole conjurer's cup as the moonlit night gathers the visible world into a smaller and smaller circle.

Dawn begins. The drums go on, their singing,
the shouts that can bend iron. I get up from bed to
stare at white dusty hills and gullies, Pine Ridge,
these badlands my father called *terre-mauvais,* as if
they were hell, as if they were *un pays malheureux,*
as if a killing thirst were their least terror.

I promised to finish my tale and keep my
bond to give you all the particulars.

To resume: What haunted Red Cloud all
those years had finally come to live in my own
house. When he stepped inside our floored cabin
at Laporte in 1877 the property was no longer
clearly ours. We were fixing to rent it to Mr. Garbutt for his use in growing hay. Red Cloud was a
changed man from that day in 1844 First Elk
Woman and I were married, though it was not
age alone that lined his face or slacked his broad
mouth.

Perhaps it was so much talk, year after year
with "Peace" Commissioners, trying to salvage the
Powder river lands and the *Pahasapa* from being
taken. Perhaps it was Crazy Horse's ghost. I did
not say much. What was there to say that had not
been said many times before? My old friend, by
now you have known for a long time you cannot
win a war with these whites? You may win battles,
but every Oglala who dies becomes a price too
high to pay for victory over Major Fetterman's
command or with Custer's men at Greasy Grass?
They wear you down? No, I kept silent. There
was nothing I could say that he did not already
know past knowing.

Red Cloud was worn down. His face looked
flattened, nearly hammered, so much so First Elk
Woman could scarcely look at him without tears.
It had begun in earnest at Sand Creek, now nearly
thirteen years before. Since then his braves had
fought Connor to a standstill, wiped out Fetterman's troop at Fort Phil Kearny, and held their

own until at the Wagon Box fight the federal troops used repeating rifles. Since then we'd twice traveled by train to Washington to meet with President Grant.

He was long past being awed by cities or by the big howitzers they rolled out and fired down the Potomac River five miles just to show him what power could be brought against his warriors in a pitched battle the way he was in 1871 when first we traveled together by private railcar from east of Cheyenne to Omaha, Chicago, and then to Washington City, where he quarreled so bitterly with Spotted Tail because by custom the older band of the Brulé always came before Oglalas in council that I shut them both in a hotel room together to work out their dispute.

When they finally came out, Spotted Tail told us he would allow Red Cloud to be the main chief of all the Tetons for the sake of peace.

The federal commissioners were so happy they gave Spotted Tail and his chiefs horses. The Brulé were well satisfied, and dashed about the capital city in their finery while Red Cloud and his entourage had to sit with their knees together being driven from place to place in broughams which he regarded as little better than the black hearse he'd seen once in Cheyenne.

He was shrewd enough now to reckon they had no way to cart those huge cannon out onto the wild plains of Wyoming where he'd call the tune. He'd been driven around New York to meet Quaker groups and speak to them at Cooper Union Hall at a meeting of their Indian Peace Party. I had read newspaper articles to him about it back when he didn't know what writing or newspapers were, and I had to tell him it was pictures in words of what the white men all were dreaming. If some dreamed of making peace with the Sioux, it went into the dream council to parley with dreams of war. Who knows but whether peace tongues might not have the force to quiet war tongues? Who knows if he could gather enough *wakan* to reach into pages of that common dream and right the balance the white man's coming had knocked off kilter? Holding the red-stone sacred pipe of the Sioux nation in his hands on the stage, he sang this prayer, *There is room in this pipe for you, Grandfathers.*

The Oglalas still could not trade furs along the Moonshell, though the 1868 treaty promised that right. Nick and I felt equally betrayed, for the treaty provided for trade along the north Platte. All this swam in Red Cloud's eyes with the ghosts who stood among Sand Creek's burning tipis. He may have swaggered as a young man when first he sought to be chief. But as the winters grew on him he saw what befell one tribe would befall every tribe.

He stood between the U.S. Army and Spotted Tail's Brulé, who never once admitted what they owed him. Spotted Tail tried to persuade his Brulé to ranch in the Dakotas, taming their old free roving life. Red Cloud kept peace, unless some new law threatened first the lands between the Big Horns and the Black Hills, then the Black Hills themselves, then what was called Red Cloud agency near Fort Robinson in Nebraska, then Pine Ridge agency along the White Earth River here in South Dakota territory, squeezed down to smaller reserves, every year it seemed, and how I could help him I flatly did not know. His eyes said he did not want to go another time to Washington. He said he would not go unless good men were around him. When he at last asked me to interpret for him in talks with President Hayes, how could I refuse? This was before Pete and Willie had been killed, and I still believed my sons had a future.

To be ushered into the White House East Room was more awesome for me than him. I could barely speak for slack-jawed gawking when I rendered Red Cloud's words in English.

We don't want to go to the Missouri country, he said. That is the bad whiskey road. I am afraid for my people. Some men will come like little white mice to eat away the grain until there's none left to fill Sioux bellies.

President Hayes merely knocked his cigar ashes into a cutglass tray. You should learn to farm, he said.

I wondered how I should interpret that to Red Cloud. Should I say, He does not think your little joke is worth responding to. Instead, he says again that you must take your people east to the Missouri or starve? No, I could not. I could only translate, word for word, or all would be lost.

What good I could do was advise Red Cloud what to ask for—three kinds of wagons to work with, mowing machines, cattle enough to raise to last winter after winter, one sawmill, one grain mill, a school with a priest like Father DeSmet for teachers—all that I had learned from watching Joe Mason build up Fort Collins and make it work.

If you will get your people to travel east to the Missouri this year, the President said, next year you can choose another place more to your liking, somewhere on the White Earth River, though not the Tongue.

Red Cloud replied, We know *now* where we want to settle—the place where White Earth Creek forks into the White River.

We'll see, the President said, excusing himself on other urgent business.

And so the meeting closed, the ladies in their Paris finery drifted out on clouds of silk. We left with a good prospect for the future, if Hayes was to be believed.

From then till now Red Cloud's chieftainship has been a long circling descent like some redtail hawk's. Dr. MacGillacuddy's one shrewd customer. First he broke the position me and Nick held at Pine Ridge as subagents. Then he broke Red Cloud's hold on the Oglala by bringing the *akicita* tradition back.

He hired Indian police dressed in mocassins, leggings, and Army tunics and led by Sword to enforce the rules of the camp and dole out monthly food. It had come full circle, back to a time when strong chiefs held the bands together ended just as for the whites a human wave following the sun had washt across prairie and mountain pass led by one Moses after another, their fleets in a weaving line like railroads that followed them and then rested, waiting for the next shift in tides.

My map of California and the northwest shows a coastline that looks bitten off, as if some huge mouth opened from the Atlantic ocean and the world beyond and stretched until it found its like, and closed, though time will tell if these appetites be not infinite, be not the gods we lie to and appease, be not the gods we give the power of the invisible to, their appetites and the need to call them something else unless they should seem beyond our control rising from the same underwater world whose springs are the soul, rising through its tangled roots. If the soul's roots lay exposed like a cottonwood fallen on the south bank of the Poudre were mined, what nuggets might be sluiced from its clots of gravel and dross?

Would that all were quite as well in my affairs, for I faced a long rail trip back to Fort Collins to sign papers and give up my land in Laporte. It was not in my nature to follow an impulse such as to fight Henry Arrison or any soldiers who came to urge me off the land, though it was a bitter moment when I found myself cleaning my pistol and staring blackly into the lamp that first night of my return. I had counseled Red Cloud many a time not to think he could win a fight to hold his land, but never before had I tasted how bitter those words are.

A man named Tobe Miller was to come and look the land over. He knew I had to leave soon whether I would or no to take up land at Pine Ridge if I did not want to be separated from First Elk Woman—and I did not—and he could name his price.

That was a long sad trip we took, First Elk Woman and I, with our surviving children, as we bid our last goodbye in 1878 to Bellevue and the Poudre. I walked every inch of that land, from the river, swollen with another June rise that wound its way through limestone crowned hogbacks, down the willow-hung sandbar First Elk Woman called "the love spot," up the banks where I showed Ab Loomis the pit my father had dug to cache the poudre, those long groves of cottonwoods and box elders, the cherry trees I planted that shed dappled light on the long grass, more like a park than a homesite, that spread northward and west, the tribal council grounds where as a youth I made my first speech before the Oglalas.

It remained the loveliest spot I had ever seen, except for one, that place within First Elk Woman's eyes, and now we must load our wagons, empty the cabin of our beds and belongings, though later we discovered First Elk Woman left her red sandstone corn grinder back on the hearth.

We reached that point on the Cheyenne Rim where the foothills sink below the line of sight. We stopped there, much as, thirty years before, my father and I had stopped at what he called First Sight, to look at the blue hump of Pike's peak I had imagined for so many years as a boy listening to my father's tales and building them in my mind.

Then First Elk Woman and I we turned our eyes north into Wyoming, across the Chugwater, Horse Creek, the Laramie I first knew when I visited Fort William, named for Sublette, my father's friend, leader of the Rocky Mountain Fur Company. I showed First Elk Woman where Pete and Willie's bones now lay, on a hill among a few cottonwoods above Fort Laramie. She sang a slow song, had me drive a length of lodgepole pine into hard-packed ground to serve as soul-post and had me place a buffalo robe on it. Then all of us surviving hugged it and said one prayer of goodbye, not asking the gods to grant the boys short stay in Purgatory but that their free souls speak well of us in the spirit world so we too one day could hope to enter those high forests where we'd hunt the spirit elk. I at last bid my farewells and felt their deaths lift off me.

Crossing the north Platte to Pine Ridge we watched a storm gather the skies, not with thunder but as if we headed into the mouth of hell, with me poling us across on the wagon now turned to raft. I would take the job of subagent at Pine Ridge until my health would break, as I have related.

This letter, as I look it over, seems one long tale of travel. I knew why Red Cloud called the road east the bad road, for I had gone back—once to gather my wild sons' bones, once to enter another part of my life that has nothing to do with Poudre valley where I found so much that was good those early days, learning to live in the wilderness with my father, my marriage to First Elk Woman, my dream of Colona, then Laporte, the town where every child was a living bond between white and Sioux, my island surrounded by rivers that wasn't ever mine.

Perhaps some clear summer night with the bitten moon and the Milky Way to guide you, you'll be sitting on the wagon seat on a trip up Poudre canyon to talk with some Methusaleh about early days for your book. You'll let your horses have their heads, and they'll curve south following that river to where the first tall stands of lodgepole timber the gulches where the people used to get their tipi poles. Perhaps you'll stop to light a pipe and a lantern to hang from a spike driven into the board end of the wagon where it will tilt as the trail dips and rises, the Poudre will hollow the canyon with its endless back of the throat hum, and you'll pause to reflect that some accounts are never settled, and you'll sense that somewhere in those pines there are eyes looking at you. If I get my last wish, those eyes will be me.

June 6, 1889
Pine Ridge Agency